DEDICATION

To Vera and all the other good women

DISCLAIMER

Dancing with the Devil is a work of fiction; any resemblance to any person living or dead or to any actual event is unintended or coincidental. The premise of the story is just that—a story. Considerable fictional latitude and invention was employed to create a "reality" of persons, places, dialogue, and actions. But, remember, this is a novel, a creation of the author, and not reality.

BOOK TWO OF THE TROJAN HORSE
IN THE BELLY OF THE BEAST TRILOGY

DANCING
with the
DEVIL

A Novel of the
Iran Nuclear Weapons
Interdiction Project

A Novel by

CARL DOUGLASS

Former Neurosurgeon Turned Author
Who Writes with Gripping Realism

PO Box 221974 Anchorage, Alaska 99522-1974
books@publicationconsultants.com—www.publicationconsultants.com

ISBN 978-1-59433-460-3
eISBN 978-1-59433-461-0
Library of Congress Catalog Card Number: 2014936141

Manufactured in the United States of America.

BOOK TWO

Dancing with the Devil

Oh, East is East and West is West, and never the twain shall meet,
Till Earth and Sky stand presently at God's great Judgment Seat;
But there is neither East nor West, Border, nor Breed, nor Birth,
When two strong men stand face to face, though they come from the ends of the earth!

-The Ballad of East and West
by Rudyard Kipling-

CHAPTER ONE

Niavaran Palace, Northern Tehran, Iran, Thursday, October 3, 1996

Roshanak Rahimi, herself, greeted the four visitors at the front door of the family residence, a singular honor for men a tier well below her husband's station.

She did not smile. Roshanak—wife of the Supreme leader—never smiled at anyone but family. She was actually one of three wives; but the other two were only *nikah mut'ah* [temporary] wives from long ago, and were now long gone. They were never mentioned by Rahimi or his wife. Although Roshanak was very much under Rahimi's thumb, she had considerable power, because she had been placed in charge of choosing husbands and wives in Rahimi's home.

Even these extremely rich men were always a bit awed to come to Niavaran Palace. The palace complex is rich in history and consists of several buildings and a museum. The Sahebqraniyeh Palace—from the time of Naser al-Din Shah of the Qajar dynasty—is located within the complex. The main Niavaran Palace—completed in 1968—was the most splendid and primary residence of the departed Shah and the Imperial family until the Iranian Revolution in 1979.

The Ali ibn Abi Rahimi family used all of the former Shah's homes; and all of them were of surpassing beauty and splendor—the palaces at Lavasanat, Jamshidiyeh Palace, former palace of Ardeshir Zahedi, Feish Ghola Palace, next to the Caspian Sea, and the Vakil Abad Palace in Mashhad with its 300,000 square meters of grounds. Niavaran Palace was the favorite residence of its current occupant, the Supreme Leader, the Grand Ayatollah, Agha Ali ibn Abi Rahimi, in part because it represented the great power of the Iranian leaders, the supreme among them able to dominate the world of Iran from the favorite home of the former powerful Shah. When Ali ibn Abi Rahimi walked through its halls and held audiences and met pilgrims there, he was rubbing the arrogant—now dead—Shah's nose in it.

"Welcome, why have you come?" Roshanak asked the standard formal question of all applicants who sought an audience with Grand Ayatollah Ali ibn Abi Rahimi.

"We are going on a pilgrimage, Mrs. Ali ibn Abi Rahimi."

She nodded and admitted them.

"May your pilgrimage be accepted by God."

They walked behind her to the great doors of the Supreme Leader's audience room. The door opened, and five *bazaaris* [businessmen] exited, making one more humble bow before they fully left the room. They had each paid the "lease"—500 million *toumans*, about $500,000 USD, on their guest slot— their twenty-minute pilgrimage. It was well worth their time, because even a nod from the chief of staff or especially from the Supreme Leader himself would result in a ten-fold return on their pilgrimage investment.

Roshanak muttered to herself as she walked away from the pilgrims, "*groveling, fawning liars and traitors.*"

Ali Hosseini Mejazi, Rahimi's chief of staff, and a significant imam—a man possessing a divine wisdom and esoteric knowledge, called *Hikmah*—himself, held the door for them and asked again, "Why have you come?"

Again, the four new supplicants bowed slightly and replied, "We are going on a pilgrimage."

More than anyone else in the Supreme Leader's household staff of 12,500, Mejazi insisted on the maintenance of the reverential reply. No one in Agha Rahimi's office is allowed to say he is going to meet Mr. Rahimi or has a meeting with him.

"Gentlemen, a brief warning: the Agha is not in a good mood. This morning, several people from this very household were arrested on charges of being magicians and invoking *djinns*. That does not auger well for the rest of today's business. Shaytan is constantly trying to undermine our Supreme Leader, and he wearies of the struggle."

"We understand," the president said with a sad expression.

"Enter, the Agha will see you."

All four men were well known to the chief of staff and to the Agha since— after the household staff, especially the 500 in the first tier—they were the most important men in the government of the Islamic Republic of Iran. Grand Ayatollah Ali ibn Abi Rahimi did not suffer people who were tardy;

and he certainly would not tolerate anyone from the government who was unprepared or a fool, Rahimi's favorite word for anyone with whom he disagreed. No one in his right mind disagreed with the Supreme Leader.

None of the four was anyone's fool, and they were right on time. They were Mohsen Shahamatdoost, President of the Republic of Iran, Yazid ibn Sarrafzaadeh, Chief of Staff of the Armed Forces of the Republic of Iran, Moqtada al-Benizir, head of the Atomic Energy Organization of Iran (AEOI), Mullah, Ali Salar Omidyar, director of the Ministry of Intelligence and Security (MOIS), and Behrouz Omidi, director of the Ministry of Intelligence and National Security of the Islamic Republic of Iran (MISIRI) or VEVAK.

Seated on a replica of the jewel encrusted Peacock throne—symbol of the power of the Shah, and believed by many to have been stolen from India—Agha Rahimi gestured for the men to come forward. His taciturn face gave no hint of his mood of the day. He took a sugar cube from a small ornate bowl at his side and dropped it into his coffee.

"Your brief was well written and to the point, President Shahamatdoost; and your subject is one I find of critical importance to the republic. Please proceed."

"Yes, Agha. Thank you for accepting our pilgrimage."

Rahimi gave a slight nod.

"This is a technical report, and I think it would be best for Mr. al-Benizir to present our progress to date."

He looked to the Agha for permission. Again, there was a slight affirmative nod.

The head of the AEOI focused his full attention on the Supreme Leader and began a brief and to-the-point presentation. He knew that the Agha had little interest in technical details of science and that he saw the world from a higher spiritual plane. Accordingly, he abbreviated.

"Agha, may Allah continue to guide your righteous hand. We servants of the revolution have been very active this past year and have made some progress. First, a little history to bring us up to date. You are aware that our nuclear program was originally launched in the 1950s with the help of the Great Satan as part of the Shah's Atoms for Peace program and of the great help we have been receiving from A.Q. Khan since the revolution. Because of provocations from the polytheists in India, our Pakistani brothers in Islam began to focus on nuclear weapons development in January 1972 under the leadership of Prime Minister Zulfiqar Ali Bhutto. Bhutto delegated the program to the Chairman of Pakistan Atomic Energy Commission [PAEC], Munir Ahmad Khan, a nuclear engineer. The program has been moving forward with great care and with speed. It will not be long before our Muslim brothers will answer the provocations of the polytheists from their surprise nuclear test in 1974, which the kaffirs called Operation Smiling Buddha. Our brothers have informed us that they will be ready to hold a formal nuclear weapon test within two years.

"Of most importance to us, China—which gave important assistance to Pakistan—is in negotiation with us to provide raw materials, instruments and machinery including weapons-related material such as centrifuges, known as *Pak-1*—and experts to further our own program. The foremost expert is Abdul Qadeer Khan, who established a network through Dubai to smuggle URENCO technology to engineering research laboratories in several cooperating countries, including Iran. I am pleased to report that A.Q. is in Bushehr as we speak and is providing crucial technical assistance to the revolution."

"I understand that much of Mr. Khan's information and expertise based on the technology that A.Q. Khan brings from Urenco is based on first generation civil reactor technology and is filled with many serious technical errors," Agha Rahimi said, surprising the four officials with the depth of his interest and information.

"That is true, but the information has proved to be authentic and provides a vital link for our centrifuge project. In that aspect, we are well underway, and can successfully portray to the world that we are engaged in nothing more than peaceful nuclear energy development. Our principle problem—as of today—is to procure enough raw materials to make serious progress. As you are obviously aware, Agha, we must proceed cautiously to avoid the West from learning our sources and secrets. That secrecy is an impediment to progress."

"How long?"

"We have three phases of work. To answer your question, we anticipate accomplishment of gathering scientists and technicians who can manage the work over the next six years. It will take eight or nine years to produce a safe and secret manufacturing apparatus. Purchase of sufficient Uranium-235 to make a workable bomb will take ten years. We should be able to produce the delivery systems concurrently. All of these predictions are based on the maintenance of secrecy—especially the prevention of Great and Little Satan finding out about our work and introducing counter measures—our ability to attract competent nuclear scientists and engineers, and a very great deal of money. As you know, many of Iran's best scientists became traitors to the revolution and have left the country for the more lucrative West. We are seeking to entice some sympathetic people back, but it is a tedious process. Pakistan has developed a very effective clandestine route to purchase tens of thousands of nuclear centrifuges and is willing to share—for a price. We have concrete plans to work with the godless ones in North Korea to obtain their expertise;

but, of course, those *kaffirs* do nothing without a substantial reward. The decision regarding money is yours, Agha. We stand ready to operate at your pleasure. Will you consider giving full authorization to the project?"

Rahimi paused. He fingered one of his favorite pipes from his collection of 200 while he ruminated on the information he had received.

"Yes. President Shahamatdoost, meet with me at the Pasteur Street residence in two week's time. I will have the political and legislative apparatus in hand then, and you may begin this holy work in earnest. Do this, but don't let the people find out."

With that catch phrase, the four men knew that the audience was concluded.

"Yes, Agha," the highly placed government officials chorused.

Each of them had met with the Supreme Leader many times in the 5,000-square-meter anti-nuclear protective bunker built under Rahimi's city residence at a depth of 60 meters. The significance of such a meeting at that place was that it would be all business, entirely secret—their lives would depend on that secrecy—and would involve a princely sum of money for funding the nuclear weapons project.

The Agha was out of sorts and had been all day. The men he had caused to be arrested as magicians had been found out by information that came from the VEVAK office. He constantly listened to remarks made against himself. His practice was to listen to 20-30 minutes of recorded conversations between political opponents, officials of the government, and military officers before going to sleep. He also listened to the newest negative commentaries at intervals during the day, which made him constantly hyperalert and depressed. When he awakened at four a.m. for prayer, he was certain that no one but Allah loved him and that he was surrounded by sycophants who protest their loyalty—like the bazaaris—in order to attain more power and greater wealth, or just to avoid his anger.

He started the day with his nagging wife—who sometimes listened to the recordings—giving her opinion that the Iranian people were fawning liars, useless drains of the economy, and maybe even traitors. The Agha loved the obeisance paid him. He was amused and flattered when he walked past a place on his way to a pilgrimage, and his followers kiss the ground he has walked on; but his shrewish wife had little patience for the daily groveling of the people. She spoiled his mood. A whim came over him; he handed President Shahamatdoost the bowl containing his sugar cubes, knowing that the bowl and the cubes would become sacred—and highly valuable.

The news that the nuclear weapons program would take a decade or more before Iran could face the decadent West as a nuclear power on equal terms with them was galling. Perhaps, he thought, some heads should roll.

§§§§§

Institute of Atomic Energy (IAE), Pyongyang, Democratic People's Republic of Korea [DPRK-North Korea], Saturday, October 5, 1996

As they waited for the supplicants from Iran, the select members of the IAE sipped Belgian hot chocolate and enjoyed a Sacher-Torte. They commented favorably on the announcement in the *Rodong Sinmun*, North Korea's state newspaper, that the DPRK's vaunted atomic energy pioneers had successfully carried out a successful nuclear fusion reaction test. The paper was enthusiastic—as it always was—over the Great Leader's newest triumph—"Our Dear Leader has led the nation to a magnificient triumph and our beloved nation now leads the way by rapidly developing cutting-edge science and technology that will guarantee safe, inexpensive, and environmentally compatible new energy sources. The people have thronged the streets to shout their praises for the Great Leader..."

The Great Leader's security forces had taken every possible step to prevent the people and the IAE personnel from seeing less enthusiastic commentaries from the *New York Times, The Times of London*, and *Le Monde*, all of which quoted scientists who scoffed at the idea that anyone had discovered the secret of producing nuclear fusion even experimentally, let alone as a practical source of energy.

Gen. Gangjon commented to his two top aides, "Soon we will see steam coming out of the smoke stacks of our newly reconstructed nuclear reactor in Yongbyon as we resume production of plutonium for our magnificient nuclear arsenal. We will dedicate that day to our Dear Leader, of course."

"Of course," the two deputies sang in a duet. "And the paper-tiger America will not do a thing about it," they added reflexively.

There was a soft knock on the door to Gen. Gangjon Chung-a's inner office. The head of the institute touched a button on his desktop; and a demure girl—eyes on the floor—ushered in three senior Iranian officials.

"Gentlemen, welcome. Please make yourselves comfortable," the general said.

"We are honored to be here," Ali Muhummad Sharifi, the Iranian Foreign Minister, said with a deferential bow.

"Bring coffee, Haneul," Gen. Gangjon said to the young secretary.

She glided silently from the room and returned in less than a minute carrying an ivory inlaid tray and six tiny cups of thick, bitter hot chocolate.

"This is the favorite of our Great Leader," Gen. Gangjon said meaningfully.

None of the six men in the room gave any evidence of distaste for the almost acrid drink. Fortunately, the cups were small, and it was unseeming to drink all of the offering. The Iranians had been forewarned by their protocol officer of the custom and of the extreme deference that must be paid to the very name of the Great Leader. The officer told them that it was much like the Islamic custom of adding a note of praise after the name of Muhammad—the equivalent to "the Prophet Muhammad, may Allah bless his faithful messenger forever" was "Park Young Hee, our esteemed and beloved Great Leader."

When the obligatory ingestion of the scalding hot chocolate was done, Gen. Gangjon said, "May I present my colleagues, Col. Dockko Yong-Jin, and Dr. Soung Hong-jik of the Institute of Atomic Energy."

Each man gave a short bow but did not speak.

"And it is my pleasure to introduce the atomic energy experts from the Islamic Republic of Iran, Dr. Moqtada al-Benizir, director of the AEOI and Mr. Esfandiari Razizadeh, his deputy," said Foreign Minister Sharafi.

Like the two junior North Korean officers, al-Benizir and Razizadeh responded with small bows.

"You have come a long way, Mr. Foreign Minister, and you must be tired. I regret that we will not have time to chat—the press of the nation's business, you understand—and that our Great Leader, may he continue to promote the glory of our homeland as did his father and grandfather before him is unable to attend.

He bears the burdens of his great office and must take care of issues of the people in the north on a matter that involves our dear friends in the Peoples Republic of China.

"We recognize your desire to further Iran's honest endeavors to become independent in energy matters. Our Great Leader has smiled on your efforts and wishes to be of assistance. After all, we, too, have borne the weight of unjust and warlike actions of the Americans. Please summarize what you need, and how we can supply that need."

"If I may, General, I will direct your questions to Dr. al-Benizir, our nuclear energy expert."

Gen. Gangjon nodded.

Dr. al-Benizir handed the general and his two aides a copy of a list of nuclear energy manufacturing needs neatly written in formal hangul Korean. The three Koreans studied the documents quickly; they were already fully familiar with the requests from the preparatory information sent to the Great Leader from Iran's Supreme Leader.

"We have given considerable study to the matter, Dr. al-Benizir; and I am pleased to tell you that we can be helpful in almost all respects. You are well aware of the stumbling blocks and hazards posed by the Americans for such transactions and of our need to be very circumspect in how our business is conducted. I am sure you will understand that the costs of doing such business have escalated in recent years. Perhaps those who prepared the financial aspects of your submissions were not quite up-to-date on such matters. Here is our revised estimate of the payment that we must receive."

He handed the three Iranians a slip of paper on which was written only a number, $2,000,000,000. Although he was too polite to say so, his countenance said, "Take it or leave it."

The Iranians had to exercise great inner control to avoid gasping. The figure was double what had been agreed upon in the preliminary discussions.

"That is more than our Supreme Leader understood would be the costs, General," said Minister Sharifi.

Gen. Gangjon shrugged, indicating that it was out of his control, "The costs and risks are as they are," he replied with finality.

The Iranians came from a nation of hagglers with a history of prolonged negotiations for matters as minor as the price of rice. They knew better than to haggle on this occasion.

Al Sharifi gritted his teeth and nodded his head.

"Let us shake hands then," Gen. Gangjon said and spat on his right palm.

The Iranians and the other two North Koreans did the same, and the deal was sealed.

Dr. Soung Hong-jik produced a document for all to sign.

Al Sharifi looked slightly perplexed after the signatures were affixed.

"I must have missed the section in the documents regarding shipping," he said quietly.

"Ah, yes, my omission. Forgive me," said the tough little Korean four-star general. "I am afraid that the risks of shipping in DPRK vessels or with DPRK crews has lately posed an unacceptable risk. Our foreign ministry and that of the Republic of Korea are locked in delicate negotiations over the seemingly unsolvable issue of cross-border visitations between families unfortunately separated by our ongoing conflict. The Americans and the Chinese will be meeting with the two sides in Panmunjon this very week. We cannot have an incident on the high seas. I am sure you understand. I am afraid that Iranian ships will need to make the transports."

It was apparent that the imperious North Korean had no intention of making the issue into a discussion. The Iranians had to lose face with equanimity and hold their tongues. The shipping issue was the lesser of their problems. The greatest hurdle in the entire process was that payment had to be in gold bullion with an interest rate of 22 percent. That was usury, and such usury was deeply offensive to the religious sensitivities of the devout Muslims.

"I must contact my superiors, General. Much of this is unexpected, and I will need formal permission."

"We have computers with minute-to-minute encryption protection in the adjoining room. Miss Park can direct you there, if you wish."

The Iranians had no real choice: they were beggars at the feast, and the North Koreans held every advantage. Al-Sharif e-mailed the information and the recommendation that there was no alternative but to acquiesce to the exorbitant demands.

Hamid Hejazi was on duty in the Supreme Leader's office. He decrypted the message and rushed it to the Supreme Leader's office. The Grand Ayatollah's face contorted into a wrathful mask.

"Bandits and pirates!" he said.

"Shall I reply, Agha?" Hejazi asked softly.

"Yes, may Allah pitch them into the everlasting fire. Tell al-Sharifi to go ahead. I will personally gouge the treasury to find the gold and will send it by jet tomorrow."

And Hejazi knew that more Iranians would go without for the cause of Project *Jahannam Adur*. He did not use all of the Agha's colorful language, but sent the message back to the foreign minister five minutes later.

When the Iranians left, Gen. Gangjon toasted his two subordinates, "A fine day's work, comrades. We have just funded a department of nuclear physics being opened at Pyongyang State University, and a nuclear reactor technology chair at the Kimchaek Polytechnic University, to say nothing of the boost this will give to the officer corps of the armed forces."

They all drank hearty draughts of *Munbaeju*—the traditional aged distilled 80 proof liquor made of malted millet, sorghum, wheat, rice, and *nuruk* (fermentation starter). It originates in the Pyongyang region and is noted for its fragrance, which is said to resemble the flower of the *munbae* tree. Only the favored few in the government and military can afford such an extravagance.

After his shift on the security detail of Agha Rahimi's office, Agent-Ex sent the officers of the Iran Nuclear Interdiction Project an ultra-secret e-mail detailing the Iran-North Korean deal, a ship's manifest, and the name and route of the ship and its course.

CHAPTER TWO

Fort Detrick, Fredrick, Maryland, Satellite Office of the Deputy Director of the Defense Intelligence Agency, Saturday, October 6, 1996

The small sign on the office door read simply, "DDDIA," for the deputy director of the DIA. Rear Admiral Neal Daastrup—known by most of his associates as 3D—sat in his comfortable old swivel chair at his government-issue steel desk. He rested his feet on the desk while he reread the report from Agent Ex in Tehran. He was perplexed; and if confirmation came in, he might escalate that to outright concern. The office was stark, with less furniture than what his secretary next door had in her office. He had a forty-five-year-old coat rack that was still perfectly serviceable, a safe that was bolted to the floor, and four utilitarian metal chairs with overly worn black seat pads. There were no pictures of the admiral with ranking officials, although he could speed dial many of them and be answered promptly, including the president.

Despite the unimposing appearance of the office and its occupant, Adm. Daastrup assists the DDIA's management of a workforce of more than 16,500 military and civilian employees worldwide. His leadership includes the Defense Intelligence Enterprise, which handles all Defense Intelligence Community organizations within the Department of Defense with an intelligence mission and/or function, plus all their stakeholders, civilian, military, and governmental, involved in creating, sustaining, and enhancing mission capacity for the protection of the United States.

Daastrup maintained this office for certain special meetings that he did not want to conduct in the main DIA Headquarters at Joint Base Anacostia-Bolling in Washington, D.C., because his visitors might be seen by eyes that

16

should not see them. The Fort Detrick office was obscure; it was swept for electronic eavesdropping devices; and his four bodyguards and driver were ensconced in an unmarked room directly across the hall. He needed only to press a button and five of the toughest senior enlisted men in the United States Armed Services would be inside his office—guns drawn—in less than ten seconds.

The DIA is the nation's premier all-source military intelligence organization. It provides the nation's most authoritative assessments of foreign military intentions and capabilities. The agency's four core competencies are: human intelligence, all-source analysis, counter-intelligence, and technical intelligence operations. Its goal is to enable military operations while also informing policy-makers at the defense and national levels. DIA's mission is unique, and no other agency matches its military expertise across such a broad range of intelligence disciplines. DIA also employs a limited number of medical intelligence analysts, support professionals, and support assistants at the National Center for Medical Intelligence, located at Fort Detrick; and Adm. Daastrup often took advantage of the seemingly innocuous titles and settings afforded under the medical rubric.

This was an important meeting. Adm. Daastrup had asked for the attendance of his most trusted confidants and some of the most effective intelligence agents in the world. Unlike the CIA, DIA agents are soldiers and seamen who have proved themselves on military duty and are thoroughly familiar with the defense departments and military operations of the United States, its allies, and its enemies. Neal was on a first name basis with his counterparts in the CIA, MI6, Australian security forces, the Mossad and IDF intelligence, and a host of official and unofficial agents from Europe, Asia, Canada, South America, the Middle-East, and Africa.

Today, he would meet with the CIA, the president's national security advisor, State Department Intelligence, Mossad, SAS, a representative of the Jewish *Sayanim* with contacts among the bazaari in Iran, and even a man from the Israeli Mafia.

Every individual with substantial knowledge of the Iran Nuclear Interdiction Program was required to have an Ultra TS/SCI [Top-Secret, Sensitive Compartmentalized Information, i.e. "above Top Secret"] clearance rating with SSBI [Single Scope Background Investigation]. Nevertheless, special cred-pack IDs were required of everyone who entered the complex at Fort Detrick. Every agent on that particular day had been given federally issued identification to enable them to enter the Fort with the least inconvenience or security scrutiny. They traveled separately from Dulles and Reagan Airports in Washington D.C., BWI Marshall in Baltimore, and Newark Liberty International Airport in New Jersey. They all stayed overnight in separate Baltimore hotels then rented nondescript economy cars for the trip to Fort Detrick. The beautiful scenery in Frederick County is a colorful backdrop against which the county's rich history has been played. It was originally settled by German and English immigrants in pre-Revolutionary War era. The county is Maryland's largest and is located in the backyards of Washington, D.C. and Baltimore. Frederick County enjoys its historical heritage and cultural diversity. At the northern end of the county, not far from the sprawling fruit orchards and a roaring waterfall, nestled in the Catoctin Mountains, is Camp David—the private retreat of every U.S. president since Franklin D. Roosevelt. At the county's southern end, on the banks of the Potomac River, sits Brunswick, an example of a nineteenth century railroad town in all its grit and glory. Between these two extremes are miles of open farmland, four wineries, several state and national parks, a Civil War battlefield, and thirteen towns of varying sizes and personalities.

The invitees drove in their separate cars at separate time intervals on I-695 around Baltimore to I-70 West to Frederick. There, they turned on exit #53 to Route 15 North then to the 7th Street exit. They turned right, went four blocks, and arrived about fifteen minutes apart at Fort Detrick's Main Gate, where they were expected. Each car was escorted by a DIA driver to the parking lot of Building 810. Each car was parked well away from all of the other invitees' cars; then a guide from the administrative assistant's office escorted them to the antiterrorism office. A second guide directed them to the unassuming DDDIA office. No one spoke.

Daastrup's secretary, Abigail Wynne, ushered each invited guest into the small conference room and offered them coffee or water. Neal Daastrup was all business, and he did not believe in having meetings of any degree of substance over food.

"Welcome, Zwi, I'm glad you could make it."

"It was a good time for me. I was in San Francisco for a meeting with a couple of important *Sayanim* for some mutual business ventures in our favorite country. Yesterday, I was in D.C. for a CIA/Mossad/MI6 gathering. I'm pooped, I have to admit."

Abigail admitted Randall Caruthers from State, Annette Redstone from the CIA, Carter Miller-Partridge for the SAS, Gideon Rothsberger III, the Sayanim, Lincoln Magalini, the president's national security advisor, and finally Moise Levinsky, the businessman from Tel Aviv. Neal raised an eyebrow at General Rosenstein when the Israeli Mafioso joined them. Zwi responded with a small wry smile.

"Welcome. Let's get started. Everyone here is on a need-to-know basis; but today, we all know the same thing; and we all need to talk a bit about the news we picked up. To come right to the point, our Agent-Ex in Iran is an unimpeachable source. He—or she-has never steered us wrong on anything. He—or she—does not ask for money or favors. And he—or she—is in a perfect position to know.

"Very recently, the Supreme Leader met with President Mohsen Shahamatdoost, General Yazid ibn Sarrafzaadeh, Moqtada al-Benizir, and Behrouz Omidi from VEVAK at the Niavaran Palace in Tehran. Our agent is one of the invisible helper bees who are presumed to hear no evil, see no evil, and speak no evil. But the agent's parents were murdered by Khomeini's thugs in Evin Prison; and he—or she—has not forgotten. The agent hates the corruption visited on Islam by the killers who took over the country; so, Agent-Ex was willing to communicate when we asked him or her to do so. He or she actually refused our money.

"This is what agent-ex learned—we have a recording for anyone who is a Doubting Thomas—the evil cabal reported to his magnificent holiness on the progress they are making towards building a nuclear weapon."

There was a moment of silence, a breath holding silence.

"I see that I have your attention. Basically, we have learned three things: the Persians are going to build a bomb for Allah. They are going to lie about it and insist that it is just peaceful nuclear energy—after all, the U.S. gave them most of what they needed to start with. There was a slight miscalculation—the Shah was given the stuff; and the Shah is gone, replaced by religious fanatics. Lastly, we know that they are not just zealots. They have a comprehensive and sensible plan. They know it will take upwards of a decade, and they know that we over here on Satan's side will do everything in our power to prevent them from getting a bomb. Questions?"

"What are we going to do about it?" asked Lincoln Magalini.

"Let's start with a plan that has short and long range goals that are specific and doable. This is not going to be nice, lady and gentlemen. There will need to be murder most foul, kidnapping, extortion, betrayal, entrapment, and if need be, war."

"I would add, preemptive strikes," said Zwi.

"And stealing," added Moise.

"And this will put us in a dance with the devil, don't lose sight of that," said Miller-Partridge. "We will do whatever we need to do. Those idiots cannot be

19

allowed to get very far down the path they have chosen. We will have to keep secrets like no one has ever done before."

"I have written out some specifics. I will give each of you your copy. Read it and shred it. That will be our record keeping mantra. So, let's start with Mr. Rothsberger since his role can start tomorrow morning. Gideon, this project of our Iranian friends will need funding—a great deal of it. I have here preliminary agreements from the Bank of China, Macau, Commercial Bank International PSC and HSBC Bank Middle East Limited—Headquarters branch, both in Dubai, Attijariwafa Banque, Casablanca, Morocco, Deutsche Bank, Frankfurt, and Landesbank Berlin Holding AG, both in Germany, all awaiting the Rothsberger & Company Bankers and Gideon Products Universal direct loan before sealing the final financing. The central bank of Iran has guaranteed the loans with gold bullion as collateral and has agreed to a 13 percent yearly compounded interest rate. In short, they are desperate.

"There is huge profit for you and the rest of the banks and that is priceless for the United States and Israel. We will guarantee the loans so as to keep you in play from beginning to end. Am I authorized to make that guarantee, Lincoln?"

"You are. Only the president and I know of the real purpose. The networks are so labyrinthine that it will appear to be business as usual for the stake placed by Washington and Tel Aviv. That investment will appear to be a bank bailout for the other banks and nothing to do with Iran."

"One more thing, Gideon. It is no secret to you that we have been grooming your son and Aaron Schmuel to work with the DIA and the Mossad once they finish their educations—which should be late this year or next year. Gideon needs to enter banking, and he needs to be the service agent for this huge loan. That will give him a reason to travel to Tehran regularly and to be apprised completely with the financial aspects of their project. We do not want him to be anything more than an analyst, but he will have such intimate access to the nuclear program's computer system that he may be able to use his knowledge and access as a weapon if or when the need arises. Are you in agreement with that?"

"Yes. Gideon is enthusiastically involved in learning clandestine work and is already applying his incredible mind in that direction. He will be thrilled to have a well-defined role. You can count on him and on me. We will use any of our contacts that are needed, as well."

"Thank you."

"Now, Moises. Here is where you come in. The Iranians are utilizing a completely illegal purchase and transport system to move parts and natural materials into the country. Criminal elements of all stripes will be involved—all for a hefty price. The Mossad will see to it that you are in the loop, and you can give feedback to them. Once Aaron is ready, he can be the agent on the ground to shepherd this along. Remember, this is a waiting game. We will follow the progress of every facet of their endeavors from the beginning to the end. Aaron will be there all the way. He and Gideon are good friends, and they can coordinate activities. It will be a tightrope act. They will be facilitating the manufacture of nuclear weapons, and almost everything they do in that regard will be rooted in lawbreaking on an international level. It will take all of their smarts and all of your contacts to keep this from blowing up. You will have to use Levi Schmuel, Aaron's father, as the principal liaison. Do we have an agreement with you and your business associates, Moises?"

"You do. I will have to check with Zeev on the details, but I foresee no problems. I will be in contact with Zwi tomorrow morning."

"Good. Now, the messy stuff. That is the bailiwick of you, Zwi, Randall, Annette, Carter, and Lincoln. Between now and that possible eventual day, all of you must have a viable military option in place that is flexible enough to mold to the changing times. Israel cannot allow the Shi'ites to have a bomb and a delivery system; so, the action may well have to be preemptive. You five and I will be the only ones with the complete intel and will be responsible to convince our superiors to be on board quietly from here on out. There will be new presidential administrations, new military hierarchy, new opinions, new problems, and new options. We will have to control them all. At the close of business tomorrow, a *lettre de marque* and reprisal—to use an old term from the days of privateers—will be issued by the current heads of state, the foreign ministries, and the directors of their respective intelligence services of the United States, the UK, Israel, and Zeev Rosenkranz's business conglomerate to grant a free hand to the intelligence, cyber, and military forces when they are needed. Guard that fact and any documents as Top Secret, Eyes Only state secrets. Our lives depend on the ultimate in discretion."

When the co-conspirators were gone, Neal rubbed his tired eyes and mused to himself, *"So this is what the rest of my life is going to be: a life-and-death cat-and-mouse game with religious bigots out to destroy the world in the name of their god. I have had enough for today, I am going home to my birthday party."*

21

CHAPTER THREE

Aboard Das Deustchland Küstenwache Zollboot, *Kalkgrund* [German Customs Ship, *Kalkgrund*], Baltic Sea, Off the Coast of Sweden, March 29, 1997

Korvettenkapitän [Commander Junior-grade (JG)], Deutsche Marine, Heinrich Kunstler, was in his second week of duty on his first command ship. Technically, as captain of the ship—the customs vessel *Kalkgrund*—he was the *Kapitän zur See* [captain at sea]. He took seriously his responsibilities as a naval officer. He, his ship, and his men were on the Baltic Sea exercising their general mission to protect German and Allied territories. Specifically, they were ordered to interdict ships deemed to be suspicious and to carry cargo that presented a danger to NATO and to the German homeland.

The signals petty officer rushed a decoded message to the bridge, and the captain read it at once. It was labeled "Top-Secret, Top-Priority," a level of communication Captain Kunstler had not before encountered in his short career as a naval officer. The message was transmitted from the German Naval High Command but originated from three American officers: Randall Caruthers, State Department; Annette Redstone, CIA; and Lincoln Magalini, National Security Advisor to the president. Unknown to Captain Kunstler, all three were also operatives in the ultra-secret Iran Nuclear Interdiction Project, which is what prompted the call to action from the Germans.

His orders were simple: "Halt and board cargo vessel *Ayatollah Mazariah*, flying colors of the Islamic Republic of Iran, inspect cargo for nuclear materials and equipment. Confiscate if found."

The operation went smoothly. The captain and crew of the Ayatollah Mazariah obeyed the customs officers and turned over the list of officers and

22

crew and the cargo manifest without protest. The manifest listed petroleum industrial equipment from Siemens of Sweden and iron ore originating from the LapCooperative Mining Consortium of Northern Sweden and Norway being shipped to Pyongyang, DPRK. Captain Kunstler's crew found that to be a completely false listing of the contents of the cargo hold and the eventual destination, which was first to Pyongyang and then on to the port of Bushehr, Iran.

The industrial equipment consisted of finely machine tooled technical instruments, €46 million worth of turbocompressors, €476 million worth of heavy aluminum tubing built to long-range missile specifications bound ultimately for Iran via Pyongyang, and €69 million worth of ultracentrifuges. The "iron ore" turned out to be readioactive and was ultimately identified as €280 million worth of highly enriched uranium [HUE]. German investigators concluded in their report to NATO that the equipment and uranium ore could have been used in Iran's WMD and missile program.

The ship and its cargo were confiscated; the crew was released to find their own way home; and the CEO, CFO, and COO of Siemans were summoned for a tense meeting with the *Bundesministerium der Justiz* [Federal Ministry of Justice]. A terse diplomatic message was sent to the atomic energy and foreign ministries of Iran and North Korea. Siemens and the two governments denied all knowledge and involvement.

§§§§§

Messages between the Offices of the President of the Islamic Republic of Iran and the General Secretary of the Workers' Party of Korea and Chairman of the National Defense Commission of North Korea, April 12, 1997, 0900-1015

0900: IRI-Be advised that the agreed upon shipment of goods from the DPRK to the IRI has been confiscated on the high seas by NATO authorities and minions of the United States.

0921: DPRK-Most regrettable. We are disturbed at the losses your nation has sustained.

0933: IRI-We regard the responsibility for the loss to be upon the DPRK since the shipment never arrived in the IRI.

0941: DPRK-That is not our understanding of the contract. The losses on the sea occurred on an Iranian registered ship. You may recall our conversation regarding the inherent risks. While you may regard this as an act of war on the part of NATO and the United States, it is a matter between your nation and those entities.

0950: IRI-We demand return of the $2 billion in gold we sent for the products we have not received.

1002: DPRK-While we regret your losses, we have no responsibility under the contract. Our part of the contract was fulfilled when the goods were loaded on the Iran registry ship, *Ayatollah Mazariah.*

1012: IRI-That is unacceptable. Our government and armed forces may have to resort to military measures should your attitude fail to improve. Not only have we suffered monetary loss, but we consider your approach an insult to our nation and your holding the gold as theft.

1013: DPRK-Be informed that the DPRK does not receive threats with any degree of latitude or forgiveness. Our nation follows a policy of *Songun* [military-first] in order to strengthen the country and its government. North Korea is proud to be the world's most militarized country, with a total of nine and a half million active, reserve, and paramilitary personnel. The General Secretary of the Workers' Party of Korea and Chairman of the National Defense Commission of North Korea—our Great Leader—will prepare the nation to meet any threat. We may accept your apology, but only if it is proffered in acceptable form and transmitted immediately.

1015: IRI-Transmission

§§§§§

Offices of the Supreme Leader of the Islamic Republic of Iran, Islamic Republic Street—End of Shahid Keshvar Doust Street, Tehran, Iran, April 12, 1997, 1143

Grand Ayatollah Rahimi screamed. His communication was incomprehensible; and the president, generals, security personnel, and atomic energy officials cowered. While they could not understand the words coming from the furious Supreme Leader, the message was nonetheless clear. Someone was

24

a traitor; maybe everyone in the room was a traitor. Someone would have to pay and pay dearly. The insult, the frustration, the dreadful monetary loss were beyond the level that Allah would accept; and there would be retribution for this major setback in the atomic energy program. Unlike some meetings with the Agha, there was no banter, no *gadeh* [idle chat and vulgar jokes as in gatherings with mullahs], and no routine discussion of business—just deadly implacable seriousness.

He had had just sufficient time to calm down to be willing to accept the execution of deputies, staffers, and the ship's crew as expiation enough. The Agha's wife feared that her husband would have a stroke and got the pale-faced senior officials out of his office as soon as she could. In all, 273 men lost their lives in Evin Prison by torture then hanging to atone for the transgressions against Allah.

At 1622, Agent-Ex sent an ultrasecret e-mail to the officers of the Iran Nuclear Interdiction Project:

Loss of uranium ore and weapons manufacturing equipment from IRI ship considered very grave and injurious to the Project *Jahannam Adur*. Relations with North Korea severely damaged; threats were exchanged.

Signed, Agent-Ex

CHAPTER FOUR

Home of Daniel and Brenda Daastrup, 1210 Potomac St. NW, Georgetown, Washington, D.C., January 20, 1999

Afsoon B. Daastrup had assumed that identity the second she boarded the flight from Basrah, Iraq, to Dulles International Airport in late 1996. Her name preserved her identities: She was still herself, Afsoon—the charm, a spell, and a bewitchment in Farsi. She had a middle initial that meant she was Brenda's although—at Neal's request—they did not include the whole name. And, she had a last name for the first time in her life and a documented legal identity and citizenship. She was a member of the Daastrup family. That had been the easiest thing in the world and yet had posed a real difficulty. The day Afsoon walked into the magnificent Georgian manor at 1210 Potomac St. NW between N and M Streets NW in Georgetown, one of the first things she saw was the large family photograph with professionally posed images of Brenda and Daniel, the parents, and their six children—Daniel Jr., who was a year older than Afsoon, and Abigail, Mary, Ruth, Evan, and Michael, who were younger. They ranged in age from two years to fourteen years that day. Mischievous Michael was the baby of the family at two. He was now five.

There were small yearly pictures of all of the children surrounding the large most recent photograph. The photos were beautiful, stunning to Afsoon who had never seen a family photograph, and disheartening because she was not included in a single one of them. She put on a brave face and decided she could not complain because she was being treated so well that it was like a dream, and she should not get her hopes up for everything.

That cause of lingering doubt and apprehension faded quickly. She stopped hoarding food after three months. It took almost a year for final legal adoption papers to be signed. The process was not as complicated or tedious as it is for some families, what with the director and the assistant directors of the DIA, the president's national security advisor, and his chief of staff, and the undersecretary of state running interference. Afsoon understood the difference between being well cared for, being the ward of a guardian, and being a full-fledged adopted daughter; but it was not until her picture was included with the rest of the family in the yearly portrait that she knew she belonged. Brenda and Daniel fudged a little. The new portrait was four months early; it was taken on the day the adoption was final.

Two weeks after Afsoon settled in at 1210 Potomac St. NW, and before her offensive bodily odors could become a family problem, a very important guest came to visit. Egyptian feminist physician and surgeon Nawal El Mubarak gave an impassioned speech against FGM in the United Nations General Assembly in New York the week Afsoon arrived, and Brenda was able to get her an audience with the president in return for examining and treating Afsoon.

Afsoon obediently submitted to the kind woman's probing fingers although it was painful.

"My dear," Dr. El Mubarak said gently, "we can repair the damage, but we cannot make you perfect again. I can repair the injury where your bowel movements come out through your vagina, and I can get rid of some of the scar tissue to make your life better. Do you understand?"

She had been prepared about the concept of surgery in advance by Brenda; so, she said simply, "Yes."

"You will be sick for a while afterwards, and there will be some pain; but this time, the pain will have a purpose—to make you better. Do you want me to do the operation, child?"

"Please."

Her trust in Brenda was so complete that she knew it was for her good. At this point in her life, Brenda was the only person she truly trusted.

Dr. El Mubarak had to be back in Cairo in a week and then was scheduled to go on a whirlwind lecture tour of France, England, the Netherlands, seven African countries, and even one stop in Morocco at the medical school there. The operation had to be done in the next few days; and Brenda turned heaven and earth over to get the hospital, the operating room, and the nurses all to agree to have Dr. El Mubarak do the corrective surgery even though she was not a licensed physician in D.C., or anywhere else in the United States, for that matter.

The postoperative pain was terrible, but Afsoon had known worse. With medications, it did not compare to what she had had to endure when the FGM was perpetrated on her. She healed quickly, and was overjoyed when she finally was able to believe that she would never again have that dreadful odor coming from her female parts.

Before she left, Dr. El Mubarak sat down with Afsoon and her mother.

"My dears, I know you have had to be brave about all of this, but there is one more thing. I am afraid that it would be too dangerous and far too painful for you to have a baby. Even sexual intercourse will be almost unendurable. It is probably best that you decide early in life not to permit that. I'm sorry, but what those monsters did to you in the name of their religion has done you permanent harm; and you will be better off to treat the area between your legs as forbidden territory."

Afsoon was too young and inexperienced to grasp the full implications; but Brenda did; and she cried. Afsoon appreciated that a woman would cry for her. She did understand that she could never again be touched by a man in that way. It was fine with her.

She repeated her mantra to herself when Dr. El Mubarak finished—"*Never again.*"

Afsoon healed and found she could live among people as an ordinary girl. No one needed to know what she had been through. It was private between her and Brenda.

To accommodate everyone's complicated schedules, Afsoon and Brenda agreed upon January 20 as her birthday; and the family had celebrated the day each year with a huge party. Her fourth birthday as a member of the Daastrup family—and her nineteenth of her life as near as she could remember—was today; and family, extended family, distant family, and hundreds of friends were streaming in. They all headed for the tub of hot chocolate; it was a bone-chillingly cold day. Afsoon had acculturated into American society with ease and enthusiasm. She was not quite as giddy as her contemporaries—too much water had passed under the bridge for her to be an altogether typical young woman—but she had best friends, fun acquaintances, and was popular at Georgetown University as she had been when she went to Georgetown Visitation Preparatory School, an upper class private school fifteen minutes away from home.

Brenda and Daniel had been successful in keeping Afsoon's introduction into American life and schooling from being overwhelmingly confusing. They were unsuccessful in keeping Uncle Neal from getting his camel's nose under the tent flap to steer her in the direction he wanted her to go. Brenda

28

and Daniel knew the bright girl was very much a potential asset to the intelligence community, and about all they could do to slow down the juggernaut was to set some limits. Afsoon's priorities—as set by her new parents—were to become a completely bonded member of the family, then to have a successful educational career—she had to start from scratch—then to get into Georgetown University. She would then be a full-fledged adult, and they would not be able to hold Neal back from her. Given her remarkable experience, talents, and fund of knowledge, they were more or less inclined to accept that their little girl was going to be a serious intelligence agent for the United States one day.

Sixteen-year-old Afsoon started the first grade at Georgetown Visitation Preparatory School. Three weeks later, she finished grammar school; and a year later, middle school and junior high. She graduated with her age appropriate class and barely missed being valedictorian because she had to become thoroughly familiar with English reading, writing, and spoken language while her contemporaries could devote most of their energies to other subjects. The subject in which she excelled was mathematics; and before she finished high school, Afsoon Daastrup was a National Merit Scholarship Finalist in mathematics and was offered full-ride scholarships to every Ivy League university in the country. She chose Georgetown University at the urging of her parents because of their conviction that she needed a bit more time to adjust to family life and American ways.

A new and wonderful world opened up for Afsoon Daastrup the day she entered the university. The vibrant Georgetown neighborhood is located north of the Potomac River just across the Francis Scott Key Bridge. It is filled with quaint tree-lined old cobblestone streets, eighteenth and nineteenth century architecture, and upscale shops, bars, and restaurants. Many of the current homes are 200 year-old restored row houses with beautiful gardens. The neighborhood is a blend of old and new, history and progress. It was founded in 1751 as a tobacco port town in Maryland forty years before the planning for Washington D.C. to be the new nation's capital was begun, making it D.C.'s oldest neighborhood. It has served as home to a long list of famous residents, including former U.S. Presidents Thomas Jefferson and John F. Kennedy. Georgetown remained a separate municipality until 1871, when the United States Congress created a new consolidated government for the whole District of Columbia. A separate act passed in 1895 specifically repealed Georgetown's remaining local ordinances and renamed Georgetown's streets to conform with those in the City of Washington.

Afsoon came to love the university as much as her fellow students. She had no money problems and could concentrate on her studies and on enjoying the vast rich cultural activities afforded by the neighborhood and the capital city. She was able to live in an apartment with four other girls at 33rd and N St. N.W. between N and M streets and bicycle to school in fifteen to twenty minutes depending on traffic at 37th and O Streets, N.W.. That gave her a secure base and a happy home—near enough to Brenda—so that she could begin the explorations of her new world.

Much of Georgetown is surrounded by parkland and green space that serve as buffers from development in adjacent neighborhoods, less upscale areas, and provide recreation. Rock Creek Park, the Oak Hill Cemetery, Montrose Park and Dumbarton Oaks are located along the north and east edge of Georgetown, east of Wisconsin Avenue—all near her home, and all great walking places. The neighborhood is situated on bluffs overlooking the Potomac River; so, there are fairly steep grades on streets running north-south, which added to the exercise Afsoon thrived on. She was in good shape and was getting better every week.

She made friends, almost all of them female. Together, they had study nights, hikes, shopping and restaurant outings, and strolls through the history of the nation as seen in microcosm in Georgetown. The neighborhood in the 1850s had a large African-American population, including both slaves and free blacks; and there was a considerable ethnic diversity in the neighborhood when Afsoon did her undergraduate work.

Slave labor was widely used in construction of new buildings in Washington, in addition to providing labor on tobacco plantations in Maryland and Virginia. Slave trading in Georgetown began in 1760, when John Beattie established his business on O Street and conducted business at other locations around Wisconsin Avenue. Slave trading continued until the mid-nineteenth century, when it was banned. Other slave markets—pens—were located in Georgetown, including one at McCandless' Tavern near M Street and Wisconsin Avenue, where Afsoon and her friends spent time absorbing the nation's history, even its worst periods. Fortunately, Afsoon concluded, Congress abolished slavery in Washington and Georgetown on April 16, 1862. When she first learned of the shameful and dehumanizing practice of slavery, Afsoon was disappointed in her new country; but her friends assured her that evil has existed everywhere. The positive thing about the U.S. is that it has enough diversity with enough political power to put to right evils like slavery, polygamy, child and female abuse, and discrimination. The new country compared very well against the one she had left.

Georgetown is home to world-renowned Georgetown University, the oldest Catholic and Jesuit university in the U.S. and the safe-haven for a combined student population of more than 28,000. The campus was located a relatively easy walk from the Daastrup's home. The main campus occupies 100 acres and includes 58 buildings, student residences capable of accommodating 80 percent of undergraduates, athletic facilities, and renowned medical school. Most buildings are of an eighteenth-nineteenth century collegiate Gothic brick architecture. There are inviting campus open green areas including fountains, a cemetery, large clusters of flowers, groves of trees, and open quadrangles. Afsoon and her friends developed their friendships between classes as they gathered on the main campus Dahlgren Quadrangle or Red Square.

Decades later, Afsoon would look back on her time in Georgetown and her studies at the university as the best in her life. She and her friends spent off hours in the shops at Georgetown Park, a shopping mall of about 100 stores with a wide selection of goods and fun, including women and men's fashion, children's fashion and toys, jewelry, accessories, books and cards, electronics, music, etc. Georgetown Park has no department store; and the smallness, the coziness of the university, the mall, and the neighborhood allowed Afsoon to put her past where it belonged—in a hidden compartment of her brain.

Her past did catch up with her in the form of Adm. Neal Daastrup, her uncle—Brenda's brother.

CHAPTER FIVE

CYCLOTRON NUCLEAR LABORATORY, 44 Oxford Street, Cambridge, Massachusetts, February 19, 1999.

Gideon E. Rothsberger IV, M.S., M.S., Ph.D.—newly appointed associate dual professor of nuclear engineering in the Division of Applied Sciences, and banking in the Harvard Business School—had an appointment to meet Neal Daastrup at the laboratory office of the division's director, Dean Narayanamurti, in the Harvard Cyclotron Nuclear Laboratory. Despite his obvious youth, He had finished his two-year stint as an assistant professor at MIT, then transferred to Harvard's Division of Engineering and Applied Sciences (DEAS) with a promotion. The division had been upgraded in 1996 when Gideon was finishing up his Ph.D. work, and he had been heavily recruited. His understanding with Harvard was that he would work three months at the university then three months at his family's bank—the Rothsberger Family Bank in San Francisco—repeating the cycle for a contractual three years, which would finish on graduation day at the end of May 1999. The unusual appointment was offered by the Faculty Appointments Administration because of Gideon's demonstrated genius and worldwide acclaim in mathematics, his pioneering doctoral work on computer science applications in world banking, and his ongoing research in nuclear engineering. Not to be ignored was the multimillion-dollar contribution towards the creation of the future Harvard School of Engineering and Applied Science (SEAS)—a department level school within Harvard University's Faculty of Arts and Sciences (FAS)—by Rothsberger Global Enterprises and the United States Department of Defense, which were closely linked when negotiations

32

took place between Gideon, the university, the Rothsberger financial empire, and the U.S. government.

At MIT, Gideon had been a member of a faculty group that coordinated a major study of the future of nuclear power with a study group from Harvard. He was to be one of the featured speakers for the group at the annual Harvard Harvey Brooks lecture scheduled in ten days. The subject of his paper was Nuclear Engineering and its Partnership with Funding Institutions Worldwide. His father, G.R. III, was on the agenda to discuss his bank's relationships with the large banks of the world, including Europe, the U.K., India, and the Middle-East—Saudi Arabia, Syria, and most recently, Iran. There was considerable interest in the symposium because—for the first time—it appeared that there may be practical avenues to begin the establishment of safe and efficient nuclear energy engineering programs around the world.

Underscoring the significance of the symposium and its proposals was the fact that it was sponsored by MIT's Office of the Provost and Laboratory for Energy and the Environment, the Harvard DEAS, and major private and business contributors from among the visionaries who believed in the technology as an important option for the United States and the world to meet future energy needs without emitting carbon dioxide and other atmospheric pollutants. Representatives of the Group of Twelve [G12], actually thirteen, industrially advanced countries—whose central banks cooperate to regulate international finance and operate hand-in-glove with the International Monetary Fund—were to be present and to participate in the group sessions scheduled after the lectures.

Gideon got off the underground at the Harvard Square T Station and walked briskly for eight minutes to the Cyclotron Laboratory on Oxford Street. Whenever Adm. Daastrup requested a meeting, Gideon knew he was likely to be in for something of a life-changing experience. He was always a bit anxious before a meeting with 3-D—the DDDIA—but the meetings thus far had always been to his considerable benefit, and he had no reason to doubt that this one would be the same.

He knocked on the door to room 12, and was admitted by a ruggedly handsome man who towered over him. The man had short-cropped blond hair, mildly cauliflowered ears, and a neck that seemed to Gideon to be twice as big around as his young thighs. When he smiled, his facial and jaw muscles appeared to be as developed as most men's six-pack abs. He had muscles on his muscles; his arms would have made a meek man of Goliath; and he was intimidating in all respects to the scholarly boy of nineteen.

"Please spread your legs and hold your arms out to the side, Sir," the giant requested in a low rumbling voice.

Gideon knew the drill and complied with alacrity.

"Are you carrying any weapons, anything that might cut me or poke a hole in me? I wouldn't like that," he said.

Gideon certainly did not want to give any offense.

"No, Sir," he replied.

The man's hands would have been able to encircle halfway around a basketball, and he used them expertly to frisk Gideon. Gideon had learned long ago to have almost nothing on his person when he met either Adm. Daastrup of the DIA or Gen. Rosenstein of the Mossad. A second, smaller but equally intense man watched Gideon with hawk's eyes, missing nothing. He was cradling an uzi like a Tea-partier dad meeting his daughter's prospective boyfriend.

"Clean," the giant announced, and stepped aside.

"Sorry about all of that, but paranoia is a necessary part of my business. I'm sure you understand," Adm. Daastrup said by way of greeting.

Gideon nodded. No other commentary was necessary.

"I have some news and some specific assignments if you are up to it."

"I'm ready."

"All right. First, you have to sign a contract and start the process for official top secret clearance, because you are going to be privy to some of the most closely held secrets in the history of our country. It is a responsibility with consequences—as you well know—and there is no allowance for your tender age. At least you are old enough to vote and to drink beer."

Gideon looked at the stack of papers.

"Can I take them home to fill out?"

"Nope. Take your time today. At the bottom of the stack is a pile for the IDF and the Mossad. They trust me to verify your signature and to vouch for you. I am sticking my butt out, and would be made very unhappy if you were to turn out to be a serial killer, a drug lord, or a traitor. I trust you; get to work."

It was tedious; but with Adm. Daastrup's help, they got through the pile in two hours.

"It'll take a few weeks to get official clearance. As I have said before, everything we talk about is secret; and today, I'm going to give you a big one. I have been working on the concept for quite a while, and it is so hush-hush that I haven't even contacted the person we are going to discuss today. We and the Mossad cousins have found it to be extremely important to get humint

34

from the very cautious and very dangerous Iranian religious fanatics who run that poor country. One of our foremost goals has been to find an effective agent with unimpeachable credentials, who speaks the language as a native, and whom we can count on never to betray us. The person must be extraordinarily brilliant—a math, theoretical physics, computer, and nuclear science genius. That sounds like the wishful thinking of a loonie, but I believe we have found just such a person."

"How do I fit into the picture?"

"I'll get to that; one thing at a time. My sister Brenda discovered the person I described a moment ago. She is young and a diamond in the rough, but I am convinced she is perfect; or that she will be once we get her a cover story that no one can penetrate, and once she learns what she needs to learn from us spies. Here's where you come in. She needs to be put on the fast track to learn everything she has to over the next four years. That will be a herculean task on both of your parts, but I am convinced that she is up to it. I am equally convinced that she will be enthusiastic to help hurt the present regime in the Islamic Republic, especially with regards to its offensive nuclear weapons program."

"You mean the nuclear research for peaceful purposes being touted by President Shahamatdoost, the kindly friend of Israel and the United States?"

"Gideon, with no intent at levity, we know for a fact that the president and his Supreme Leader and their closest religious zealot co-conspirators are planning to make a bomb. Others speculate that the Iranians could possibly be contemplating making an offensive nuclear bomb, but are lukewarm to the proposition. I repeat: we know for certain. The other thing we know is that they have a timeline, and they are doing fairly well at keeping to it."

That was sobering news to a young man with a future. He had no illusions about what would happen if the unthinking Iranian zealots got a bomb and the means of delivery; it would be World War III.

"The potential agent I spoke about is a girl named Afsoon Daastrup. She was adopted by my sister. You need to be a crucial part of preparing her for perhaps the most important intelligence mission of all time. Here is a dossier. It is a thick one; so, you can take it with you. Don't let it out of your sight or mention her name anywhere to anyone until we finalize a public purpose for the two of you to get together. Right now, today, we have a problem with her that we have to nip in the bud. I think I can get her cooperation; then I'll get back to you; so, we can work out the details of her training."

§§§§§

35

Birthday party for Neal Daastrup at Neal and Ruth's home—3522 Orchard Lane NW, Georgetown, February 23, 1999.

The Daastrup clan gathered in force for Adm. Daastrup's birthday, as they did every year. It had become the glitziest and most important social event for the family, and the family business always got a positive boost from the get-together. The Daastrups were an important family, and the men and women who attended were connected. There were three state senators, a member of Congress, seven flag officers of the United States Navy, and three or four people who did not share with others what they did.

The Daastrups' Georgian house was built in 1811 during the regency period—the de facto reign of George, the Prince Regent, who ruled while his father, George III, was declared incompetent. The house was classical Georgian, and Ruth had had the old house renovated and updated with loving attention to the detail of the post-colonial era when the house was built for a wealthy planter—and slave owner. The magnificent handmade red brick home was notable for its authentic proportion and balance—twin chimneys and square symmetrical shapes with paneled doors centered in the front facade. The interiors were as rich and beautiful as the outside was elegant and imposing. The waxed wood floors gleamed under the light of the huge entry hall chandelier.

The spouses and children of the non-sharing relatives simply informed anyone who asked, "My dad/mother/aunt/uncle/brother/sister, etc. works for the government." Everyone who was anyone knew that Neal Daastrup was the 3D and was involved with the defense intelligence agency—another way of saying that "he works for the government."

Afsoon had been a bit afraid of the stern navy officer when she was first introduced to him at her own first birthday party the month she had arrived in the United States, January 20, 1997. He won her over with ease. He was a gentle man despite all of his gold braid and medals, and he had a sense of humor that kept her laughing. So, the new immigrant came to be fond of her new uncle while still being awed by him. Once Neal got to know her better, the feeling of awe was mutual.

After the raucous dinner where everyone talked at once and vied for attention; and, after the presents, it was an unspoken agreement that Neal would retire to his study, close the door, and send for the family members who needed something or sometimes even had something to give. This year, he asked to speak to Afsoon first.

36

Afsoon was always awed by her uncle's special place—the former drawing room of the house's golden age. It was ornate and simple at the same time—less fussy and confusing, but more elegant than that found in later times in the Georgian era—and richer than any palace she had seen in her perusal of picture books when she lived in Kurdestan. The tall windows—designed to maximize the views out to the gardens—ensured that the room felt light and Airy, and the gardens were resplendent with color in the spring, summer, and fall, and were still fairly green in the winter. The symmetry of the home's external and internal layouts resulted in a sense of balance and harmony.

The tall ceilings had wide decorative gleaming gilded white plaster moldings in an acanthus pattern that accentuated the height and importance of the princely room. There was a classical ceiling rose in pale pink that drew the viewer's eyes upward. The window sills were lined with white marble, and the centerpiece of the room was a magnificent white marble fireplace with a break fronted shelf. The fireplace burned natural gas for the efficient and wood for the purists. There were no hanging photographs or paintings. The room was dominated by a single fresco mural of a Daastrup ancestor leading a small band of rag-tag colonialists against a larger force of redcoats.

Afsoon took a seat on the cream white and gold sofa and reacquainted herself with the walls and the ceiling. The only other furniture was a pair of winged arm chairs with a striking damask striped pattern and Adm. Daastrup's mahogany desk. The lower wall section of chocolate brown wood paneling stopped at a dado rail about two and a half feet from the floor. The tall middle section was hung with *eau de nil*—pale yellowish green colored—silk hangings, which was all the rage in the Georgian era—1714-1811.

"How are you getting along in school, my dear niece?" he asked as she came into the pleasant Georgian room.

"More than fine. In fact, I am scheduled to give two lectures—one here in Georgetown and the other at Harvard under the Georgetown, MIT, and Harvard's Enhance Learning on Campus, Global program."

"That's great, Afsoon. What are your lectures about?"

"At Georgetown, the subject is the maltreatment of women; the focus is on Iran. I don't think anyone has a better right to speak up or knows the subject more up close than I do. At Harvard, I am speaking to a worldwide collegiate audience on evolution—specifically on how it is one of the four pillars of biological life."

Neal already knew that from his sister, Brenda; and that tidbit of information spurred him to put forth a serious offer. The Georgetown subject would not fit into his plans, however intensely Afsoon felt about excoriating the Iran regime. There was a pregnant moment while he carefully considered what he would say next. Afsoon was well aware that her uncle was struggling with a decision; so, she waited patiently.

Neal templed his fingers on his forehead, then he straightened up and held Afsoon's eyes with his.

"Afsoon, I had intended to wait a while longer before bringing up something to you. Are you aware of what I do?"

"I think so. You are the deputy director of the defense intelligence agency. I presume you are a spy or a master of other spies. I don't know what sorts of things you do, really, though."

"Well said. So, I will not beat about the bush."

Afsoon frowned slightly.

"It's another one of those pesky English idioms. It means to avoid coming directly to the point by just hinting at the idea in the hopes that your listener will catch on."

"It's a way of lying," Afsoon said, ever the straightforward woman.

"Yes, and that is part of what I am going to talk to you about. I am going to tell you some things, and everything will be the truth. I promise never to lie to you, and I want you to promise me the same thing. The promises we make have great meaning, Afsoon; I want you to know that."

"I trust you Uncle Neal. What is it?"

"Where to begin?... I know you feel deeply about the women's issue. Your experience is almost beyond comprehension for any of us who have not endured or even seen such things. I also know that you hate the governing regime and Islam as it is practiced in Iran, and I could not agree with you more. But I have an even more serious concern. This is the secret I am going to share with you. You know that I work for the intelligence services of the United States, and what I learn has to stay a secret. You must not ever let on to anyone that you know, okay?"

"Yes, Uncle," she said, her mood matching his deadly serious expression.

"I can't tell you how I know, you understand; but the evil regime in Iran has set in motion a detailed plan to make atomic bombs and a long-range delivery system. They will be ready to launch in five or six years, no more than ten. It is my job to see to it that they can't. I am working to interfere with them in every way possible. That is where you come in."

"Me?"

"Yes, Afsoon. You have a unique set of qualities that makes you a perfect weapon to use against them. Frankly, they don't care if people criticize them. They believe their god has ordained them to murder every last unbeliever in their evil construct of Islam, and they intend to do it with nuclear weapons. You may be able to make the most important difference in stopping them. First of all, we have all kinds of electronic surveillance equipment; but we do not have effective people—spies, if you will—on the ground and among them who can get us the information we need and may even be able to sabotage their efforts.

"You are Iranian and know the country and several of its languages better than anyone we know about. You hate them for legitimate reasons; and frankly, that's a good thing, because it is a catalyst that can keep your mind in focus. They must stop harming women. They must stop murdering innocents by supporting terrorism. And—most important—they must never get their hands on a nuclear weapon. They will plunge the world into World War III if they do. You are a genius. You can learn nuclear physics, nuclear engineering, and computer science enough to be able to infiltrate their research and development system and hopefully disrupt it."

"How, I'm just a girl? What do I know about how to do all of that?"

"Afsoon, that is one of the things I like best about you. You are humble and teachable. You have the brains; we just have to fill them up with the information you need. I have resources beyond your imagination and can make you an undisputed expert—an expert the Iranian government will not be able to resist."

"What would you want me to do ... exactly?"

"That is the perfect question. Let's deal with the answer one step at a time. First—and I know it will be a disappointment to you—I need you to cancel your talk on Iran and its maltreatment of women. We need you not to be on record anywhere as opposing the monsters in Iran. In fact, we want you to begin to pretend—as your cover alter ego—to become radicalized, to support the regime. Afsoon Daastrup doesn't need to do that, as strange as it sounds. We have put into motion a way for you to be a different Afsoon—a new name, a new history, a new family, a new education—in short, to have a cover story that the Iranians will never be able to unravel. Do you understand the idea of a cover story?"

"I read spy novels and undercover cop books. I understand the idea pretty much, I think."

"Great. That means you will have to learn to act and to learn your cover story so well that it is real for you. If you are questioned, your answers will be perfectly believable, and we will make them supportable. We have four or five years to do that. You will need to begin at once to lead two lives—one as Afsoon Daastrup, lovely young coed working on her major in mathematics and nuclear engineering, and the other as Afsoon Mouradipour, a California Jewish girl who—despite all of her family's hopes and dreams—becomes radicalized and aspires to go back to help her former homeland develop its ultimate weapon against the unbelievers—the corrupt and decadent West."

Afsoon reacted with a contemplative silence. She was being faced with a profound life-changing existential choice. It was too much for anyone to ask of her; it was unfair. To this point, she had not spent much time in self-pity; but she had suffered the agonies of hell at the hands of the religion and the government of Iran. She had—by a miracle named Brenda Daastrup—escaped from the land of misery and fear to a place of calm, safety, and joy. To ask her to leave all of that wonderful life and possibly return to live for a time in the Islamic Republic of Iran was the height of cruelty.

On the other hand, Afsoon was consumed with hatred and a profound desire to get revenge. Two years ago, she would have been content to limit her revenge to a brutal retaliation against Ahriman, Fereshten, and Hassanzadeh Shakibaie, Imam Ali Abedi and the black shrouded women who held her down for the FGM, the jailors at Piranshahr prison, and the Dashnaksutyun bandits. Now, she was being offered the chance—supported by the most powerful nations in the world—to wreak a soul-satisfying vengeance on the regime and the very religion that had been the architects of her suffering. And—beyond her own trials and limited satisfaction at getting her revenge—she would be able to make women free in a world where they could not be free owing to the presence in their lives of the religion of Islam.

The crisis of conscience being faced by this sensitive girl of tender years was not lost on Adm. Neal Daastrup, nor was he unsympathetic. His own moral qualms were set aside, however, because the geopolitical issues at stake were more important than his own, Afsoon's, or any individual's personal needs.

Afsoon tightened her lips.

"I'll try," Afsoon said with careful and deliberate determination.

With that, Neal knew he had her. For the next hour, he explained the main elements of the DIA's and the Mossad's plans for her. The last part of his presentation was to have her agree to meet Gideon Emmanuel Rothsberger IV the following week to begin her new educational enterprise.

40

CHAPTER SIX

Harvard University Nuclear Engineering Building, Room 181, 33 Oxford Street, Cambridge, Massachusetts, February 28, 1999.

Afsoon and Gideon communicated by telephone—pay phones—several times to facilitate her acceptance as a full-fledged member of the Harvard/MIT committee on the global future of peaceful nuclear energy power production. It was an immediate goal of Gideon to give them an excuse to meet occasionally and apparently accidentally or for other purposes than for playing the spy game to have her be involved in similar projects as his. The involvement of Afsoon's school, Georgetown University, posed no problem because it had a mutually beneficial arrangement with Harvard on several levels, including nuclear physics and nuclear engineering. It was something of a greater stretch to convince the arrangements committee of the symposium to put her on the program, since she was only an undergraduate student. He was able to get her an appointment with the project vice chairman, and he and Afsoon stayed up nights prepping her for questions on everything to do with nuclear energy production. The effort paid off, and Afsoon Daastrup was taken on as an intern whose assignments were more than just running errands and serving coffee.

Gideon's coup was to get Afsoon a brief spot on the project's symposium designed to launch the new program. The program was set to begin the following day, and Afsoon was scheduled to give her presentation on the day after as one of the last speakers. Lesser lights in university programs are given the last or next to the last slot on the agenda when most of the attendees have departed for work or home. Afsoon was, at least, not last—she was third to the last. It was a start anyway.

41

The two of them prepared a paper, largely written by Gideon; and Afsoon chafed at the idea of someone else doing her intellectual work. She rationalized that it was for the good of the cause, and she was willing to bide her time. Gideon chose the topic of his former research into computer science algorithms as they applied to banking statistics and planning. He and Afsoon worked out a program related to taking the group's project to the countries of the Middle-East, and particularly to Iran. The clincher for the two of them and for the chairperson and the symposium director was Afsoon's direct personal knowledge about Iran, Islam, several of the Iranian languages, and the nuts and bolts of nuclear engineering. The latter came largely as a result of the fact that both of them had a rigid work ethic, and Afsoon had a brain that was nearly equal to Gideon's. He gave her full credit for that and willingly pushed her as hard as either of them could tolerate. She was ready before the time for her talk, but barely.

§§§§§

Gideon lectured to a packed house. Part of the attraction was curiosity about what a young man not yet twenty years of age could have to say to a roomful of the world's foremost experts in the production of nuclear energy and the financial considerations that the young man was to insist would see a profit for investors in twenty years. In the lectures preceding Gideon's, distinguished speakers outlined practical arguments that this nuclear engineering technology should be considered a crucial option for the United States and the world to meet future energy needs. The nuclear option was outlined as a preference to the status quo because of its increased efficiency, renewable energy sources—some 20,000 years of use just from the raw sources in the United States alone. Carbon sequestration options were included in the package as an adjunct to the nuclear option so that a successful greenhouse gas management strategy could save the planet and its people.

Gideon's lecture was addressed to government, industry, financial, and academic leaders. Speaking both as a Ph.D. in nuclear engineering and as a major banking executive, he discussed the complexities of the interrelated technical, economic, environmental, and political challenges of a worldwide cooperative effort. His take-away thesis was that the world was facing an eventual failure to provide the energy sources required to maintain even the current level of energy use. Nuclear energy—established on an efficient and cooperative global basis—would solve the problems. However, an all-out effort on the part of developed nations would be necessary to overcome the present hurdles of environmentalists' success in thwarting progress by ramping up the legal and political impediments to establishment of new plants. He presented a detailed program for manufacture of new plants and maintenance of all current and future plants to keep them both safe and efficient. He admitted that proponents of nuclear energy faced a significant uphill series of skirmishes to bring about an increase in global nuclear power utilization over the next fifty years and beyond.

Some came to scoff at the temerity of an adolescent presuming to lecture his betters. Some came to find the flaws in his and the rest of the lecturers' reasoning. Others—the environmentalists—came to the symposium as avowed enemies of nuclear energy. Gideon's answer to them was that the nuclear option of energy production should be advanced precisely because it is an important carbon-free source of power; and its dangers to the world were—by history—miniscule in comparison to the benefits to the earth and its population. However dubious they were when they entered the lecture hall, all of the attendees left with the impression that having fresh leadership in the world of nuclear engineering and finance might well make the difference, and that Gideon Rothsberger was going to be one of those leaders.

Afsoon's lecture lacked the wide appeal of Gideon's and of the other recognized stars of the nuclear energy world. It was not intended to be the object of acclaim to such a wide world. She limited her discussion and proposal to the Middle-East market, and particularly to Iran. Afsoon spoke to the delegation from the Islamic Republic as if her talk was for them alone. She was flagrant in her praise of the progress seen since the 1979 revolution, and the Iranian delegation conveyed in glowing terms back to the flattery-loving leadership of the country the importance of developing nuclear energy production throughout the nation. The religious leadership was well ahead of their delegation on that conclusion.

There was no need for the Western restrictions and impediments; the Supreme Leader could whisk them away with a sweep of his hand. Afsoon gave salient portions of her lecture in Farsi and in Arabic to underscore the interest the Harvard/MIT committee and the world's financial giants had in doing business with Tehran.

In the Supreme Leader's office at the Pasteur Street residence, the delegation's reports were enthusiastically received—particularly the information that funding could be obtained without compromising the tenets of the revolution—and this Iranian girl named Afsoon was discussed seriously as a person to bring back into the revolutionary fold. Agha Rahimi assigned the task of recruiting this girl—this rising Iranian star—to the revolutionary cause to a joint task force co-chaired by Moqtada al-Benizir, head of the Atomic Energy Organization of Iran (AEOI), and Behrouz Omidi, director of the Ministry of Intelligence and National Security of the Islamic Republic of Iran (MISIRI) or VEVAK. The first problem for their recruitment was going to be to learn her family name and where they lived. In their haste, the Iranian delegation to the conference had failed to gain any more information than that her given name was Afsoon, and that she was an expert in nuclear engineering.

The day after Afsoon's talk, and after they had a little while to cool down from the stress of the preparation and delivery of their crucially important talks, Gideon finally broached the subject of the spying they were about to add to their already complicated lives. They were sitting in one of Neal Daastrup's safe houses in Boston to throw off any potential watchers from the hostile world.

First, Gideon and Afsoon set up a schedule for him to tutor her in a crash course in advanced nuclear physics, related computer science, nuclear engineering, and the economics of building nuclear facilities. Much of the tutelage would take place in secure rooms at Rothsberger & Company Bankers where Gideon was now a senior vice-president. Then, he got down to the elements of the clandestine work they were going to do.

"Afsoon, your uncle, Neal, and some of his friends have asked me to talk to you about the overall plan to infiltrate the Iranian nuclear industry without raising suspicion. Are you okay with the idea?"

"Neal told me a little. It involved a family in California named Mouradipour. I'm okay with what I've heard so far."

"All right, let me fill you in on a few details. The important people in the project that is now called the Iran Nuclear Interdiction Project—including little you and me—are going to meet with the Mouradipour family sometime in June. This is what we are going to ask of them and you."

He laid out the plan in considerable detail, but stressed that it was still in the formative stage; and everyone involved with it would have to be able to be flexible. Afsoon was willing but still keeping a measure of reserve to be sure that her own interests were not completely eclipsed as the great Iran Nuclear Interdiction Project swept over them all.

CHAPTER SEVEN

Chancery of the Embassy of Sweden, 2900 K St NW, Washington, D.C., June 18, 1999.

The Chancery of the Embassy of Sweden is in House of Sweden located at the intersection of Rock Creek and the Potomac River in Georgetown. The ambassador, Jonas Zillacus, was selected by the Swedish government because of his extensive trade and economic relationships with the United States and despite his misgivings—bordering on outright hostility—towards the military adventurism of America. He especially disagreed with the overt antagonism emanating from the United States towards the Muslim world—lately so actively aimed at the Islamic Republic of Iran. That was one reason why Adm. Neal Daastrup chose the House of Sweden to be his site for clandestine meetings about his project to interdict any and all plans of Iran to export terrorism and its nuclear development program. It was highly unlikely that any Muslim nation—including Iran—would suspect that a Swedish embassy could be a hotbed of hostile intrigue against them or their enterprises.

The other reason was Ali Nylander, the consular agent in charge of trade and economic affairs. Ali was the Swedish official with the most comprehensive knowledge of Swedish interests as they related to economic and trade policy of the United States. He served as the Swede in charge of the links between Sweden, the World Bank, and the Inter-American Development Bank. He had two other attributes that made him the perfect partner for Neal Daastrup. Firstly, he was by nature a soldier having served two hitches in the Armed Forces Intelligence and Security Centre [*FMUndSäkC*], a training and development center for national and international intelligence and security services within the Swedish Armed Forces before entering the diplomatic service.

Secondly—as Ali's first name implied—he had a family history with Iran. His paternal grandparents were from Isfahan, Iran, and had been driven out of the country along with the many professionals who were employed by the Shah when the Islamist regime took over the country and elected to decimate the ranks of the educated. That alone would have engendered ill-will on the part of the Jobrani family, but the facts that their entire life's savings held in Iranian banks had been stolen from them by the holy Grand Ayatollah Khomeini and his minions; and as a parting gesture, Grandmother Maryam—a sheltered and protected woman of fifty-five—had been taken to Evin prison where she was raped because she was a Christian.

Iran is a relatively large Middle-Eastern country—slightly larger than Alaska. Although it is located in the Middle-East, Iran historically has had much in common with European culture. The original inhabitants of Iran were Indo-Europeans, or Aryans, and the linguistic roots of Farsi are the same as the roots of English, German, Spanish, Latin, and French. Over centuries, there has been a large cultural exchange and mutual influence with Europe, especially under the Shah. Many familial and business alliances were established. Making good use of the Jobrani family's contacts, Maryam and Kourosh made it to Sweden where they prospered. Their eldest daughter married a Swedish diplomat named Petter Nylander. To please the grandparents and his wife, Petter permitted the name of his firstborn to be Ali.

A powerful legacy of hatred persisted within the Jobrani family, but it was not spoken about outside the close family because of Sweden's antipathy regarding America's attitudes towards Muslim terrorists—a term not used in polite Swedish society. To have expressed such an attitude would have resulted in failure for Ali's budding diplomatic career, and he held his peace—with the exception of confiding in his friend, Neal Daastrup, one evening when both were in their cups. It turned out that Ali knew several like-minded Swedes in the embassy who were not averse to aiding certain American enterprises that were not approved by the Swedish government.

Adm. Daastrup got off the metro at the Foggy Bottom Metro Station with the hordes of tourists and demonstrators coming into the city for the first gay rights demonstration on the Mall. Three or four hundred thousand supporters of same-sex marriage were expected to pack the area by ten a.m.; and already, the police presence was massive. Neal flowed with the sea of people as he made his twenty-five minute walk—which should have been only fifteen—to the Swedish embassy. By prearrangement with Ali Nylander, he was able to enter the compound through an obscure rear entrance. The craggy-faced blond guard checked his identification and admitted him. His bodyguards and their guns were given comfortable seats in the guardhouse and were politely and carefully watched while their boss went inside. At the door of the chancery, Ali met Neal; and they exchanged hearty handshakes.

Ali's genes apparently had come from his father's side since he looked more Swedish than the imposing white-haired fifty-three-year-old king of Sweden, Carl Gustaf Folke Hubertus [Carl XVI Gustaf].

"Hi, and welcome, Neal. We've set aside a room—actually one of the corporate apartments in the Icelandic section—down the hall from my office; and on this chaotic day no one will pay any attention to our cloak-and-dagger shenanigans; and there won't be any log-ins or other records."

"Thanks for everything, Ali. I wouldn't have put you in a compromising position if it was not so important."

"I know, and I'm glad to help. Let's meet the others."

Like the rest of the chancery, the room was crisp and efficient—no frills or flounces. There was a gorgeous view of the Potomac waterfront, and an assortment of the handsome uncomfortable wood furniture for which Sweden is famous. There was a small blond wood coffee table but no conference table or any other accoutrements of an office. The Embassy of Sweden in Washington, D.C. is one of the largest Swedish legations in the world. The Chancery—The House of Sweden—is owned and managed by the Kingdom of Sweden through the National Property Board and consists of the Embassy of Sweden, the Embassy of Iceland, and nineteen corporate apartments.

There were four other Swedish diplomats already seated in the room. Ali made introductions.

"Ladies and gentlemen, let me introduce Admiral Neal Daastrup, the deputy director of the Defense Intelligence Agency of the United States. Everyone calls him 3D."

The assemblage nodded their welcome.

"Neal, this is Dr. Arvid Bergström, counselor for Swedish defense—mainly an information service here in the embassy—and is the liaison hub between Swedish and U.S. defense authorities."

Neal and Arvid shook hands.

"This is Counselor Ms. Sanna Kullberg, special advisor, Homeland Security Affairs; this is Mr. Magnus Bielvenstram, minister-counselor, Trade and Economic Affairs; and this fine looking young man is Johannes Hjerdstadt—I think—he is the undersecretary for embassy affairs—whatever that is. Everyone knows that his real bosses are in the *FMUndSäkC*. We don't talk about that," he said with a conspiratorial smile.

Neal smiled back and shook everyone's hands.

Ali went on, "Everyone here is aware that we are on touchy ground, and knows at least that it has to do with our friendly counterparts in Iran. Neal, I trust all of these people as I would my own father. We are here to help, and we don't divulge secrets."

"Good enough for me, Ali. Ladies and gentlemen, for a number of purposes, let's keep our communications to first names. I won't telephone you directly. All of us will need untraceable satellite world phones. I will need all of the numbers, but you each should know only mine and Ali's for the sake of security. I will sometimes send a coded message to the main embassy e-mail—ambassaden.washington@gov.se—using only your first name; so, be on the lookout for something related to the project I am about to divulge. After today, I will keep communications on a need-to-know basis. That way, you can never divulge anything you don't know. Not to be melodramatic, but the Iranian VEVAK are as nasty as people get; and the secrecy is for your protection as well as for the success of the enterprise we call the Iran Nuclear Interdiction Project."

Everyone nodded their understanding.

"I don't need to tell you that the world would be in peril by the Iranians having offensive nuclear capability. You are all aware of the suggestions swirling around in the media that Iran may or may not have peaceful nuclear capability, and they may or may not have a program to develop atomic weapons. I know—from our most reliable sources—that Rahimi's regime is well on its way to perfect a nuclear program and to bring it operational. They are spending a fortune that is—to some degree—impoverishing their people in order to get the raw materials, to bring in the necessary sophisticated equipment, to build a secure facility, and last, but not least, to attract expert nuclear scientists and engineers to push the work forward. That is where you all come in. We need your help to embed an expert who can pass every test they throw at him or her. Would that it was different, but we have only one candidate; and we need the assistance of the Swedish people to make her as genuine as it is possible for an agent to be."

"Aren't you nervous about having all of us know about her, Neal?" asked Johannes.

"Not to the extent that I am going to share—again on a need-to-know-basis, Johannes. And most importantly, I trust you; and the United States trusts you as friends even if Zillacus has a public front disagreeing with almost

48

everything the U.S. does in its relationship with the misunderstood governments of the Middle-East."

There was a careful knowing laugh among the occupants of the room.

"I won't keep you all day. We will leave the details until another day. In fact, although I have the agreement of the prospective agent, I have yet to contact the main people who can make this happen. Their agreement is crucial; and I am confident that I can get it; but I have to admit that—in this case—failure is a possibility.

"Her name is Afsoon. She is a former Iranian national who now resides elsewhere. If everything pans out, several of you will meet her in person. For her own reasons, she has a personal stake in bringing down the evil regime and to prevent them from gaining the power of life-and-death over much of the world that they would have with the possession of nuclear weapons to use as an extortionate club to leverage their neighbors, to threaten Israel, and to put all of us in peril.

"Afsoon has some very remarkable attributes: she is young but a certified genius and is presently on the fast track to become a real expert in theoretical physics, computer science, and nuclear engineering. She knows the country and speaks several Iranian languages with fluency; and as I alluded before, she is a determined—albeit clandestine—enemy of the Rahimi regime and Iranian brand of Islamic justice and terrorism."

Surmising what a young Iranian girl must have been through to become so opposed to the regime and sympathetic to her, Sanna Kullberg asked, "What do you want us to do?"

"I thought you would never ask," Neal smiled. "We want two things: Firstly, we are working on an elaborate cover identity for her, one VEVAK cannot break, and won't even suspect. We intend to have nice American girl, Afsoon, be radicalized and to have to seek asylum in the more friendly atmosphere of Europe, most notably Sweden. We need you to move her—or rather her alter ego's—application for Swedish citizenship along as efficiently and quickly as possible. Secondly, we need her to be independently wealthy in her own right, and to have unimpeachable credentials in the nuclear power world—again, especially in Sweden—and to be a real power in both the financial and the technical side of nuclear power production, despite her youth. That is where you come in, Magnus. Lastly, in the end, this will be a military intelligence operation and may turn into a limited and targeted military operation in conjunction with the Israelis. That is where we will need you throughout the planning, analyzing, and facilitating phases, Arvid and Johannes."

49

"All right," said Ali, "but you know we can't ever have it known that Sweden is involved."

"I most certainly do," Neal said, "and it is the last thing on earth I want to become public knowledge or for the Iranians to have the slightest inkling about. I know you are busy; so, I will take off. I will be in touch with specifics as the need arises. Thank you in advance for your help."

Ali said, "Yeah, we have a big day; this afternoon—despite all the hullabaloo going on at the Mall—we Swedes are going to hold our fourth annual VASA Bike Race to advertise Sweden's legendary Vasaloppet ski race. The embassy—together with Washington Area Bicyclist Association—is going to jump-start the summer season by inviting bikers for the annual race, and we all have to be there. The riders get to choose between 56, 28, or 14 mile routes. All finishers received the traditional blueberry soup in the same cup as the skiers get at the Swedish VASA race—yoo-hoo. It is hot today; and the race will be grueling; we are going to bike around Bethesda, Silver Spring, Rock Creek Park, Georgetown, Chevy Chase, and end up back at the Potomac River. Tonight, the ambassador is holding a party for the new mayor of Minneapolis, the first Swedish American—John Walfriedsson—to become a mayor of a big U.S. city. We are going to have the Swedish House Mafia—a Swedish electronic dance music trio consisting of three house disc jockeys—a group you might not be too familiar with, Neal, as the lead entertainment. Can't you just feel the excitement mounting?"

"I certainly can, Ali; and I hate to have to miss it. But duty calls. Have a great time."

They all laughed, stood up and shook hands again, and went their separate ways with a lot to think about.

CHAPTER EIGHT

Home of Daniel and Esther Mouradipour, 375 Trousdale Place, Beverly Hills, California, June 24, 1999

D r. Daniel Mouradipour sat in his favorite easy chair—upholstered with soft red Moroccan leather—feet up on the well-worn ottoman reading the latest issue of *Heftah Bazaar: A Persian Weekly Magazine* with no particular interest, his mind wandering to the arrival of the expected guests. His wife, Esther, was watching Channel 1 with somewhat more interest. It was beamed from a room above a dentist's office and was only one of the 25 Farsi language television stations in Greater Los Angeles targeting Iran. The subject of the talk show—the ever pressing, omnipresent issue—was the standoff over Iran's nuclear enrichment program, which was followed more closely in the Los Angeles' Iranian-American community—Tehrangeles— than anywhere in the world.

On the panel of the show, the representative of the People's Mujahedeen argued that the many exiles in Tehrangeles and New York should urge Washington to work harder to harness Iranians' widespread frustrations; so, they can force their newly embraced government to change the nuclear crisis— as presented by their lobbyists—and which has garnered some support in the Congress but is seen by many Iranians as an Islamic-Marxist cult. The supporter of the Iran Democracy Project was arguing caution—that the United States, by playing the role of a distant, yet supportive and vocal uncle—could galvanize the younger generation in Iran to widen the fissures in the government and change the country. He was able to argue that recent antigovernment student demonstrations at the Friday prayers at Tehran University were evidence of the success of their methodological war of attrition on the hated

51

regime and urged patience. As the debate did every night, it turned into an acrimonious and, at times, a vociferous and discourteous free-for-all with nothing settled. Esther—unlike her husband—was frustrated that nothing concrete was being accomplished and that the expatriate Iranian movement was being fragmented into an ineffectual debating society entirely comparable to the Cuban expatriate opposition to Fidel Castro's communist regime.

After years of heated arguments, a distinct split emerged within the Persian diaspora throughout the world. A majority opposed any military attack, convinced that it would only cement the mullahs and ayatollahs in power and repeat the chaos that occurred in Iraq on a far bloodier scale. People in that group pushed for a rather subtle approach that they hoped would collapse the repressive government of the Islamic Republic from within. They fretted aloud that subtle diplomacy had become a lost art in Washington.

Others considered the talk about diplomacy as no more than idle dithering. They advocated a more aggressive approach on a continuum from using the vast wealth of expatriate Iranians to defeat the Iranian government's commercial efforts to outright subversion of the economy; and finally, there were firebrands who wanted to supply armed commando and sabotage units to destabilize the country. The most extreme advocates of action were not averse to mounting a terror campaign on the order of the one being practiced by Hamas and Hezbollah against the West.

Esther was interrupted by the insistent buzzing of the gate security alarm. Daniel nodded to her to answer over the intercom and to open the electronic locking system to the gated architectural estate from the comfort of her chair by pushing a button. Esther got up to investigate to be on the safe side. There were two new black suburbans parked in front of the wrought iron gates of the entrance, which was not particularly unusual given the importance of the people with whom Daniel did business. Esther nodded at Daniel.

"Go, ahead, dear. It's them," Daniel said.

"I certainly hope so. They look like some very serious men to me."

They were speaking their at-home language, Dzhidi (Judæo-Persian).

She pushed the button to open the gates and said, "Come in, please," over the intercom.

The suburbans drove up to the front door and parked in the oval driveway with their fronts pointed back at the street. Six powerful looking men stepped out and inspected the area then walked to the second vehicle and stood around it. One man stood on each side of the closed suburban and opened the car's doors. Three middle-aged men, a young man, and a young woman, stepped out and were escorted to the front door of the house. Before they could ring the doorbell, the doors were opened by a pair of liveried servants; and they were admitted into the imposing entry hall.

"Good morning, and welcome," said the master of the house and offered his hand. "I am David Mouradipour, and this is my wife Esther."

The newcomers all shook hands with the Mouradipours, and Neal introduced everyone, "Mr. and Mrs. Mouradipour, I am Neal Daastrup. We talked on the phone. And this is Gen. Zwi Rosenstein of the Israeli Defense Forces; this is Ali Nylander of the Swedish diplomatic corps; this young man is Gideon Emanuel Rothsberger IV, a senior vice-president of Rothsberger & Company Bankers; and this beautiful young Iranian girl is Afsoon Daastrup. As time goes on, we will talk a great deal more about her."

The Mouradipours were pleased to see Gideon in his yarmulke and were particularly impressed with the stately beautiful Iranian girl.

"*Naeaam lahaker outcha*," [Hebrew: Pleased to meet you], Mr. and Mrs. Mouradipour," Gideon said.

The Mouradipours were very pleased to hear the mellifluous language of their beloved religion.

"*Az didare shoma khosh vaqtam*" [Farsi: I am most pleased to meet you], Mr. and Mrs. Mouradipour," Afsoon said.

The Mouradipours replied with genuine happy smiles to hear the language of their native country from a new guest. Gideon's and Afsoon's replies broke the ice.

Ali also replied in Farsi, Zwi in Hebrew, and Neal in English and any remaining tension of unfamiliarity for everyone in the room evaporated.

Daniel led them into the spacious sitting room full of handsome Persian furniture and memorabilia, and the floor was covered with antique European Abusson and Savonnerie carpets. Esther left briefly and made tea for everyone and served the hot beverages herself, an unusually familiar gesture in the Mouradipours' home.

When the tea and obligatory pleasantries of nonbusiness chatting dwindled, Daniel came to the point, "Well, Neal, I take it you have more important business to impart than the results of the football game between the league from Beverly Hills and those unprincipled scoundrels from down there in Westwood. Esther and I are on the edge of our seats to learn why such an important delegation should come to our humble home."

"It's complicated; but Daniel and Esther, there are two related ways in which you and your family could be of real help to a cause we think is important to you. It certainly is important to our country. Please believe me when I tell you that we have every desire and intention to respect and to protect your family in the plan I am going to lay out for you. But there is some possibility of risk."

Esther gave her husband a small sidelong glance of concern. He put up his right hand in a soothing gesture.

"So, I will get right into it. First, you know from the start that you do not need to enter into the project at all. You can say no, and that will be the end of it. However, once we present the plan, you will have to sign the official secrets act; and that carries some serious responsibilities and consequences. Daniel and Esther, are you all right for me to proceed?"

Daniel looked at Esther, who nodded.

He spoke for both of them, "Yes."

"You have met Afsoon. That is her real name. It cannot be lost on you that that is the same name as the daughter you lost in infancy in 1980, shortly after you arrived in the United States from Iran after the fall of the Shah. Our Afsoon lived in Iran until she was sixteen. I won't go into all of it, but the religious zealots who run the country and who poison the minds of its people inflicted terrible injuries on Afsoon. As a result, she is willing to aid in the cause of interrupting the march towards nuclear weapon capability sought after by the Supreme Leader and his ... subordinates."

"How do you know that they are working at making nuclear weapons? Here in Tehrangeles, we debate the question endlessly. I was watching a program as you pulled up to the house just this morning where the question came up again. President Shahamatdoost has said over and over that their intentions for nuclear energy are peaceful, only peaceful," Esther said, almost pleadingly.

Daniel said, "And they don't allow the IAEA in for a full inspection."

"I can't tell you how I know. That is a top secret piece of information that men have died to get and to protect our source. But believe me, it is so—Iran is well on its way to building nuclear weapons of mass destruction. We are here because they must be stopped, and you can play a key role in that effort."

"Who are we that we have all of a sudden become so important?" Daniel asked.

"You are expatriates from Iran in its worst days. You have come to the United States; and like the majority of your fellow escapees, you have done extremely well. You are a world renowned professor of obstetrics and gyne-cology. The two of you contribute heavily to Iranian causes including sending money to well-vetted charities in Iran. Make no mistake; they keep track of such things. Ob-gyn is a much neglected specialty, and there is a crying need for experts to go to Iran to help. You have never been a public critic of the regime since you came to Los Angeles to live."

"We are terrified of the VEVAK. We know they send agents to assassinate dissidents here. We have friends who have learned that to their dismay."

"If you agree to help us, we will assign secret agents to augment your personal security. We are at the point now where I can't go forward unless you sign the official secrets act. It is simple: will you help in the project and keep its secrets under penalty of treason, or will you stop now; and we will be on our way with no hard feelings."

"We will sign. The ayatollahs ruined our beloved homeland. They raped our wives and daughters, and they drove Persia back to the ninth century. They export terrorism all over the world. Do you think there is a Jew living that is not aware of the horrors they have perpetrated against us? If we can be of service to our country, save a Persian woman or a jew, and rid the world of their nuclear madness, we will do whatever we can."

This time, Daniel did not look at Esther. He assumed his patriarchal role, and his word was final. In any case, Esther was in full agreement—her father, now dead, was a general under the former Shah, protected after the revolution by family members connected to the new Islamic government. She had a great deal to bring to the table, and with that, a history of serious experience with the infighting at the top of Iranian society. Neal handed the papers to the Mouradipours, who signed them with alacrity.

Neal continued, "The plan is this: you allow us to use your daughter's name as a cover for our Afsoon here. That will mean that we have to invent childhood experiences that could have happened but didn't. She will have to have gone to Beverly Hills High and to have excelled. She will have had to be one of the valedictorians, a National Merit Scholar, and a mathematics prodigy. She will need a different birth certificate—one that has her living to the present day. She will need a driver's license and a passport that has been current since she became twelve. She will have a social security card, work credentials, graduation certificates, and everything else that will make her be alive and active today. We can do all of that for you. The certificates will be genuine.

"You and the rest of your family will have to be in on the secret and will have to memorize the cover story with all of its invented memories and accomplishments so that no one will ever slip up. You are right about the VEVAK; they will come, probably as wolves in sheep's clothing, but they will come. We will all have to be patient; this will take years; but Afsoon's cover story must be unimpeachable. You will have to be consummate actors in a most serious drama."

"You are a lovely girl, Afsoon. I hope you will come to think of us as your family as you play your role," Esther said to Afsoon, who had remained quiet throughout the presentation.

"Thank you, Esther, you are most kind."

"Afsoon must have memories, real ones. She needs to live with you for months at a time, attend school in California and graduate from Berkeley with honors. She is brilliant and can do her part, but she lacked schooling in her early years. You will have to take her to meet family, friends, business people, and members of the active Iranian community. She will have to become more Persian Jewish than the rabbi. She will have to see and to feel people, places, things, and events to be able to recall them without difficulty. She will be the star actress because she will have to be Afsoon Mouradipour in all respects. The VEVAK will question her one day, and she cannot reveal the slightest crack in her cover. It will cost this girl her life, and probably yours."

"We will help. Our family will help. Tell us what to do, and we will do it. Our hatred for the monsters in Iran who have perverted our entire homeland is boundless. We are only too happy to help to bring them down," said Daniel.

"Now comes the first of the hard parts. It would be expected that you and your family would hate the authors of the Islamic revolution with every fiber of your being. But your daughter, Afsoon, must be something of a rebel. She must convert to Islam in a mosque with radical sympathies and must become radicalized herself. We have set in motion a plan for her to go to Sweden with a lot of other liberals and semi-radicals and to establish herself there as a zealot hijab-wearing woman who despises Western Civilization. She will be a woman who has intentionally immersed herself in nuclear physics and engineering studies in the hope that one day, she will be discovered and will be able to go to Iran as one of the new order, determined to bring down the West and bring Persia back to its former glory. She can make history by assisting to make a bomb that will annihilate the Jews of Israel and to purify the Muslim world throughout the Middle-East."

Daniel and Esther shuddered, but nodded their understanding and acceptance.

"The second of the hard parts is, of course, what she will really be doing is throwing a monkey-wrench into their nuclear works at a strategic point in the developmental process—and hopefully before they have a functional and deliverable weapon. You will need to help her in active ways that carry some danger. Dr. Mouradipour, you can become a contributor to Iranian causes, especially by helping to build an obstetrical and gynecological system to train new doctors and nurses in real science unhampered by their religious

56

nonsense. Some steps are already underway under the aegis of some liberal European governments, businesses, and charities. We want you to travel to Tehran with a delegation from Sweden and to link up with physicians there to further the work. It so happens that there are some Persian Jews who have rejected Israel and have remained faithful Iranians who support the revolutionary regime. Some of them are not quite what they seem, and they are prepared to help all they can. The Mossad has established agents among them; they are called the *Sayanim*. I am sure you are familiar with the term. You have had a lot to absorb today, and Gen. Zwi Rosenstein of the Israeli Defense Forces will return tomorrow to meet with you and a few very select members of the Tehrangeles synagogues who are willing to help you meet the right people and to learn enough tradecraft to convey messages and the like while remaining undetected and safe."

He nodded at Zwi, who gave a small hand sign to the Mouradipours.

"The last thing today is to let our poor patient Ali have his say. He is helping in ways that his government would not approve. I will let him explain his role, then we will let you have a rest. It is a lot to take in in one day."

Ali took the lead and explained the Swedish role in the Iran Nuclear Interdiction Project. Using his contacts, Ali would have Swedish passports, visas, identification papers and fake school credentials—all entirely authentic—made for Afsoon. She would have naturalization papers that made her a dual citizen of Sweden and America and passport stamps that show her as a world traveler as a Swedish citizen for the purpose of pursuing her education and for lecturing on nuclear energy issues. Ali was clear, concise, and to the point. He offered Daniel and Esther the opportunity to ask questions, but they had none. They were making a real effort to take it all in, and finding that they would need more time to absorb the details and to make the life-changing adjustments that these spies were requiring of them.

When the three men left, they promised to get back in touch soon. Afsoon was invited to stay and to start her life as part of the family and to learn all there was to learn about life as a Persian Jewess transplanted to Beverly Hills and Tehrangeles.

CHAPTER NINE

Tehrangeles, and Beverly Hills, California, June 24, 1999

The expatriate Persian subculture in the United States is a close-knit interrelated people with a diversity of religions and ethnicities—Muslim, Christian, and Jewish. The closeness and cooperation is intensified the more narrow the focus. The Persian Jewish community is particularly tightly intertwined owing to their history of persecution in Iran, the difficult circumstances that brought them out of the country over the past century, and the uniquely successful culture that has evolved. The diaspora resulting from the 1979 Islamic revolution in Iran particularly brought an educated, skilled, successful, and cohesive people to America by the thousands, where their numbers increased several fold and where they flourished. On the west coast, the result has been the establishment of what has come to be known as Tehrangeles or Irangeles. That title has been loosely applied to the wider Iranian/American culture; the usage of the terms have become so common that they are generally taken to refer to the larger Persian-American subset of Iranian immigrants, many of whom are now second and even third generation American citizens and are proud to be full-fledged, flag-waving Americans. The local Los Angeles Persian area center has been officially recognized by the City of Los Angeles as "Persian Square."

When Afsoon and her spymasters came to visit the Mouradipours, the United States was home to nearly 80,000 Iranian Jews, most of whom have settled in the Greater Los Angeles area and in Great Neck, New York. Those in metropolitan Los Angeles settled largely in the affluent Westside cities of Beverly Hills, Santa Monica, the Los Angeles Westside neighborhoods of Brentwood, Westwood, and West L.A., and the San Fernando Valley communities of Tarzana and Encino. A third of the student body of Beverly Hills High School was of Persian origin.

The area is recognizable by its Persian businesses and Farsi language signs along Westwood Boulevard in South Westwood—"Little Persia" or Persian Square—where the Persian community originally gathered. The epicenter of Persian life—at least in California—has remained in the Westwood neighborhood—between Pico Boulevard and the edge of the campus of UCLA. On the wider map, it is between Beverly Hills and West Los Angeles. The area is full of uniquely Persian shops and restaurants, Persian media including magazines, newspapers, radio, and television stations. Iranians make up at least a fifth of the resident population of Beverly Hills, and the large majority of them are Jewish. Along many streets throughout Tehrangeles, almost every sign is in Persian. In Greater Los Angeles, there are more than 300,000 people of Persian extraction, of which nearly 30,000 are Jewish. There are only about 87,000 Jews left in all of Iran. By some estimates, there are almost two million Iranians living in the United States.

Neon signs in Persian decorate the windows of the Tehrangeles Markets. "Kabob" may glow in bright red, "Iranian Market" in intense green, and "Persian Emporium or Persian Restaurant" in a rainbow of colors. This corner could as well be in Tehran as Brooklyn Heights could be a part of Mexico. Restaurants advertise an enticing blend of Persian and Middle-Eastern flavors—beef tongue sandwiches, kabobs, polo, stews, and desserts like saffron and rose ice cream.

At the Encino Town Center, two of six movie screens show Iranian movies. Young educated Persian adults—many of them students at UCLA and USC— pack cafes—beckoning to them in both English and Persian where they can smoke water pipes and debate long into the night. The Ketab Bookshop in Westwood is a nightly hub for intense discussions on sanctions versus military action against Tehran.

Nowhere else in the United States is the standoff over Iran's nuclear enrichment program followed more closely than in Los Angeles's Iranian-American community. It is impossible to avoid hearing snippets of animated conversation on the subject during a leisurely stroll along Westwood Boulevard. The nuclear crisis—which gets scant attention elsewhere—has prompted many exiles, as individuals or as organized groups, to urge the government in Washington to work harder to harness Iranians' widespread frustrations. The aim—whatever the philosophy espoused by the disparate elements of the expatriate community—is to force the government to change its apparently lackadaisical disinterest in the subject that is so intense in Persian Square.

Groups as different in approach as the People's Mujahedeen have received some tacit support in Congress, but the Mujahedeen is seen by many Iranians as an Islamic-Marxist cult and lacks widespread support or influence. Supporters of the Iran Democracy Project wish to see a more interested American government but only want the United States to play a role of a distant, but supportive and vocal uncle that could galvanize the younger generation in Iran to widen the fissures in the Islamic government there and to bring about real change in the country. No one in Tehrangeles or in the diaspora of people of Iranian extraction wants to see a calamitous all-our war between the United States and Iran. They fear the extremism of the ruling body of Islamic Iran because they might just set the spark off.

The wealthy family, business associates, and co-religionists of the Mouradipours were of a decidedly more proactive bent in comparison to many other interested Persian groups, in large part owing to their keen memories of what they consider to be fringe Islamic extremists' overthrow of the legitimate government of Iran, the imposition of a radical and iron-fisted Islamic cultural philosophy that dominates the peoples' lives, and the flagrant persecution of the Jews. For that reason, when David Mouradipour discreetly asked the Persian Jews of influence from around the country to come to Tehrangeles for a serious gathering that might make a difference in the status quo, they came willingly and in secret.

The Mouradipour nuclear family arrived on June 26 to stay for a week at the family mansion. They were the first to meet Afsoon and to learn of her mission. Daniel and Esther had insisted that the family and their most trusted friends be made part of the project to upset the Iranian nuclear timetable. Their argument was cogent—the project would not work without the worldwide contacts of the Persian Jewish community of the diaspora, and the vested interests of their close confidants would prevent dispersion of the knowledge of the plan to the wrong persons or groups. Neal and Zwi had reluctantly agreed, and a meeting was set in the Hebrew school in Persian Square for the twenty-eighth.

During the four days following the first meeting of the Mouradipour patriarch and matriarch, Esther took Afsoon all around the Jewish world of Tehrangeles. Gideon Rothsberger took a week's leave of absence from the bank and joined the two women so that Esther could feel confident in the wide security screen that enveloped the courageous young woman from Iran. It was also important for Gideon to get to know the cover identity—Afsoon Mouradipour—and the visual and human elements of her life.

The tour was not particularly about seeing great synagogues, statues, or impressive libraries. Rather, it was an immersion in street life, the kind of things that might be asked of Afsoon or even of Gideon when a VEVAK agent tested her cover story. They sauntered along having brief conversations with Esther's friends in the Elat Market on west Pico and the Amiri Travel Service on Westwood Boulevard. They sampled tidbits at the Falafel King Restaurant on Broxton Avenue, and at the Charlie Kabob on Pico. They enjoyed tiny cups of *kahvaye turk* coffee at the Zinio Cafe on Westwood. It was thick, strong, and only semi-sweet. It was served hot in a small steaming cup, and it was expected that everyone drink it down in one scalding swallow because that was the custom in Iran. The three "locals" walked through the Damoka Persian Rug Center and had tea and biscuits with the owner. He was enthusiastic for Esther to see his new selections of Persian, Indian Agra, Turkish Oushak, Chinese Peking, Caucasian, antique European Abusson and Savonnerie carpets, and tapestries. Esther assured him that she would come back when she had more time to consider purchases.

At each stop, she took the risk of introducing Afsoon as her daughter who was off to school at Berkeley. Since the people they were encountering were largely acquaintances rather than intimates, no eyebrows were raised about what could have been a surprise daughter as might be seen on a silly American daytime soap opera. Knowing nothing of Farsi or any other Persian language or the written Persian or Perso-Arabic, which is based on the Arabic script, Gideon appreciated the occasional respite from the pervasive Persian when they encountered on Pico-Robertson, Persian grocers who sold almost everything, from groceries to electronics to music and movies—all with a distinctive Persian accent. Throughout the day on every street, the store aisles were lined with the carts being pushed by fervent shoppers. At least some of the business signs in this strictly observant neighborhood were written "glatt kosher" in English in conjunction with the larger size Farsi lettering; so, Gideon did not have to feel like a child being dragged around by his mother holding his hand.

They took a taxi into the heart of Los Angeles to see the La Brea Tar Pits and a new synagogue, Ohr HaShalom, popularly known as the Downtown Synagogue, and the Hollywood Temple Beth-El was known by locals as the "Temple to the Stars." The sun was beginning to descend towards the horizon when they made a stop at the Laemmle Music Hall in Beverly Hills, which was to be part of Afsoon's cover, because Afsoon Mouradipour's favorite movies—featured Farsi-language films—are often the day's fare. They spent considerable time walking around and through the Nessah Synagogue, the largest traditional Persian Jewish congregation in the United States. The center—located in the heart of Beverly Hills—keeps the traditions and customs of Iranian Jews according to Orthodox, Sephardic Halacha as practiced in Iran. The Nessah Educational and Cultural Center is popular among Persian Jews who observe the traditional form of Judaism practiced in Iran, and Afsoon had to be thoroughly familiar with it.

The final stop on their tour was out in San Fernando Valley at the Eretz-SIAMAK Cultural Center in Tarzana. It is the oldest Persian Jewish organization in California and the largest in the San Fernando Valley. Its importance to the growing cover story was that it was one of the Mouradipours' favorite charities—an important and highly networked institution that subsidized living expenses for hundreds of poverty stricken Persian families who find their way to the U.S. from the persecutions of the Iranian Islamic regime—and Afsoon Mouradipour was to be a personal benefactress. The rabbi in charge had been approached by a Mossad operative because he was a dedicated member of the *Sayanim*. He readily agreed to be part of the embellishment of Afsoon Mouradipour's cover even without knowing the reason why. She was already listed as more than a benefactress; she was an assistant editor of the institution's publication—the *Iranian Jewish Chronicle Magazine* (known better by its Persian name, *Chashm Andaaz*). Afsoon took time to memorize the names and faces of the charitable workers.

The tour ended with dinner at the Shamshiri Grill in Westwood. They were famished; so, daintiness aside, they feasted on an assortment of Persian and Mediterranean cuisine. The dinner included stew, lamb kabobs, and the Shamshiri specialty—Shirin Polo, which is basmati rice with saffron—to complement their meat and seafood dishes.

$$\S\S\S\S\S$$

Back at home with the Mouradipours, Afsoon spent the evening being quizzed by and learning from the nuclear family members who had traveled to Beverly Hills for the purpose. Daniel and Esther directed the full disclosure of the Iran Nuclear Interdiction Project to only two of their children, with a more limited version being given to the rest in order to limit the spread of the secret.

Abraham—the eldest Mouradipour son, and scion of the family's future—warmed to Afsoon as soon as they met. She took his enthusiastic acceptance of her as a concerning—but short of an outright—threat. It was silly, she knew; but the Berkeley senior looked too much like her rapist, Hassanzadeh

Shakibaie, for comfort. He was nothing less than a gentleman, and largely won her over before the evening was done.

As they gathered in the great room, Ruth—the youngest Mouradipour daughter, and the only one still living at home—provided the ice-breaker for the family and made a proposal that was to revolutionize the way the conspirators could communicate in what appeared to be an innocent, even vacuous way. She was six years younger than any of the four other children and was the darling of the entire clan. She was a beautiful high-schooler, a cheer leader, and was full of enthusiastic stories from her day that charmed everyone. Ruth talked to everyone. The fourteen-going-on-fifteen-year-old ninth grader at Beverly Hills High School had 432 friends. She knew that with precision because she was an expert in the new ideas of using social media via the internet.

Ruth had a dial-up computer when she was eight, the gift of her indulgent and amused father. CompuServe became a computer service provider for the public in 1969, and was well established in the late 1980s when Ruth began to develop an interest. She began to accumulate her large list of friends—real and virtual—by the time she was nine-and-a-half. E-mail started in 1971, and was a must for Ruth Mouradipour and her affluent Persian-American friends as they learned that it was trendy. Her grandmother had insisted that a cultured young woman learn to write letters and that she should keep up a lively correspondence with people who mattered throughout her life. Ruth took that to heart to a degree that would have amazed her solicitous grandmother had she had the faintest idea of e-mail, the internet, or how to turn on a computer. She and her friends spent no less than two hours a day sharing their hearts, trivia, and drivel with each other.

In 1978, two Chicago computer hobbyists invented the bulletin board system [BBS] to inform friends of meetings, make announcements and share information through postings. It was the rudimentary beginning of a small virtual community that, by 1997, became an integral part of Ruth's everyday life. By then, her parents were beginning to worry that their youngest daughter was spending too much time on the computer; but the ever indulgent father presumed that it was a fad that would pass; so, Ruth blithely went ahead with her ever increasing sophistication with the burgeoning world of social media. In 1979, Usenet was created as an early bulletin board that connected Duke University and the University of North Carolina; and it became part of Ruth's life, along with the 1984 Prodigy online service that had millions of subscribers in 1997, Ruth and her friends were introduced to THEM. The America Online [AOL] service opened in 1985, the year Ruth was born; and she was an enthusiastic user by the time she could read—she and several million other children.

Ruth and her widening circle of friends took advantage of every new internet service as it became into common use. In 1989, British engineer Tim Berners-Lee began work at the European Organization for Nuclear Research, in Switzerland [CERN] on what eventually became the World Wide Web; in 1992, Tripod opened as a community online for college students and young adults; and Ruth, despite her youth, was one of the early subscribers. In 1993, CERN donated the WWW technology to the world. That same year, college students at the National Center for Supercomputing Applications [NCSA] at the University of Illinois at Urbana-Champaign gave the world the first graphical browser—*Mosaic*—and Web pages were born.

Ruth had her own website when she was ten. By then, there were over 200 Web servers online. In 1997, blogging began, SixDegrees.com let users create profiles and list friends, and AOL Instant Messenger let users chat in real time. In 1998, Google opened as a major Internet search engine and index; and in 1999, Friends Reunited was founded in Great Britain to relocate past school friends and went on to become the first online social network to achieve prominence. That year, 70 million users were connected to the internet.

Daniel Mouradipour recognized his daughter's sophistication and that the web and its social media was not just a fad, but was, in fact, a relatively untapped gold mine. He became a willing early investor in 1994 when an almost unknown Beverly Hills Internet company—BHI—started GeoCities, which allowed users to create their own websites modeled after types of systems already in place in other urban areas. GeoCities passed the one million member mark by 1997 and five million a month before the family meeting where Ruth was to make her contribution. By then, there were well over 35 million user Web pages on GeoCities throughout the United States, and Daniel was able to spearhead the company's expansion into the foreign market, including into a nervous Iran. As in everything else his Midas touch contacted, the Mouradipour family brought in enough money for several families to retire on. The internet and social media had caught on so enormously that the web was now being called the information superhighway.

Having heard the proposal to help Afsoon, her country, the Jewish cause, the female cause, and to rid the world of the Iranian nuclear threat, the ninth-grader made a proposal that bewildered the grandparents, astounded the parents, and met with enthusiastic approbation among the younger set.

"We can talk to our friends all over the world—including Iran—anytime we want and anyway we want. I can control how we talk by getting all of these friends on board; and it will be a way to get Afsoon's name out as a scientist, a nuclear engineer, and someone who might be leaning towards the Iranian regime's way. Daddy said that we needed to be cautious and not to let people become suspicious. We also had to have a way to get those horrible VEVAK agents to recruit her. Well, my dear family, the social media are the way. I can bring anybody up to speed who wants to work with me to use it. It is going to be the future, and we can start using it to our advantage now."

The family voted to let Ruth head up a committee to pursue the idea. Later, when Neal and Zwi learned about her proposal and her expertise, they provided money and computer science experts to make it viable. Gideon Rothsberger joined the group and used his expertise to make it a viable way to communicate vital intelligence in the innocuous language of the social media to further the aims of the umbrella Iran Nuclear Interdiction Project.

The wider extended family meeting was too large to be accommodated at the Mouradipour home. Family members had come in from all of the major centers of Persian-American concentration; the United States is home to 80,000 Iranian Jews, most of whom settled in California. Representatives of the areas where large numbers of Iranian Jews settled in the aftermath of the downfall of the monarch—New York, New Jersey, Washington D.C., Maryland, Virginia, and Texas. A large contingent came in from Great Neck, New York. By mutual agreement, the large family meeting was to take place in the Chabad Persian Youth Center, 9022 West Pico Boulevard, Los Angeles. It was likely to be the site of a very lively discussion.

CHAPTER TEN

Chabad Persian Youth Center [CPY], 9022 West Pico Boulevard, Los Angeles, California, June 28, 1999

Daniel and Abraham arranged for an unobtrusive stay for their privacy conscious guests at the Best Western Plus, Carlyle Inn on South Robertson Boulevard, six blocks away from CPY. They reserved the entire hotel for a week even though they were only going to use it for three days. To avoid encountering people moving in and out of the hotel's parking lot, they left the hotel vacant for the first day they paid for. The prominent sign on the pillar facing the boulevard and a conspicuous sign on the front entrance read NO VACANCY. RENOVATIONS IN PROGRESS. Whatever inconvenience the owners may have perceived in the arrangement was dispelled by a handsome overpayment. It was not a particularly significant concern to either party to the contract because Elijah Adamson was an Orthodox, Sephardic Halacha member of the same congregation as the Mouradipours—the Nessah Synagogue. One hundred fifty of the closest confidants of the Mouradipours checked-in on the twenty-seventh. The accommodations were below the standards the wealthy Persian Jews usually enjoyed, but they recognized and accepted the need for relative anonymity. In that regard, they all agreed not to be driven to the hotel by limousine, another small sacrifice for the cause about which they knew very little. The one thing they all had in common besides their Persian Jewishness was their universal complete trust in Daniel Mouradipour.

There is no parking at the CPY; so, visitors must park on the street. That was unacceptable to any of the security and privacy conscious attendees or their bodyguards. Anticipating that problem, Abraham arranged beforehand to have the important visitors delivered by private buses. Most of them had never been on a public bus, and they chose to treat it as an adventure. Security service vehicles were parked unobtrusively at strategic locations along the route from the hotel to the youth center. Unknown to the arrangers, the attendees, or their private security services, some of the most efficient guardians in the world were watching as well. Mossad, DIA military police, and twenty-five Kosher Nostra soldiers sent by Zeev Rosenkrantz were scattered along the streets, in buildings overlooking the travel route, and walking incognito along the main streets, side streets, and alleys. The security could not have been tighter if a U.S. president was happening by for a political photo-op.

There was no reason for outsiders to take notice of the gathering crowd of Orthodox Jews at the youth center; it was a common occurrence. The Chabad Persian Youth Center and Hebrew School on Pico and South Wetherly Boulevard is a well-known religious organization center devoted to bringing lapsed or inadequately educated Jews back to Judaism and is very active in community services. The cornerstone of its Chabad-Lubavitch philosophy is its focus on education and study for men, women and children, regardless of affiliation or background—including gentiles. Rabbi Hertzel Ezekialson, the director, was more than happy to open the center to the Mouradipour party. He knew well that the attendees would be the crème de la crème of Jewish society and no doubt would be a robust addition to his roster of donors.

Everyone was seated at six-forty-five, and the gavel came down at seven p.m. on the dot, a signal to all of the Jewish business grandees that this would not be a waste of their time; and it was not for anyone's entertainment.

Daniel stood at the lectern and watched the clock. He made three strikes with the gavel, then began to speak.

"My fellow Persians, my friends in Judaism. Much has been said about the current regime in the land of our heritage and its provocative outbursts threatening nuclear holocaust against Israel and the *Kalimi*—our beloved *k'lal Yisrael*—in the past several decades. Tonight we are meeting because there is something we can do besides talk. We are pleased to have in attendance the mayor of Beverly Hills, one of our own, Billy Kermanian. He is under the press of the business of his office, but he has generously agreed to give us a few minutes of his time."

There was enthusiastic applause for the popular politician. He stepped up to the lectern unabashedly wearing his famous campaign button with its message conveyed only in Farsi and waved his somewhat garish election brochure—also written in Farsi—to the admiring audience.

67

"*Salam aleykom* and *shab bekheyr* [Farsi: greetings and good evening]," he shouted.

The audience answered back in Farsi. Kermanian presumed that everyone in the audience spoke the mother tongue; so, he did not even give a nod to English-only speakers.

"Let me tell you why it is great to be a Persian-American. I have thrived in America like most of the rest of you and our people. The per capita income of Iranian-Americans is 50 percent higher than the national average even though many of us—like me—arrived in the country penniless. A little less than 40 percent of you have a college degree. I somehow got by without one. Comparable to the minority from the Indian subcontinent, Persian Jews who emigrated from Iran form one of the wealthiest and best educated waves of immigrants to come to the United States ever in its history. There are some 80,000 of us Iranian Jews settled in the Greater Los Angeles area and in Great Neck, New York. I'm pretty sure I see some old friends out there from New York; *Khosh amidin* [welcome] to Tehrangeles! Enjoy yourselves.

"I know you have weighty matters to discuss; so, I won't take up any more of your valuable time. Let me wish you God's protection and *movaffagh baashi* [Farsi familiar to friends for: success]."

He received a standing ovation and gave a vigorous two-armed farewell wave all the way of the podium and out the door, followed by his retinue of bodyguards and assistants.

Daniel stood again and introduced Neal, as a U.S. agent, Zwi, as an Israeli government agent, Ali, as a Swedish diplomat, Gideon as a major Jewish banker, Levi Schmuel as an Israel businessman, and finally, Afsoon, as the daughter of the Mouradipours and the focus of all of the effort that was to constitute the Iran Nuclear Interdiction Project.

"I will tell you somewhat about our daughter Afsoon, then each of the others will give a short description of what they will accomplish as we keep a hawk's eye on the goings-on in the Iran nuclear industry. After those introductory remarks, we will split up into groups. You have all been given a card with a number printed on it and a room number here in the CPY. Please go there promptly. For the security of the project and its eventual success, and for our own and our families' safety, we must maintain a policy of need-to-know. Please do not discuss anything that goes on in the room to which you are assigned. If you need to know something from time to time as we proceed, Zwi, Ali, Gideon, and Levi will assess the need and let you know what you need to know. Afsoon is personally entirely off limits. You will never know her whereabouts or what she is doing; so, she can move freely and without attracting the attention of the VEVAK.

"We have come to love Afsoon. I can let you know that Esther and I had a daughter who died shortly after birth whose name was also Afsoon. As you know, Afsoon means charm, spell, bewitchment. It is one of the most common of Iranian names for girls; so, it is unlikely to attract attention in and of itself. My family and I are going to make a great personal sacrifice, which is why we feel no qualms in asking you to make similar contributions to this important effort. These agents shall erase all official records of our birth daughter and substitute the Afsoon you see here today as a living girl who grew up in our home, attended our synagogue and schools, and is being educated in the university of our choice. What she is learning is Top Secret, and we are forbidden to divulge the nature of her mission. Her life depends on our complete discretion. I ask you today to provide appropriate photographs and documents that could be helpful in establishing an unbreakable identity for this lovely and brilliant girl. The government will create truly authentic documents such as driver licenses and the like. We need to be able to create family albums, yearbooks, and records of family interactions that will have to be as real as if she had actually lived her life with us. Please get together with our second son Isaac to correlate that work.

"Now, a little about Afsoon. Trust me when I tell you that this girl with the courage of Esther in the books of the prophets has weathered the flames of hell and came out of them a dedicated part of our new interdiction program. Her personal background—including language skills—will mark her as a genuine Iranian citizen of the present generation. Her experiences have guaranteed that she will see the project to the end. You and I have our own reasons to dislike the Islamic regime, but hers is more intense and burned in more internally and deeply. We will support her as she puts on the best Oscar winning acting performance in the history of theater. She will have to be better than Artemis Pebdani, Sarah Shahi, Bahar Soomekh, and Mozhan Marno all put together; and we will have to play serious supporting roles as we are called upon from time to time. Do not tell your friends or your family what you do in this enterprise. It is trite, but 'loose lips sink ships' applies with a vengeance here.

"Now, let's hear from the officials running this show, then get to our separate rooms and to work."

Neal, Zwi, Levi, Ali, and Gideon each impressed the audience of leaders with their unspoken credentials and knowledge. Each spoke in the language of his specialty, and each conveyed a concise message about what was his area of responsibility and basically what he would expect from the Sayanim with whom he worked. After those short presentations, they broke for lunch. The afternoon was made free of distractions for the important and taxing committee work that lay ahead. The meal was catered by the Javan Persian Restaurant on Santa Monica Boulevard. It consisted of light offerings of blends of Persian and Middle-Eastern flavors. The unique dishes included kabobs, polo, stews, fresh Sangak, ground beef koobideh, barg, must o khiar, and a variety of desserts, all of which were certified to be both kosher and Persian.

The committee meetings extended until eight in the evening. Daniel allowed bathroom breaks, but refused to provide any more food until the work was done. The intensity of that decision was not lost on any attendee. When they gathered for a last group handshake, over $100 million dollars had been pledged. The most secret and sacred family connections were served up to ensure the success of Afsoon's long-term effort. There WAS FREELY PROFFERED expertise of religious rabbinical scholars, business tycoons with international networks, the wisdom of men who had grown up in or still visited Iran. Many of the men were able to conduct business in an uneasy relationship with the Muslim overlords of Iran who made no bones about their hatred for everything Israeli, Zionist, or Jewish.

They went their separate ways, and the economy of Tehrangeles experienced a major boost over the next four days as they ate, worshipped, and consulted—all with the utmost discretion and conspiratorial zeal. One hundred fifty new converts left the immediate area with their heads brimming with ideas and hope that, at last, something concrete would come out of their huge backlog of talent and experience.

Every man was well aware of the dangers posed by his decisions that day, and no one took them lightly. Rumors of danger have been whispered about on Westwood Boulevard since the first Persian Jewish emigrant arrived there. It is the truth that for more than two decades after the Islamic revolution, VEVAK hit squads have roamed Europe and the United States, sent by the regime to silence opposition leaders. More than one assassination took place in the Persian Jewish communities of America and throughout Europe. Not many were brave or foolish enough to go public with aggressive criticism or regime change rhetoric. In secret, these men were sure they could effect change; and not one of them wished for fame or notoriety. The intrigue and potential for violence and retaliation goes both ways in Tehrangeles. The Council on Foreign Relations of the United States issued a secret report citing Tehrangeles as one of the places the CIA sees as a potential fertile source of intelligence and recruitment. The men of the Mouradipour family were dedicated closet spies by tne end of the day.

CHAPTER ELEVEN

28314 Terrace Drive, Saint Francis Wood nabe, San Francisco, California, July 1, 1999

Afsoon awakened in a beautiful four-poster bed in a high-ceilinged room surrounded by comfortable chairs, a writing table, and a small but to-the-point library of Orthodox Judaism. The only familiar thing in the room was her beloved *Fereshte*. Even the little rag-doll angel from Nassir was different. It was clean. Afsoon had been asleep for seventeen hours, the product of exhaustion from the whirlwind events in southern California the previous week. Some real angel had lovingly washed Afsoon's one enduring possession—the first time it had been cleaned since Nassir had given her the most important birthday present of her young life. It took a few minutes to orient to her surroundings.

She was in Gideon's house, the house of a strict Orthodox Jewish family that was similar in function to the Persian Jews she had left in Beverly Hills, but less Middle-Eastern and foreign. She was about to begin a crash course on how to be a Jew, and then she would have to learn how to become a Shi'i Muslim. She had to accomplish all of that, get a masters in computer science, and a doctorate in nuclear engineering—all in four years. What Afsoon did not know was that she was just starting in the massive learning project designed to save her life and to make her one of the foremost American spies of all time.

Gideon was off to work at the bank. His responsibilities took him away from home more than half of the time. He was the head of the international division of the bank; and he traveled to meet and make deals with large primary banks in the U.K. (Barclays Group), Canada (Royal Bank of Canada—

71

RBC), Germany (Deutsche Bank and NRW Bank), France (BNP Paribas), Luxembourg (Banque et Caisse d'Épargne de l'État), the Netherlands (Rabobank Group), Spain (Banco Santander), the Vatican (APSA, the Administration of the Patrimony of the Holy See), Israel (HSBC Private Bank), Belgium (KBC Bank), Qatar (Qatar National Bank), Japan (Shizuoka Bank), Singapore (DBS Bank), the PRC (China Development Bank), and Switzerland (Zürcher Kantonalbank).

All of the banks with whom G.R. IV did business met the strict criteria of G.R IV's superiors—G.R. II and G.R. III—who refused to do major bank business with any but the safest banks in the world. An additional criterion was that the bank's intelligence division was satisfied that Tehran would agree to do business with the bank. That, of course, ruled out any mention of business with HSBC Private Bank or any other Israeli bank, but did not exclude Jewish bankers who did not have affiliations with Israel. The final criterion for the Rothsbergers, the U.S. government, and the Mossad was that any chosen bank had to agree to become involved in worldwide nuclear energy funding.

His current trip was to Tehran, where he and the head of the Deutsche Bank in Bonn were exploring the first major investment by Europeans and Americans in the fledgling Iranian peaceful nuclear industrial efforts. There had been considerable opposition from the Department of State towards any American investment in Iran's nuclear ambitions, and even towards the Germans who would be breaking the sanctions agreement between the U.S. and its allies. Support for the proposed American-German-IRI venture came from an unexpected source—U.S. President Howard Ryan, whose vote of approval overrode all naysayers. Gideon recognized the hidden hand of 3D, and probably the CIA in that machination.

The demands of such high level banking took a huge toll on Gideon. When he was home, he had to cram study German, French, and Farsi for starters. He burned through Rosetta Stone study discs feverishly, and the bank hired the best language tutors for him. Afsoon served well to help him with street Farsi, but he required the services of banking confidants of the Mouradipour family for more sophisticated financial language help. It was an uphill battle even for a linguistic genius like G.R. IV.

He made time to help further Afsoon's nuclear and computer studies at both Georgetown and Berkeley, but he was spread too thin to be her tutor in the nuances and intricacies of Orthodox Judaism. His visit to Beverly Hills and Tehrangeles had convinced him that he could not master the subtle differences between his family's brand of Jewish orthodoxy and the Persian Orthodox Judaism practiced by the Mouradipours. The solution was highly satisfactory as it turned out. His vivacious fifteen-year-old twin sisters entered into a rambunctious and infectiously fun partnership with their counterparts in Daniel and Esther Mouradipour's family. Afsoon and the four Jewish girls swapped Hebrew and Farsi language instruction the way little children learn; they ignored written or other visual means and concentrated on learning by reading or hearing and translating. Afsoon had several years to learn to write Hebrew; she was already facile with written Farsi.

Gilda (age thirteen) and Aaragail (age seventeen) had arrived the previous evening from Beverly Hills, and because Afsoon was so tired, spent most of their evening watching television with the Rothsberger twins, Tahmineh and Leila (age fifteen). Their educational day started in earnest with a shopping spree in the morning, followed by a tour of U.C. Berkeley campus in the afternoon. They were on their own for the shopping; but the trip to Berkeley was under the guidance of Chava Rothsberger and her mother, Rebecca Hershowitz.

Both women were thoroughly familiar with the Berkeley campus, were heavy contributors, and had serious influence with the administration. It was delegated to them to convince the university president to create a shadow university career history for Afsoon Mouradipour that would result in a B.A. in physics with a major in nuclear physics, a masters in computer science emphasizing the use of computers in nuclear engineering, and a Ph.D. in nuclear engineering—all over the next four years, and all in the interest of national security. Liberal Berkeley would be hard to win over; but a letter from the president and from the Deputy Director of the Defense Intelligence Agency would go a long way towards getting what the Rothsbergers, the Hershowitzes, and the Mouradipours wanted.

For Afsoon, it was one of her few days of pure joy. She giggled with the Mouradipour and Rothsberger girls, spent money frivolously and with more abandon than she had ever dreamed possible in her childhood. Wealthy as Daniel and Brenda Daastrup were, they had a frugal side that guarded against Afsoon being spoiled and becoming a rich teenage brat. On this getting-acquainted day, Afsoon thrived on being spoiled; and all of the girls had a rollicking good time. It was fun being able to lord it over the math genius, Afsoon, as they struggled with being able to converse with her in Hebrew. By noon, however, Afsoon's quick mind and linguistic gifts allowed her to use the rudiments of the language reasonably well. She could say "Hello," "Thank you," "My name is Afsoon, what is yours?" "Where is the bathroom?" "Can you recommend a good restaurant?" "Where can I catch a taxi?" and the like. It would be a considerably more difficult task to inculcate religious terms with

73

which she was unfamiliar, but she and her newfound sisters were determined to bring her up to speed in the religion she was supposed to have spent her life in. In two days, she would return to Beverly Hills where a kindly old Persian Hasidic rebbe was going to take on that task with her.

Rebecca and Chava met the girls for lunch at the Café Gratitude in the Gourmet Ghetto neighborhood of North Berkeley. They all arrived early enough to be able to find parking on Shattuck Avenue, and to be able to have a leisurely lunch before their scheduled meeting with President Tate-Waring at two. The teenage Rothsberger girls ordered vegan food—one more way to annoy their traditionalist parents—but the two women, Afsoon, and the Mouradipour girls were confirmed omnivores; they ordered corned beef, one of the house specialties.

They finished in time to allow a brief tour of the Berkeley campus before they walked into the university president's secretary's office at five minutes to two o'clock.

The secretary admitted only Rebecca, Chava, and Afsoon to the president's office because they were the only ones scheduled, and because 3D and the other officials involved in the growing intelligence operation were searching for ways to limit the spread of the secrets.

"Welcome, Mrs. Hershowitz and Mrs. Rothsberger," President Tate-Waring greeted them. "Before we say anything else, I want to thank both of you and your families on behalf of the university for your generous gifts over the years."

"You're welcome, President," replied Rebecca, who assumed the role of spokesperson.

"So, what is it I can do for you?"

"I know you are very busy, President Tate-Waring; so, I will come directly to the point. Not to seem melodramatic, but what we are about to ask is a matter of national security; and we must have your assurance that nothing we tell you will ever leave this room."

Ms. Tate-Waring raised an eyebrow, "In important matters, I always inform the university regents and our attorneys. I have to tell you that I keep no secrets from my life partner. With that caveat, I will agree to the secrecy. I must say that I believe our government has far too many secrets."

Rebecca Hershowitz was no stranger to confrontation, and she almost never lost a contest where the stakes were high for her. Although Chava was keeping quiet, she was her mother's daughter with respect to the level of her determination to get her way when it mattered.

"In all of the years that our families have given support to U.C. Berkeley, we have asked for nothing in return. Our names do not appear on buildings; we have allowed you to take public credit without us speaking out. We have not voiced our discontent over the radicalism allowed on the campus, and we do not plan to do so today. But, Madam, I did not exaggerate when I stressed the national security aspect of what we are asking. I will explain enough to let you know why there must be absolute secrecy, even from your significant other. If then you elect to refuse to help us, you will not hear from us again. Understood?"

It was an implied threat that was not lost on the president, and she could ill afford the fallout that would come from the funding committee if she alienated two families whose combined contributions now exceeded $200 million.

"All right, convince me."

"We are authorized to inform you as a fact that Iran has made serious progress towards manufacturing nuclear weapons of mass destruction, and has plans to launch in the relatively near future."

Mrs. Hershowitz had a reputation for no-nonsense directness, and from her quiet place behind the scenes of major developments in California and the country, she was known for her absolute rectitude and, when necessary, her ruthlessness. Now, she had President Tate-Waring's attention.

"How do you know this? When do they plan to attack? Who do they intend to attack?"

"We are not at liberty to tell you any of that. In fact, we do not know. I had hoped to get your cooperation by simply asking; but since you seem bent on maintaining your liberal credentials above all else, I must produce two authorizations that should suffice to convince you of the need for secrecy from the get-go and for your full and unswerving cooperation."

She handed the president the two letters of authorization, the one from the Deputy Director of the Defense Intelligence Agency first. The university president still looked somewhat dubious.

"I must say that the board of regents would look askance at any involvement with the intelligence services of the U.S. I don't need to remind you of the debacles that came out of the Viet Nam and Watergate eras."

By way of reply, Rebecca handed over the second letter. Tate-Waring's eyes widened when she saw the White House stationery. She read the letter from President Ryan quickly, then perused it slowly in order to take in its gravitas.

"This is a serious matter. I don't know whether to consider this an opportunity to serve in a very important cause or a heavy-handed hint at extortion. I shouldn't have to tell you that—despite our political philosophical differences—I am every bit as much of an American patriot as you are, Mrs. Hershowitz," she huffed.

"Are we to proceed, Madam President?"

"I will hear your request, and I agree to keep that secret. So, yes, do go on."

"First, let me introduce this young lady. You will know her by the name of Afsoon Mouradipour. She is not a professional agent, but she has unique qualifications to allow her to be of inestimable importance to the security of the United States. You will scarcely ever encounter her again after today, but you can serve her and your country for which you are so patriotic by doing the following."

Rebecca and Chava laid out the need for establishing a false but unbreakable identity and educational experience for Afsoon Mouradipour, complete with class schedules, grades, interactions with professors, extracurricular activities, and three degrees—bachelor's, master's, and a doctorate. Afsoon was to be accorded extraordinary privileges of attendance at any necessary educational activities deemed necessary, and she was to have an unprecedented access to major professors to hasten her actual education in the areas that would be of practical necessity for her to know. The areas that mattered were Islamic studies, computer science, nuclear physics, and nuclear engineering. Rebecca assured the president that all costs for Afsoon's unusual educational program would be borne by the Mouradipour family. Her educational credentials were to indicate the date of matriculation as 1996 when she entered the university having graduated with full honors from Beverly Hills High School. The completion of all of her degrees was to be dated June, 2004. She was to receive each of those degrees magna cum laude.

"This is not as far out as you might imagine. This young lady is a certified genius, and her educational achievements are beyond extraordinary. She never entered a school before three years ago, and she is now a fully successful student in a major Eastern university. She is particularly accomplished in learning languages and mathematics. You are free to test her in those areas. Please, feel free to provide any help necessary to eradicate any deficiencies you find. However, remember that anything you do is to be done in secret. We have a list of professors who will help in this endeavor."

Chava produced the list of professors who had assisted Gideon Rothsberger during his stay at Berkeley and included Frau Miller from Saint Francis Woods Hebrew School as one of the references. G.R. III and 3D had already secured their services. As *Sayanim*, they were enthusiastic to participate in a project of material benefit to the *Kalimi*—their beloved *k'lal Yisrael*.

President Tate-Waring sighed, knowing that she was beaten.

"What can I say? I'll do it, but the secrecy pact goes both ways. My career will be ruined if this ever gets out. Can I assume that the people involved are good at keeping secrets?"

"Most definitely. And from time to time, they will extend assistance in the preparation of documents that you can use in the preparation of this elaborate deception. Your successors will never be the wiser and will never have to apologize for a predecessor who was a patriot," Rebecca said without the slightest hint of irony.

In a week, President Tate-Waring was in possession of a full dossier on the career of Afsoon Mouradipour at her elementary school, middle school, junior high school, and Beverly Hills High School. Afsoon's record was beyond reproach, which was especially remarkable in that she had spent less than a day in and around the schools. That inadequacy would be corrected as she spent more time with the Mouradipours during the next six years.

CHAPTER TWELVE

Tower of Bank Markazi, Mirdamad Building, 144 Mirdamad Boulevard, Tehran, Iran, July 3, 1999

Gideon Rothsberger IV and a committee of German bankers representing Deutsche Banks in Frankfurt and Bonn, the Landesbank Berlin Holding AG, and the NRW Bank, sat in the waiting room of the main offices of the Central Bank of the Islamic Republic of Iran waiting for an audience with the director of the Atomic Energy Organization of Iran (AEOI), Moqtada al-Benizir, and the director of the Central Bank, Ali Mohamed Mustaffen. It was presumed to be an intentional show of disrespect that the men who had traveled such a distance and who represented almost as much money as did the bank, should have to cool their heels in an anteroom.

After an annoying hour looking at the formal portraits of Ayatollah Khomeini and Ayatollah Ali ibn Abi Rahimi, they were ushered into the inner office. There was no attempt at softening the obvious: this was the office of the main bank in Islamic Iran, in the building owned by the Islamic bank, and any and all supplicants were privileged to sit under the cold hard stares of the two Grand Ayatollahs who were the first two Supreme Leaders of the implacable Islamic nation. A large well-worn copy of the *Qur'an* had a prominent place on the man's simple steel desk.

"The director is a very busy man," a stiffly polite clerk stated. "Please state your business briefly."

Gideon had been elected spokesman of the group by the biblical method of drawing lots.

"Director Mustaffen, we are honored to have the opportunity to meet with you. We are here to inform you that our banks, and several others that

78

we represent, desire to provide funding for your peaceful nuclear energy infrastructure."

"At a price, of course," the director said tersely.

"Of course. This is business, and we are aware—as you no doubt are—that financial transactions between the United States, Europe, and Iran are frowned upon, and may actually be illegal. We understand that you need to have a way to circumvent the sanctions emplaced by America."

"The Great Satan."

Gideon ignored the interjection. "And the major financial centers of Europe."

"Perhaps. Let me be clear, gentlemen. Iran is independent and can take care of its own needs. However, if you can offer a way to make the path smoother, we could possibly be interested."

Mustaffen was a caricature of the ideal Iranian. He wore a mullah's turban although nowhere was it stated in print that he was a cleric. He had bushy salt and pepper eyebrows that overshadowed his uncompromising half-lidded eyes. He wore the requisite white shirt buttoned to the top and no tie—*Allah korusun* [God forbid] that he present himself with a Western affectation. He wore an ankle-length Nur al din lightweight thobe lacking buttons, ideal for the oppressively hot weather in the city. Gideon could not see his feet, but he was certain that whatever foot covering he wore, it would look very much like Khomeini liked to wear.

There was little outward difference between Mustaffen and Moqtada al-Benizir, director of the AEOI; but the nuclear engineer lacked the cruel knifelike intensity of gaze and the forbidding downturned façade of the bank official's face. He looked every bit the scientist and managing engineer he was forced to be in costume.

Gideon replied firmly, "Perhaps, Director, we have made an error in thinking that your nuclear energy system could benefit from reliable funding in an unreliable and perhaps hostile world. We came to do business, but it would appear that we are neither needed nor necessary. We will be on our way. We will be attending the ministerial meeting of the Economic Cooperation Organization (ECO) tomorrow, and we have some preparation to finish before meeting with the businessmen of Iran. Thank you for your time."

It was a bluff, but a calculated one.

"Why have you, a Jew, come? Our president and the Supreme Leader have made no attempt to hide our contempt and disdain for Israel and its population of Jews. On the other hand, we have cordial business dealings with members of the Jewish diaspora in our petroleum and petrochemical industries, and in the transportation and distribution of raw materials. Can you work with gentiles? Can we work with *kaffirs*?"

"I am a Jew and make no apologies for being one. My family's bank and our global enterprises holding company do business with a great diversity of people and ethnicities. Our philosophy is that money does not have a country. As long as we trust that we are dealing with honest brokers, we can overlook a great many concerns that others may be impassioned about. In terms of any allegiance with Israel, our family does not recognize nor condone its existence. We are from the Haredi sect Neturei Karta, which has historically been opposed to the existence of Israel. With a little investigation, you will find that our rabbis have visited Iran on several occasions to attend to matters of consequence to Iranian Jewish families and not for Israel or against Islam or Iran."

It was a bold lie, but Gideon made the decision to take the risk that Mustaffen would not take the effort to determine if he and his family were actually members of the Neturei Karta. It was true that the sect eschewed Israel for reasons obscure to Gideon, but the lie was about his true background. He figured he was not important enough for the VEVAK to bother with.

"Well answered, young man. I believe we can do business. Are you prepared to operate outside the artificial sanction boundaries created by your hostile governments—both the American and the German and other European government cliques?"

"We will need to have assurances of mutual confidentiality, and such a level will have to be earned by both sides and, no doubt will be gradual. Our approach is simple: We lend you money at interest. You spend as you wish. You pay us back in a reasonable time, say five years. We do not care what you do with the money, but we do not accept excuses for nonpayment. Can we start a business communication? Here is my business card and those of my German colleagues. Our private communication information is contained on them and is not for public scrutiny. That much we will need in return from you, Director."

The director stood and handed Gideon five of his personal cards embossed with the official title and logo of the central bank on heavy bond gloss coated white cards. The print stood out in bold relief and was not obscured by any background design. The cards appeared to be both official and officious. By standing up, Mustaffen was signaling an end to the meeting.

Back out on Mirdamad Boulevard, the three Germans took a moment to heave a sigh of relief before asking a few pertinent questions.

"Gideon, I think you handled yourself well. I thought we were sunk when that bigot went into his little rant about Jews. I have to say, I don't quite understand why you are willing to subject yourself to the abuse. More than that, I want to know if there is more to this than meets the eye—more than profit. I think we deserve an answer before we get ourselves up to our eyeballs in a *Kartoffelsuppe* [thick potato soup]."

The reference was not lost on Gideon whose facility with German was nearly native in its fluency.

"Trust me, *meine freunde* [my friends], there is a purpose to be accomplished I cannot fully discuss; and, more importantly, there is a profit—a huge profit—to be made. You can back out any time you fail to see a profit. None of us can afford to be careless about the need for secrecy, nor can we let down our guard about the fact that *wir kommen in Bett mit dem Teufel* [we are getting into bed with the devil]."

The meeting at the Bank Markazi sobered Gideon. He vowed to get some better answers from his DIA and Mossad handlers before he brought himself, his family, his friends, and his country down. The ministerial meeting of the Economic Cooperation Organization (ECO) combined with the Islamic Republic of Iran and Eurasian Cooperation Conference, chaired by Iranian Foreign Minister Ali Muhummad Sharifi was held in Tehran Grand Hotel because it was located in central Tehran and because it was one of the few decent hotels with a conference room. It was listed as a four-star establishment, but Gideon and his German friends agreed with the other Europeans they met that it was no more than a two-and-a-half.

The conference attendees included businessmen, government officials and geopolitical and business scholars from a broad assortment of countries, including Russia, Kazakhstan, Tajikistan, Afghanistan, Pakistan, Iraq, India, China, Singapore, Saudi Arabia, France, Luxembourg, Canada, and Germany. Americans were conspicuously absent, as were women.

Sharifi was unusually frank in describing the fact that all of Eurasia was grappling with serious problems that interfered with the normal conduct of business. His list included sanctions by America and its European allies, terrorism, extremism, illicit drugs traffic, economic and political underdevelopment, ethnic, border, and sectarian conflicts, environmental problems, and political disagreements, which created problems for the stability and security of the region and the world. At the present time every issue on the Iranian official's list was inimitable to business success. He was fully confident that conditions would improve.

Gideon and the Germans had their doubts, but that was not of particular concern to them. They were there to make contacts and to begin the tedious process of finding people who were capable of making things happen and were not so far out of the legal track that they would all land in prison. They were so successful in that aspect of their journey of exploration that they went home feeling that their project could begin. In Gideon's case, he could see a real chance that the the Iran Nuclear Interdiction Project—his real reason for putting himself, a Jew, into the maw of the Islamic tiger—was more likely than he would have hoped to get off to a good start.

CHAPTER THIRTEEN

Offices of the Leader of the Islamic Republic of Iran, Islamic Republic Street—End of Shahid Keshvar Doust Street, Tehran, Iran, February 12, 1423 (Islamic Calendar), February 12, 2003 (Western Calendar)

"The Supreme Leader is not in a favorable mood today. Be brief and be exact, gentlemen," said Col. Dariush Aghdashloo, on-site commander of the Agha's private security force.

The men meeting with the Supreme Leader [SL] that day were the same inner circle who had met with the SL at the inauguration of the nuclear weapons project for Iran October 3, 1996—Mohsen Shahamatdoost, president of the Republic of Iran, Yazid ibn Sarrafzaadeh, chief of staff of the Armed Forces of the Republic of Iran, Moqtada al-Benizir, head of the Atomic Energy Organization of Iran (AEOI), Mullah, Ali Salar Omidyar, director of the Ministry of Intelligence and Security (MOIS), and Behrouz Omidi, director of the Ministry of Intelligence and National Security of the Islamic Republic of Iran (MISIRI) or VEVAK. Each of them knew exactly why Agha Ali ibn Abi Rahimi was out of sorts. Although they were not involved in the offense that had darkened Ali ibn Abi Rahimi's mood, they knew that their personal occupancy of a place of power was never certain since they served at the pleasure of a religious man with a capricious and vindictive nature.

In a few hours, they would all celebrate Eid al-Adha—the post-Ramadan feast—with the Rahimi family in the nuclear proof bunker below where they were then standing. None of them was completely sanguine about his own chances of being in attendance. Ever since the SL had lost the use of his left arm in an assassination attempt in 1981, he had been overtly and unabashedly

83

paranoid. His 10,000 strong—1000 of which were women—private security force was drawn largely from his most trusted cadre of veterans in the MOIS. His oldest friends—if the Supreme Leader of Iran's Muslims could actually have friends in the usual sense—were the directors of his personal guard. The management was conducted by Daron Naderi (head of amputee war veterans), Ayatollah Mohammad Esmail Rahmanipour (currently a member of parliament), Ali Hossein Rahnavard, director of IRGC intelligence, and Bobak Larijani, head of the guard corps and member of the Security Council. Col. Aghdashloo was second in command to Rahnavard.

The latest incident had rattled the SL because the traitor was a senior member of the Revolutionary Guard whose family was well known to him. Brig. Mostafa Khanoum had been stationed in Western Azerbaijan Province, and had been identified as a CIA traitor only three days ago. He had been taken to the Kahrizak Detention Center by trusted soldiers of the MOIS's Basij Militia where he had "freely confessed" his crimes of betraying the Revolution and *mohareb* [war against God]. This was according to a thinly-veiled opinion piece the previous day in *Sobhe Sadeq*, the Revolutionary Guard newspaper. All five visitors knew for a fact that the godless miscreant had been tortured until he named all of his accomplices, including the CIA operatives. After confessing, he was tortured to death; and his corpse was smeared in pork fat and left in the desert for buzzards.

When they entered the room, Agha Rahimi said curtly, "Sit."

They sat.

The grim-faced Agha was dressed in one of his expensive aba cloaks and his signature crown shaped turban. Two massive guards in the uniform of the private protection unit stood impassively alert behind him. Hamid Hejazi and Haji Uthman Asghar were chosen for their unswerving allegiance to the SL and to the revolution. They were—by rigorous training—deaf, mute, and amnesiac.

"Tell me why all I hear is bad news about the nuclear weapons project."

Omidyar had drawn the short straw and was the spokesman for the five men of the inner circle of Project *Jahannam Adur* [Hell's Fire]. When the Supreme Leader had suggested the name for the project, the ring leaders were immediately inspired by its appropriateness. There are nearly 500 verses—roughly one out of every twelve—in the *Qur'an* that speak of Hell. The *Qur'an* has only about 30 chapters and 114 subchapters. It is about 600 pages long depending on the specific printing edition and language. *Jahannam* [hell] was specifically created and prepared with eternal fire by Allah, so that He could torture unbelievers.

84

"Please, Agha, let us assure you that much progress has been made. Most of the statements to the contrary come from the Great Satan, Little Satan, and their European lapdogs. We have a huge underground factory in Bushehr in an atomic bomb-proof bunker. Our centrifuges are whirring night and day. The supply of raw uranium ore—while not plentiful or cheap—is arriving at a pace that we can predict with confidence that we will have a weapon ready in less than ten years, perhaps as little as eight if we can find the necessary scientists and if the Russians will relinquish the bulk of their deteriorating stockpile of highly enriched ore from the old station. We have excellent designs for the construction of an explosive device that can be salted with materials designed to create long-lasting and hazardous fallout in a wide area, perhaps all of the United States. We have sufficient cobalt to make that a fairly simple addition when the time comes."

Rahimi interrupted, "But at present, you have not stockpiled a fraction of what is needed to finish the job. I have heard nothing but promises and problems about the Russian source."

"Not for want of trying, Agha. The Western banking consortium has supplied us with sufficient funding, but we do have three problems with regards the Russian source. Firstly, the Russians fear antagonizing the Americans regarding nuclear issues. As you are fully aware, the two powers established an uneasy stalemate during the Cold War, and have reached what they both consider to be parity. For them to be caught—or even suspected—of selling their old radioactive rods and stores of highly enriched uranium would be regarded by the Great Satan as tantamount to a declaration of war. The Russian Federation is understandably jittery. Secondly, the location and climatic conditions on the Russian's Kola Peninsula create extremely difficult logistic problems even in the event that we obtain full cooperation from the Russian Federation. The place is located in the Murmansk Oblast territory, which is in the far northwest of Russia. It is a horrible place—it lies almost completely to the north of the Arctic Circle, and the ports are frozen in most of the year. The obvious third factor is the huge difficulty of buying reliable ice-breaker ships. We would come to the attention of every maritime nation in the world if we were to try to do this openly."

"Tell me you have made at least some progress."

"We have, but it has been a frustrating process of three steps forward and one step backward for the past seven years. We used the Jew's money to gain the cooperation of the *russkaya mafiya* [Russian mafia], and they went behind our back to work with the Israeli mafia from Tel Aviv. Those criminals seem not to care a whit about their religion, their country, or their people. Money is their god, so far as we can tell. We have not had any reason to suspect anything devious towards our deal. Of course, those fools still believe that we are only interested in peaceful uses of nuclear energy."

"And you trust a set of Jewish, and I should say, Israeli, criminals ... all of you?"

Omidyar answered for the group of five, "Trust would be far too strong, Agha; but we have VEVAK watching their every move; and there has never been a single suspicious move on their part. The money transfers have been as smooth as clockwork; and our agents have been able to gain access to every mover and Shaker—as the Westerners say—in the chain of delivery of raw materials and machinery we have requested. The dark hands of the criminals has been there working for us all of the way."

Rahimi nodded.

"We have had to move very cautiously to get the sophisticated machinery out of Europe, to Turkey and Armenia, and finally to us. The Americans are no fools. They are determined to enforce their sanctions, and they have thwarted many of our attempts. Still, enough gets through that Project *Jahannam Adur* advances. Our main problem—and one that we have had the greatest difficulty in solving—is that we lack enough competent scientists and engineers; and our universities are not capable of producing the required level of advanced nuclear physicists, nuclear engineers, or computer scientists as yet."

"What are you doing about that, Ali and Behrouz?" the SL asked the two chiefs of intelligence.

This time, Behrouz Omidi, head of VEVAK, answered, "We are scouring the world, Agha. It seems that the scientists are in demand and are successfully recruited to lucrative employment in the growing nuclear energy plants in the Western world. Also, of course, they fear being involved with us. Even the Believers are skittish about the American sanctions—for their livelihoods and for their very lives. We do, however, have a prospect—an American—whom we are grooming. The prospect certainly has the credentials, and appears to be leaning our way."

No one noticed the slight hint of increased interest on the face of the guard, Hamid Hejazi, standing behind the Supreme Leader.

"Tell me of your failures."

"Not to divert attention from those working in Project *Jahannam Adur,* but we have had more than our share of mishaps and instances where Allah, the All-Wise, did not seem to favor our efforts. A cargo of crucial sophisticated machine parts was intercepted by Interpol. That was investigated and appeared to have been an unfortunate combination of astute police work rather than any sort of failure in our efforts. An old rust-bucket cargo ship sank on its way from Djibouti to Yemen, apparently because it was not seaworthy. All hands were lost, and what matters is that a major load of high quality uranium ore went to the bottom of the Gulf of Aden as well. Huge amounts of *bakhshesh* [tipping, bribery] changed hands to acquire high-grade ore from the Tahaggart deposit in Algeria, the Letlhakane project in the northeast of Botswana, and the UraMin Inc. Bakouma project in the Central African Republic. We are still in good standing with those whose goodwill we have cultivated; but we will have to restart the whole process; and that will take time.

"Our finance people protested to the Western bankers that we never received either of those shipments and, therefore, should not have to pay. But the money grubbing Jew bankers demanded full payment. They had the temerity to attach copies of the pertinent parts of our financial agreement for our peaceful nuclear enterprise with them which clearly state that we must pay regardless of our success or failure. The loss of the raw materials and of the machine parts cost us more than a year of progress, and the wrangling over money cost us another eighteen months. They were deaf to our assertions of principle—we were being discriminated against because of our true faith. The Jew banks are without principle. They could only see money. In the end, we had to pay up or lose their backing. We have no other backers, Agha. We are caught in a bind not of our making."

"No evidence of sabotage?"

"None that we could find, not a hint. We are confident that these were acts of Allah, not our enemies; although we remain vigilant."

"It is well that you should. We will meet again in a year, and I will expect better news. You are dismissed."

CHAPTER FOURTEEN

Office of the DDDIA, main DIA Headquarters, joint Base Anacostia-Bolling, Washington, D.C., February 14, 2003

D DDIA Adm. Neal Daastrup received an encrypted satellite telephone message from Agent-Ex less than an hour after the conclusion of the top level meeting in the Supreme Leader's bunker in Tehran on February 13. He arranged for a conference call to be made to the major participants in the Iran Nuclear Interdiction Project. Those arrangements consumed his secretary's time for nearly four hours, which was frustrating; but finally, Daastrup's secretary, Abigail Wynne, confirmed that everyone was on the secure line.

"Hello, everyone," Neal began. "This is 3D. Let me take a minute to be sure that we have everyone, and that everyone can hear and be heard. Just answer yes when I say your name, please."

He then methodically read off the list: "Zwi Rosenstein, Israel; Zeev Rosenkrantz, Israel; Moise Levinsky, Israel; Ali Nylander, Swedish diplomat; Carter Miller-Partridge for the SAS; Gideon Rothsberger III, U.S.; G.R. IV, U.S., Levi Schmuel, U.S.; Daniel Mouradipour, U.S., Abraham Mouradipour, U.S.; Randall Caruthers, U.S. State Department; Annette Redstone, CIA; Lincoln Magalini, U.S. National Security Advisor."

There was an orderly "Yes" reply from all thirteen participants.

3D began, "I'll come right to the point. I have received a detailed intelligence report from our Agent-Ex in Iran. The agent reported a meeting at the Supreme Leader's bunker in central Tehran attended by Mohsen Shahamatdoost, president of the Republic of Iran, Yazid ibn Sarrafzaadeh, chief of staff of the Armed Forces of the Republic of Iran, Moqtada al-Benizir, head of the Atomic Energy Organization of Iran (AEOI), Mullah, Ali Salar

88

Omidyar, director of the Ministry of Intelligence and Security (MOIS), and Behrouz Omidi, director of the Ministry of Intelligence and National Security of the Islamic Republic of Iran (MISIRI) or VEVAK. Agent-Ex reports that Ali ibn Abi Rahimi was upset that a trusted Revolutionary Guards colonel had betrayed the country to the CIA. Are you aware of that, Annette?"

"Sadly, we are. Fourteen of our assets are missing and presumed dead. It is a real setback for our operations."

"Our asset went on to say that the name for their nuclear weapons project is Project *Jahannam Adur.* For those of you whose Persian is rusty, it translates roughly to Hell's Fire. Ali ibn Abi Rahimi received a detailed report about the progress and difficulties of their efforts thus far. The bad news is that they remain on track and are gaining on their requirements for raw materials and machinery. The good news is—thanks to Levi's son, and DIA agent Aaron— there have been several shipping mishaps along the way—one ore cargo sunk, and a load of fine tooled machinery was intercepted by officials on the side of the angels—our angels.

Thanks to G.R. IV, the Trojan Horse aspect of our project is well underway and has not come under suspicion. You will be pleased to learn that when the terrorists lost cargoes, they still had to pay our banks. That made them huffy about Gideon IV, but has not interfered with his continuing acceptance in their important loop members. It was reported to Ali ibn Abi Rahimi that there has been considerable trouble for them to obtain refined uranium stock-piles from the Russian Kola Peninsula. Thank you, Randall. It would appear that a bit more quiet diplomacy is in order to keep them away from all that rotting nuclear weaponry, but not overt enough to have the terrorists catch on that there is an organized covert interdiction program underway."

"We'll keep working on it," Randall said.

3D went on, "The single most important piece of information to come out of the meeting was that Omidi reported that they are circling and beginning to court a potential asset in the U.S. who has all of the educational assets and may be ripe for recruitment into Islam, to be radicalized, and eventually to become their much needed top expert in the bomb making enterprise. Thank you G.R. IV, and Daniel. To this point they do not seem to suspect that they are clearing the way for our Trojan Horse to be brought into their compound. Any questions or comments before I have our agent, Aaron Schmuel, Levi's son, brought into the conference?"

"I would like a little more update on our Trojan Horse asset," said Lincoln Caruthers. "How is our girl progressing, 3D?"

"I'll let G.R. IV and Daniel speak to that," Neal said. "Gideon, you go first."

"Afsoon is a truly remarkable human being and is the perfect choice for the task we are preparing her for. She is an all-around genius, especially in math; is juggling immersion in two lives at a level that would win her an Oscar if we gave such awards; and is to graduate in her role as Afsoon Mouradipour from Berkeley with a doctorate this spring. She already has a masters. We have had impeccable assistance from U.C. Berkeley's administration, and Afsoon has actually attended some classes that give her exposure to any intelligence agent who might have an interest. Off the record, she has been tutored by some of the finest minds in advanced mathematics, computer science, nuclear physics, and nuclear engineering in the world. They all say she deserves the Ph.D. she is going to get, even though, in fact, it is a phony. Right after graduation, she will work full-time for the Harvard/MIT consortium to promote global increase in the production and use of peaceful nuclear energy production. We understand from Ali that her work will likely take her to Sweden.

"In her real life role as Afsoon Daastrup—yes, that Daastrup family—she got her B.A. in computer science three years ago and a masters in nuclear engineering from Georgetown University last year. She has a job with a subsidiary of the Tennessee Valley Authority (TVA) deploying small reactors and using MOX fuel—mixed oxide fuel—nuclear fuel that contains more than one oxide of fissile material, usually consisting of plutonium blended with natural uranium, reprocessed uranium, or depleted uranium in LWRs—light or regular water reactors. If she actually showed up at her job, she would be working out of Little Rock. As it is, her uncle and Mr. Magalini have connections with the TVA, which make it possible for her to remain on the record as being employed and to be able to take up her position when she returns from duties elsewhere they did not want to know about. The process of creating her cover identity in all of its bona fides and her fictional radicalization is a subject for Mr. Mouradipour. I will turn the time over to Daniel."

"Thank you, Gideon. Please permit me to mention Gideon's role in all of this. He has taken considerable risks and has handled the financial aspects of the Iran Nuclear Interdiction Project with finesse, and without detection. He is altogether too modest about his contributions to Afsoon Mouradipour's education and probably to Afsoon Daastrup's. With his guidance and direction, she has become a full-blown math and computer genius; and I understand that someone from Neal's camp is going to get her to be as much of a genius in using computers for secret stuff and hacking, neither of which I understand. My family connections have made a contribution, I tell you without boasting. Abraham has been the most important in that, but he prefers that I be the spokesman.

"She has had a full pre-conversion course with the rabbis at the Nessah Synagogue, the largest traditional Persian Jewish congregation in the United States. The center is located in the heart of Beverly Hills, which may be significant to any Iranian agent who wants to take a peek. She has been there enough that members of the congregation will remember her. More importantly, Nessah keeps the traditions and customs of Iranian Jews according to Orthodox, Sephardic Halacha as practiced in Iran. The Mouradipour family and the synagogue's connections to Iranian Jewish families is very open and almost certainly well-known to the VEVAK and to Islamic organizations. Our relations with the country have always been good once our separation was complete after the revolution. We have never been known to further Israeli causes. We have close relations with families who belong to the Haredi sect Neturei Karta, which has historically been opposed to the existence of Israel. Their rabbis have visited Iran on several occasions, and through them we have established cordial—but careful—relations. We—including Afsoon—have open invitations to visit with them in Iran anytime.

"So, Abraham has seen to it that Afsoon has had a thoroughgoing introduction into the Haredi's particular beliefs and customs. Many Haredi families would recognize her on sight. We also have friends from the Muslim side. We have not told them a thing, but Abraham accidently on purpose arranged for Afsoon to visit Iranian Muslim Association of North America Cultural Center on Motor Avenue in LA. There—again in the most casual fashion—our pretty girl happened to meet some young firebrands from the Ali and the Twelve Imams mosque in downtown Los Angeles, which is Shi'i, of course. Our own information and that given us by the DIA indicates that there is a significant radical turn there and that some visits by Iranian agents takes place now and then. We are at an early stage. We are hoping to wait until she is invited to come to the mosque rather than to have her initiate the idea.

"Our family has supplied every iota of information that could possibly be of use to flesh out the life of our daughter, Afsoon. As I look at the documents and read the story of the little girl we lost, it is almost as if we have a real history of her life. Afsoon has studied the material very thoroughly. With her encyclopedic and photographic memory, she has taken it all in as part of her. I don't see her ever making a mistake about her cover story. That is all thanks to the work by the DIA, and it is still ongoing."

"Thank you, Daniel. Now, if there are no questions, I think it's time to hear from our action man, Aaron Schmuel. I'll open his connection. Aaron, are you there?"

"Yes, Sir, Adm. Daastrup."

"We've had a pretty long presentation of what is going on in the Iran Nuclear Interdiction Project. A lot of money has been spent in the program; and between you and Gideon, we have seen some return on that investment. Give us a rundown about you and your black works."

"Many of you know that my father is Levi, and he is probably on one of the lines. Hi, Dad!"

"Hello, Aaron. Nice to hear your voice."

"Yours, too, dad. At the instigation of Adm. Daastrup and Gen. Rosenstein, I joined the army ROTC in college; and after graduating, I completed basic combat training then went to OCS [Officer Candidate School] at Fort Benning, Georgia—3rd Battalion, 11th Infantry Regiment. From there, I moved on to the Ranger training at Camp Rogers and Camp Darby at Fort Benning, then to the mountain phase at Camp Merrill, then to the Florida phase at Camp Rudder in Eglin Air Force Base. Although the desert phase was eliminated in 1995 for most rangers, Adm. Daastrup got me into a special desert training conducted at the White sands Missile Range in New Mexico, Dugway Proving Ground, Utah, and Fort Bliss, Texas. As soon as I finished, Adm. Daastrup got me into the CIA training center—The Farm—in Virginia.

"Gideon and I spent some time together learning encryption, defense computer network and other signals information, and then how to be the smoothest computer hackers outside of the Russian mafia or the defense department of the PRC. With a bunch of money, they were able to bring us together with some teenage hackers on loan from the Russian mafia, and with some Chinese whose military stints were completed. The PRC would not like it if they learned that we have had such an education, but some corrupt prc officials and the Russian criminals were persuaded with lots of money. After Gideon left, I completed the agent course, which was even tougher than the Army Ranger training. I have been more or less freelancing on the Iran Nuclear Interdiction Project since then.

"To make a long story short, I handpicked a squad of regular army, CIA, mercenaries, and Kosher Nostra fighters loaned by Mr. Rosenkrantz. Hello, Zeev."

"Shalom, Aaron."

"The DIA, Mossad, NSA, and CIA supplied us intel, and we went to work doing what we did best—being pirates and spies specializing in wetwork. When we could, we staged accidents that shortened the careers of scientists, VEVAK agents, nuclear scientists, and engineers on the Islamic Republic's payroll. To our benefit, Iran never made those career-changing events known because they would have had to admit that they existed and that the nuclear WMD program existed. Nothing from any of our sources suggests that they have serious suspicions that foul play—at least on our part—was involved. My men and women are good. We sank two ships, one carrying raw uranium ore out of Dijoubi, and one in the Persian Gulf that was carrying a load of centrifuges from a factory in Belgium. Only a handful of people even knew that ship was in transit, and we doubt that even they know what happened to it. Secrecy has its downside. We captured an Iranian unit headed towards the Kola Peninsula through Norway. Norway does not have any fools in its security service. They let us keep the Iranians, and those people proved to be a treasure trove of information before they had the misfortune to suffer carbon monoxide poisoning in their tents way up there beyond the arctic circle.

We interdicted a Russian nuclear scientist and a Chinese computer specialist out there in the middle of the desert in Iran. The CIA was suspected. The Iraqi Kurdish DPIK was suspected. The Mossad was suspected. But without bodies or any other evidence, they might just have gotten lost out there in the sand; and the Iranians have chosen to accept that face-saving explanation; so, our informants tell us. We have set up more-or-less permanent communication and monitoring stations everywhere there are uranium mines, spent fuel dumps, outdated weaponry, and every place we know about that makes the machinery for nuclear weapon manufacturing. We are up and running; and no doubt, we will have more to report the next time this group meets. That's all I have. See you later, Gideon. We need to have a little Krav Maga training."

"Then toughen up, Aaron," Gideon said.

"I think that about wraps it up, my friends," 3D said. "Keep those reports coming in."

The telephonic conference ended with a choir of clicks.

93

CHAPTER FIFTEEN

Camp Peary, York County, Virginia, Armed Forces Experimental Training Activity (AFETA)—Department of Defense, February 24, 2003

Afsoon flew into Reagan National Airport in Washington, D.C. from LAX on the twenty-third and stayed overnight with Daniel and Brenda Daastrup. It was a short, bittersweet overnight. It was wonderful for the extremely busy girl but bitter as well, because it was going to be months—if not years—before they saw each other again. Since she was awarded her masters degree from Georgetown in 2002, she had only been home four times for a total of thirty-eight days.

She had been in Beverly Hills and around Tehrangeles working feverishly to learn how to be a good Muslim girl. Even that exercise had refueled her hatred of the religion of intolerance and violence and brought back fitful memories of her life in Iran. She had been tense most of the time, and it was exhausting. Besides, she was becoming discouraged that she was ever going to be contacted by Iranian agents who would have had to recognize her growing radicalism after she formally converted. Aside from a few pleasantries, she had hardly even spoken to a man other than the Imam who gave her the lessons in Islam. She arrived home tired and ready for bed. An hour of talking with her parents and another spent playing with the children—Daniel, Abigail, Mary, Ruth, Evan, and Michael—was all she could manage. Brenda tucked her in, and Afsoon was asleep before Brenda was all the way out of her bedroom. She was clutching *Fereshte* as she slept.

Gideon arrived late the same night and fell into a king-size bed at the Four Seasons in Tyson's Corner. He had spent every day since the teleconference

94

with the members of the inner circle of the Iran Nuclear Interdiction Project locked in a boardroom fight at the Rothsberger & Company Bankers main offices in San Francisco. Because G.R. II was definitely beginning to show his age, G.R. III—Gideon's father—was becoming concerned about the transition of power when the time came for G.R. II to step down or in the event of his death. He had taken most of the previous year to transfer family stock into G.R. IV's name and had come within two percent of a sufficient majority to ensure that his son would get the chair. When he presented the recommendation that G.R. IV be made the full senior vice-president—in essence the president-elect—he would be guaranteed that he would succeed his father when G.R. III had to move up to the CEO position in the global company. No one challenged G.R. III's right to the CEO position, but there was a significant mood in the boardroom to place Uncle Nathan into the president's chair because of G.R. IV's youth.

The discussion became serious, then heated, then acrimonious. Nathan showed his lust for the top job even though his long career had been lackluster at best.

"I demand a vote," he had said without having made a realistic canvass of the board members.

As usual, G.R. III had done his homework and agreed to the vote. He held his, his father's, his son's, and his mother-in-law's shares and their associated votes until everyone else on the board had voted. At that point, there were 18 votes for Nathan and 11 for Gideon.

G.R. III had looked at the stern faces of the board members. Nathan was flushed with a sense of victory coming within his grasp.

G.R. III said, "And the last votes are those of the G.R.'s. They represent 41 shares, or votes, if you prefer. The succession has been secured. Gideon, please stand so that there can be no mistake about who the next president will be, and who is—as of this date—the senior vice-president and the president-elect. I hope it will not be for many years, but my father appears to be in ill-health at the moment. We'll see."

Gideon stood and nodded at the board. Nathan resigned on the spot and collected his stock options. His office was cleared by the close of business.

Aaron Schmuel left the west coast city of Bushehr, Iran—the site of Iran's only nuclear power plant and its clandestine research and development center—immediately after the telephonic conference concluded. He had a long trip ahead of him—Bushehr to Abu Dhabi to Paris to London and to Dulles International Airport. He had to evade possible watchers, both persons and computers. He had been reconnoitering the plant, but was ostensibly a red-haired British tourist seeing the sites of the pleasant city. He was dirty, tired, and out of sorts when he got into Washington, D.C. He stayed three days at the BOQ at Andrews Air Force Base.

Elsie Silberberg made a leisurely flight from Jerusalem to London and then to Dulles International. She found a seedy little motel in Leesburg and watched television for two days. Gen. Zwi Rothstein had told her that her work at the Mossad Research Department could wait, and she should make herself inconspicuous for a few days before beginning her work in Virginia. She fidgeted the entire time.

At 0600, an olive drab army bus began picking up each of the new visitors to Virginia. The windows had all been made opaque with camouflage paint; and there were no identifying signs on the vehicle; otherwise, the bus was no different from thousands of other military busses in and around the District of Columbia. They were given box lunches—which avoided stops along the way—and, as an added convenience, the bus had an efficient and clean lavatory. For Aaron, Afsoon, and Gideon, it was not their first time in such a conveyance headed out into the Virginia countryside. For Elsie, it was her first, and she did not like the claustrophobic conditions. Nothing seemed particularly sinister; so, she took a nap and did math problems in her head to pass the time.

Camp Peary—better known as the Farm—is hardly the innocuous Armed Forces Experimental Training Activity (AFETA) that the sign on the front entrance declares it to be. Although the CIA denies it, the Farm is their training facility and has been since 1951. In that year, the U.S. Navy returned to the property of the old WW II Seabee base, secured the portion north of the highway—which was State Route 168 at the time—and announced it closed to the public. The portion of the original World War II Seabee base north of Interstate 64 is still closed.

The reason for the closure—according to the CIA—was to provide a secure area for testing and evaluation of classified materials and equipment and not as a training area for personnel. In 2003 when the four relative newcomers arrived, that was partly true. They did come to learn about classified materials and equipment—the most sophisticated weaponry of modern warfare—the computer. As Aaron could attest, the CIA had trained him at the Farm to be as effective and efficient an assassin as could be produced. There is not a single neighbor to the alleged "secret" base that does not believe that its primary purpose is to train killers. That flies in the face of the CIA's adamant denials.

Afsoon, Gideon, Aaron, and Elsie were driven to a large new building in a grove of trees well outside the main compound. Like the proverbial mystery wrapped in an enigma, that place was a secret within the most secret place in the United States. Once they were shown to their rooms and were gathered for a briefing and snacks, Gideon and Elsie renewed their acquaintanceship of the past eight summers when Gideon returned to work and learn at the Mossad's Research Department.

"Hello, Elsie. Does this place make you nervous?"

"Sure. I've fallen into the hands of the Yanks. That ought to scare anybody."

"We are just here to deal with some arcane computer problems. From what Aaron tells me, the agent training is what every sane person should fear. It makes SEAL and Ranger training seem like a kindergarten outing."

"Are we here to be tested?"

"Not in the same sense as agent training. I am pretty sure that the test will be to solve serious and genuine computer issues. I think there is already a good deal of talent here with you and me, to be less than humble. But, someone else is coming to put us in our place, I am told."

"Can't wait," Elsie sulked.

The someone elses arrived two hours after the four newcomers. It was disconcerting to all of them that even more people were going to be in on much of the secret information of the Iran Nuclear Interdiction Project. The new arrivals in the building were an odd assortment of ducks. The five people from the Sherman Kent School for Intelligence Analysis were all young—no one older than thirty-two. They had long hair, tattoos and piercings, earlobe flesh tunnels and fluorescent plugs, and were dressed in the popular casual dirty of the streets. Their persons were none too clean either. Despite CIA prohibitions, the analysts brought their own food group staples—licorice, chocolate truffles, M&Ms, and high glycemic suckable candy.

The Sherman Kent School for Intelligence Analysis is the most important training school for Central Intelligence Agency (CIA) intelligence analysts. It is located in Reston, Virginia. It was opened three years earlier and housed on the second foor of a handsome and expensive five-story structure of gleaming polished brick and smoked opaque glass. In addition to the usual weather proofing insulation, the entire building was ensheathed in special sound-suppressing materials studded with sensors that effectively prevent eavesdropping from the outside. The school's study area—in practical terms, its work area— is affectionately nicknamed "The Vault" because of its monotonous steel windowless walls and the numerous locks, alarms, sensors, and friendless guards.

The school's activities are classified. It is a crime to describe its interior. The school is under the Directorate of Intelligence of the CIA. In its broad activities, the school serves as one part of what amounts to the CIA University. The school provides a a CIA-wide, cohesive, and integrated set of training that grew out of the criticism of the nation's iconic spy agency for its failures that led to the Muslim attacks on September 11, 2001. The wake-up call required a clear and pragmatic response to the changing needs for intelligence gathering after the attacks and the growing threat of Muslim terrorism. The overall new CIA education began to include foreign language, in-depth regional studies, satellite image analysis, wiretap transcript analysis, encryption and decryption, media transcript analysis, listening technology for all sorts of auditory communication device use, and computer and other electronically generated communication devices. The mission purpose for the school was to hear, see, read, and analyze everything all the time. Along with the National Security Agency—an even more secret entity—that ambitious goal was well on its way to being fulfilled.

The four members of the Iran Nuclear Interdiction Project could well have received the message the Sherman Kent School teachers' aides had to offer at the Reston building. However, the project's leaders considered their mission beyond Top Secret and were intent on containing all information within as small a group as was practically possible. It took the signature of the president, the DCIA, the DNSA, and the dean of the school to get the five computer super-experts to leave their safe lair and to come to the Farm, grumbling all the way.

Five more people arrived after the Sherman Kent students were introduced, and assigned to their state-of-the-art computer arrays. Each of these new people had been at the Farm for several days learning about the perils of betraying secrets and about the truly handsome stipends they were each going to receive for their work. They were all dressed in the latest fashion, coifed and manicured at expensive salons, and not in the least awed by the assemblage of brains with whom they were mingling. Three of them were under the age of sixteen. They were on loan from the Russian Mafia and were needed because of their truly phenomenal capabilities to hack into any computer system around the world. They had served the United States as mercenaries previously by gaining access to the defense computer systems of Saudi Arabia, Iran, Iraq, China, Japan, and Israel.

Afanasy Fedoseev and Lyosha Demidov were children of the streets abandoned by their prostitute mothers when they became inconvenient. They were discovered by the russkaya mafiya when they were still prepubescent. Recognizing talent—even genius, when they saw it—the mafiosos had the boys educated in everything that had to do with computers. They gave them last names—Russian people began receiving surnames only about 100 years ago during the first population census of 1897. Until that time, all that passed for a last name was a nickname, and many of those in villages were absurd and even demeaning. Both boys were arbitrarily given surnames of senior mafiosos. Neither boy had a patronymic, a common middle name for Russians, because neither had a father. The boys were given status and treated well, but were more or less prisoners in gilded cages in their early years as junior mafiosos. As time went on, and they grew older, they also grew craftier; and finally, they became minor russkaya mafiya princes and were allowed considerable latitude for travel and social activities. They had three hard and fast rules of life: no drugs or alcohol in a land and industry rife with addiction, no freedom from their watchers/bodyguards ever, and no betrayal of the russkaya mafia—early on, they learned that use of their talents against their benefactors was considered to be a capital crime. Like other young hackers, they enjoyed their lives as princes and had no thought of killing the goose that was laying their golden egg. The two boys reveled in their status as top hackers in the computer underground community.

Renata Leonidovna Zaslavsky's involvement in the russkaya mafia was entirely different and foreordained. Her father—Leonid Aleksandrovich Zaslavsky—was the *vory v zakone* [syndicate boss and chief of the thieves-in-law] of the *Solntsevskaya Bratva,* Russia's largest criminal group with about 5,000 members having a global reach. Interpol described the Solntsevo district mafiya as one of the best structured criminal organizations in Europe and that it operates as a quasi-military operation. The FBI indicated that Russian-speaking criminal syndicates control a third of the estimated $12 billion global cybercrime market, and described them as the greatest threat to American security of the twenty-first century. Leonid was wanted for more than 300 murders in the United States; so, he could no longer travel there.

The U.S. has no extradition treaty with Russia; but Leonid could operate with impunity in Europe, Asia, and the former Soviet countries. He had to depend on subordinates to run operations in America.

Renata—despite her youth—was one of those. Given that she was the daughter of the *vory v zakone*, she was an untouchable. No criminal in his right mind would risk a six-week slow death by disturbing a hair on the beautiful blond girl's head. She was a genius in her own right; her specialty was the placement of network viruses that could be used to corrupt information transfer or to disrupt the function of an entire network—say, the Iranian nuclear program's computer system.

Their work on this project let the Russian hackers call themselves white hat, black hat, and script kiddies—with the white hat appellation being debatable if their victims were asked.

The other two were Chinese—one a woman, the other a thin myopic older man. She was Veronica Chiu, who had worked for the defense forces of the PRC and had been instrumental in China's infiltration of American and European defense systems and major business industries. The man was Clement Chang, former head analyst for the Ministry of State Security (MSS) and all three major military intelligence divisions of the People's Liberation Army. He was honorably retired and legally allowed to pursue his living as he chose. However, that he now worked for the CIA would certainly not have been well received by his former employers. Had they known his activities and whereabouts, his days would have been numbered. His main claim to fame was his almost uncanny ability to penetrate and disrupt computer and communications systems and to embed viruses and worms for any of a variety of nefarious purposes.

The two former PRC computer specialists—working in the headquarters of Unit 61398 of the People's Liberation Army located off Datong Road in the outskirts of Shanghai—had headed up the Chinese hacking campaign, which they called Night Dragon. It had affected more than a dozen companies in the energy industry of the U.S., and the instigators became the object of an intense recruitment effort by the DIA. Up to that point in time, the U.S. military had neither the specialized expertise, the capacity to establish a sophisticated cyberdefense system, nor to launch effective cyberattacks that could not be easily traced back to the DOD. In order to correct those deficiencies, these former senior Chinese computer analysts were now being paid a king's ransom by a variety of agencies of the United States government to wage the silent cyber war that was now gripping the world—the equivalent of the now defunct Cold War.

As soon as lunch was done, they got started—no time for idle chit-chat. The first order of business was to divide up into groups to deal with separate issues of the computer-based project. The divisions were natural: the three Russians, with their russkaya mafiya interconnections, assigned themselves the task of hacking into the many Iranian computer systems and preparing a fertile bed for the introduction of the viruses and worms; the two Chinese chose their particular area of expertise, that of developing new and unique viruses and worms to be introduced into the systems made vulnerable by the Russians; the Sherman Kent School students presented a letter from U.S. President Howard Ryan, and countersigned by the DCIA, DNSA, and the

Senate Majority Leader, Tom Bradshaw, which authorized the work of the group and a preemptive cyber strike subject only to final approval by U.S. President Howard Ryan. In the law—which was cited as the legal premise for the letter—the president was given the broad power to order a preemptive strike if the United States detects credible evidence of a major digital attack looming from abroad under the president's authority to conduct covert action. They set to work grinding out the software data that had to be put into place over the next several years in what they dubbed the Trojan Virus—which would be a composite of many worm and virus infections.

After their announcement, the CIA University team set to work on a specific target—the slowdown, then complete destruction of centrifuges at Iran's Natanz uranium enrichment facility. Iran uses P-1 centrifuges at Natanz, the design that A. Q. Khan stole in 1976, took to Pakistan, and later sold to the Islamic Republic of Iran. They also took on the massive task for the researchers to find and study an Iranian virus so that they could create a vaccine. They were already thoroughly familiar with the prodigious scope of their undertaking. First, the antivirus makers had to capture a computer virus, take it apart piece by miniscule piece, and thereby identify its so-called "signature"—unique signs in its code— much like bomb squad investigators studying the way a particular bomb was made, before they could write a program that would remove it. They chose to work both offense and defense. They had in-depth knowledge of their adversary that was able to produce viruses—an estimated 40 million of them in 2003—faster than the antivirus teams from government, military, and private entities in the Western world could come up with yet another vaccine; the Western protectors of their cyber systems were falling behind.

The young hackers worked very efficiently using the time tested processes of gaining illegitimate entry into what should have been private, password protected, and encrypted computer information banks. They began with a technique they called "dumpster diving." The hackers literally searched through users' garbage to find discarded documents containing information they could use directly or indirectly to help them gain access to the intended network. Next, they port scanned all ports on the targeted host machines for a response, i.e. to determine if the networks they opened were vulnerable to attacks. Open ports—those that responded—allowed the hackers to access the system. The next step for the Russians—called social engineering—was to contact the target to find vital information which will facilitate access to the system. Their finishing step was to invade the opened target and attack or steal from it. It was tedious work and took them a full three days of work to get everything ready for the CIA students, the Americans, and the Israeli woman to insert their devious little viruses and worms.

Afsoon, Gideon, Aaron, and Elsie made up a team to prepare computer inputs that would make it extremely difficult ever to determine the source of the Trojan Virus and to give it a simple start-up code and a quick trigger to send it out to the entire system. No one in the group had any illusions that they could stop the Iranian nuclear threat by a nicety like limiting the preemptive strike to the atomic energy sites alone. No, the ambitious plan was to hit Iran with the catastrophic effect that might otherwise only be possible with an electromagnetic pulse weapon. The stakes in this ever escalating stalemate were now higher than ever.

Iran had become radically paranoid and vengeful since they were attacked by a computer worm known as Stuxnet, which caused its uranium enrichment centrifuges to spin out of control and self-destruct, slowing the Iranian program's progress. The Iranians accused the Israelis and the Americans; and to no one's surprise, the Americans and Israelis denied any knowledge of the virus or the attack. In both of those countries, an explosion of activity by computer scientists and engineers took place in the aftermath of the attack, because the virus was promiscuous and poorly contained. It boomeranged back on both countries—if indeed, they did originate it—and caused widespread and serious computer system disruption.

America and Israel vowed never again to be the victim of such an attack or miscalculation, depending on whose version one accepts. Computer security— which the American-Israeli team was working on—was a paramount issue.

The four partners from America and Israel also came up with an ingenious virus—Fireball—which was able to spy on computers in Iran and to go undetected for years. They also created clever e-mail accounts that were used to plant long-lasting malware that did not interfere with computer function until the command was given. The target of this attack was to be against Iran's high-speed fiber-optic lines.

The Sherman Kent School—CIA University—team studied in detail the Stuxnet virus itself and several variants before coming up with one of their own that got around several of the flaws in Stuxnet. The previous year, a new worm—with several characteristics of Stuxnet—was found at the Laboratory of Cryptography and System Security (CrySyS) of the Budapest University of Technology and Economics. The CIA team analyzed the new malware— dubbed Duqu by the Hungarians—and tweaked it with extremely close attention to detail over the next two days. They named their version the Hungry Trojan. Their new worm was designed to capture data first such as keystrokes

102

and system information. Then the data obtained was able to be used to enable a future Stuxnet-like attack.

The Hungry Trojan virus contains a number of sophisticated aspects, one of the most important of which is code for a man-in-the-middle attack that produces a fake set of industrial process control sensor signals. This enabled the targeted system to continue functioning although infected, and not to be shut down due to detection of abnormal intruder behavior.

Such complexity is very unusual for malware consisting of a multi-layered attack—initial spread by removable USB flash drives, four-zero-day delayed CPLINK vulnerability that allowed the establishment of an alibi by the attackers and time for an in-house hacker to get away. The final layer included in the very complex new virus was to add a variant of a Cornhusker worm, which had been an annoyance in the past, but in combination with the Stuxnet component was deadly. Their insidious and toxic new malware was able to install itself on PLC devices unnoticed and sit there like a sleeper mole agent waiting for its master to give the attack command. The Hungry Trojan System servers designed to subvert Iran's nuclear program were created as "proxies" able to hide the true "mother ship" command and control server in the U.S.

It could be argued about who started the process and who deserved the blame, but no one in the group was willing to deny that what they were doing—engaging in a shadowy struggle of computer sabotage with Iran—was the start, or very near the start, of World War III—the cyber war to end all wars, and without a single bullet being fired. The groundwork plan was laid out in considerable detail at the end of the week when it was time for everyone to take his or her work back to complete the finishing touches. There was a sense of accomplishment and a vague sense of unease at where all of this might lead. How many people would suffer? How many would die? How many lives would be ruined? For the Russians, it was exhilarating. For the CIA University students, it was sobering. For Afsoon, there was a sense of foreboding.

CHAPTER SIXTEEN

Ali and the Twelve Imams Mosque, 13260, Venice Boulevard—Southeast corner of the intersection of Venice Boulevard and Walgrove Avenue—South Park, Los Angeles, March 2, 2006.

As she had done for nearly two years, Afsoon knelt in the women's section for Friday prayers—*Isha* [evening prayer]. The mosque was a strict Shi'i one, and the prayers were done on an area of stone dust rather than on a prayer rug. The stones came from the grave of Ali ibn Abi Talib, she was told by one woman, or the holy rock is "collected sand from Karbala from imam Hussain's tomb."

"We only pray on it, dear, because—according to our rules for prayer—we *should* pray on things not made by man," the old woman told her. "It is for the same reason that we pray with our hands open and not like the shameful *kaffirs*, the Sunni, who pray with their hands in a fist. It is the will of Allah."

Afsoon had converted from Persian Judaism to Shi'i Islam eighteen months ago in as public a way that Uncle Neal and Daniel Mouradipour thought proper, and had been expecting to be contacted before this. The waiting was tedious; and she was beginning to think she was simply going unnoticed; and the plan to get Iran to make the first contact was not going to happen. Her knees felt stiff as she and the other women began to stand up. She shook off the few grains of sand that had collected on her abaya. Other than being taller, younger, and more willowy than the older women around her, Afsoon had only one other characteristic that should have mattered. She seemed happy and cheerful most of the time, while the women around her seemed downtrodden and tended to look down without making eye contact.

She was dressed like they were. In a run-down thrift shop on Pico, Esther Mouradipour had found her a secondhand black abaya—the traditional wear for Muslim Women around the world. Afsoon's abaya was black—like 90 percent of the others—and covered her from head to toes. The day was warm; so, her abaya was made of soft and light fabric. Abayas are categorized in three different types, Khaliji abaya being the least attractive of the three.

She seemed not only to belong in the mosque, but to fit into the neighborhood. Her uncomfortable garment was a size too big and had one inconspicuous and slightly off-color patch over each knee. Her sandles were old, scuffed, and dust worn. She had affected the role of a devout and submissive Shi'i girl; and although she knew it was necessary to play the role well, she did not like it. The business about the sacred sand, praying with open versus closed hands, giving rote—and to her, meaningless—prayers to a god that did not exist was all magic and about as real as fairy dust. Nevertheless, she dutifully performed as she knew was required of her.

Downtown Los Angeles is the smallest region of the city by area. There had been a four-year renovation of the neighborhood, which had made the area on the north side of Venice and the west side of Walgrove into a more nearly upscale neighborhood, but east and south of those two main thoroughfares remained seedy and somewhat less safe than the sister neighborhood. Afsoon lived in a single family residence with three other working girls. There was one bedroom and one bathroom in the house of 858 square feet that was stuck in the center of a 2,500 square-foot lot. The landlord was disinterested in providing any upkeep on the house or the lot; so, over time, the grass became knee high and childrens toys, and collected garbage was strewn about everywhere. A broken plastic three-wheel tricycle was still sitting in the same spot it had occupied two years ago when Afsoon took up residence.

Early on, Afsoon let her roommates know three things about her: she was disenchanted with American life with all of its decadence and the bodily exposure by the women; she had given long consideration to leaving Judaism, and had found Islam to be more vibrant and uplifting. When she converted, she gave over her whole life to Allah. She felt that she could be of more use in the world if she could find the right fit. That was why she had settled on the Ali and the Twelve Imams Mosque as her place of refuge from the wicked outside world.

She made no excuses for being bright. She made every effort to avoid appearing arrogant; and the girls liked her; but they were awed by her brain power. Afsoon spent her free time reading heavy books and scribbling mathematical and nuclear physics equations. The other girls found her hard to understand. She was the prettiest of them all; but they were of an age when they did everything a good Muslim girl could do to attract boys; and she roundly ignored the opposite sex as if they had leprosy. In a different situation, it might have been whispered that she was a lesbian; but that was not possible since she was a member of the Ali and the Twelve Imams mosque where such a person could never be. It simply was not possible to be a lesbian and be a Muslim. The men of the mosque let it be known that they would consider it their duty to perform an honor killing to cleanse the holy mosque if one should be suspected.

As she walked out onto Venice Boulevard to make her way home to another boring afternoon of pretending to read the *Qur'an* but actually reading her math books, a man—one of the swarthy men with long hair and a full beard she had noticed on the men's side of the mosque every now and again—bumped into her shoulder.

"Sorry, Sister, it was clumsy of me."

"It was nothing," Afsoon said and started to walk on.

"May I speak with you, Sister?"

Afsoon looked about to be sure there were people nearby. The man did not miss the wariness in her face and body language.

"You have no need to fear me. I would like to have a serious discussion with you. I want it to be very proper; so, you will feel completely safe."

Afsoon unconsciously backed away a couple of steps before responding, "Where and when would you and I talk?"

"Would you feel safe in the mosque with the mullah present?"

"Perhaps. But my brothers would have to be present as well. I do not take chances of being alone with a man."

"That is to your credit, may Allah bless you for that. A virtuous woman is like a ruby to Him. I confess that I know something about you; and my friends and I are impressed with your manner. We have attended your discussions at Berkeley where you defended the faith against the unbelievers."

"You were in Berkeley?"

"My friends and I are students there. We took the trouble to find out who you are and what mosque you worship in from the directors of the seminar where you speak. I hope you are not offended."

"I don't think so. But, still, I must be careful. A woman must, you know."

"Afsoon, I remember your name from the seminar. Is it all right if I call you by your name?"

"Yes, you may."

"I have observed that you seem to pray with easiness. Do you perhaps speak the language of Allah?"

He said it in Arabic.

She replied in the same tongue, "Not very well, but I have been learning Arabic for the last few years while I was thinking about converting."

That was a lie. Afsoon's Arabic was more than fluent, it was native with all of the nuances and regional characteristics of a native speaker. She masked that fact by keeping her responses simple and direct.

Afsoon was trying not to play too hard to get; but she knew she could not appear the least bit anxious to continue the conversation; so, she let the man take the lead.

"Forgive my discourtesy. I would like to introduce myself. I am Ali— Ali ibn Massoud."

"I am Afsoon Mouradipour."

"That is a Jewish name, is it not?"

"Yes, I am a convert from a Persian Jewish family."

"Do they hate you for accepting the True Religion?"

"No, they are quite understanding. They were saddened by my choice; but they shrugged it off saying that I have always been my own person, and going off to college exposed me to different ideas. They think they should have protected me better. They mean well, and they still accept me in the family and in their home."

Ali looked at her before speaking. If she were his sister, and she converted from Islam to one of Shaytan's religions of lies, he would have killed her himself. It was the will of Allah. It was in the holy *Qur'an*.

"I am happy for you, Afsoon; perhaps you can have the best of both worlds. After all, they are *Ahl al-Kitāb* [People of the Book]."

He nearly choked on his words, but his face betrayed none of his disgust for her parents and her former religion. She had seen the light, *Alhamdulillah* [Thanks be to God].

In a few more minutes of Arabic conversation, Afsoon and Ali agreed to meet at eight o'clock at the mosque in the presence of Mullah Omar. They further agreed that he would bring his friends—two true and faithful Shi'ite Muslims, and she would bring two men from her family.

When they parted, Afsoon ran home and made two telephone calls. The first was to Daniel Mouradipour.

"Hello, Daniel … Father … I have important news, and I need your help immediately."

"Hello, my lovely daughter. You have my help. What can I do?"

She quickly related the conversation and explained the need for her to have two "brothers" come to the mosque with her that night. They had to be Muslim or at least great actors, and they had to be big and intimidating.

"No problem on either request, Afsoon. We have friends with such sons. They have considerable dealings with Iranian Muslims and speak Arabic and Farsi flawlessly. They are brutes. Sound about right?"

"Perfect. Thank you. I love you as a father."

His voice cracked, "And Esther and I love you as a daughter. Go with God, dear one."

The second call was to her uncle, Neal Daastrup, on his cell phone. It was ten fifteen in Georgetown; and he was sitting in his easy chair sipping scotch and talking with his wife, Ruth, when Afsoon's call came through.

The caller ID showed "Afsoon Mouradipour." She had a different mobile phone for her real self—"Afsoon Daastrup."

"This is a secure line," he said out of habit, as much as anything else.

"Do you know who this is?"

"Yes, dear. Go ahead."

"They have made contact."

"When?"

"A few minutes ago. I am supposed to have a meeting at the mosque at eight o'clock Pacific time. The mullah, my contact, and his 'friend,' and my two brothers. In islam."

She could almost see Neal's eyebrows raise.

"I told Daniel, and he will send two men to protect me. He says they can pass as Muslims."

"I presume you mean the mosque on Venice Avenue?"

"Yes."

"I will have agents there before you get there. They know how to be discreet and how to watch your back. Be careful, dear girl. This is beginning to sound like the big time."

"And I am scared. But I can do it."

"You are a brave and good girl. Ruth and I love you. You know that Brenda and Daniel do as well—it goes without saying. I will let them know."

"Thank you, Uncle Neal."

A large black Buick Rendezvous pulled in front of Afsoon's rental house with fifteen minutes to spare. Neither she nor the two men in the Buick saw the two black suvs following them at a professional distance. Each of the suvs had six men dressed in SWAT uniforms and were armed well enough to conduct a credible attack on a force of sixty combatants.

Afsoon hurried out to the Buick. A powerfully built young man, every bit the Arab military man, stepped out and opened the rear door. They drove to the mosque in less than ten minutes and parked in plain sight in full view of the front door. The two suvs parked on side streets. A driver was left in each car and the motors were left running. The remainder of the men disappeared into the vacant lot surrounding the mosque and took up positions surrounding the building. They were no more visible than the shades of the night.

Afsoon and her two "brothers" tapped at the mosque's door. Mullah Omar opened the door wide and invited the three of them in.

"Please. The house of Allah, may His name be praised forever, welcomes you. Ali and his friend Ibriham are already here. Let us all sit together and have some flavored tea."

Ali and Ibriham appeared from the next room, and shook hands with the men. They assiduously avoided physical contact with Afsoon as was proper and expected.

There was a short period of quiet innocuous conversation as they drank their steaming saffron flavored tea. The men sized each other up, and their wariness softened. There did not appear to be a threat. The conversation was conducted in Farsi, which Afsoon's "brothers" presumed was a test of their bona fides as Iranian Muslims.

"Do, you speak Farsi, Daughter?" Mullah Omar asked.

"*Baleh* [yes]," Afsoon replied.

She was careful not to allow the mullah or the men she presumed were VEVAK agents to suspect the full fluency she had in the language of her birth.

The conversation proceeded in Farsi.

One of the "brothers" asked, "Why have you asked to speak with our sister?"

"She seems to be one of us," Ali answered. "We wish to be sure of that and to suggest that she make a contribution of her talents to our Persian people in the homeland and in the diaspora, if that would be all right with her family. I assure you that our intentions are entirely above board."

"Brother" shrugged and nodded his head for Ali to go on.

"We have come to realize—as you as her brothers in islam no doubt also realize—that Afsoon is special. She is extremely intelligent. We are aware that she has a masters and a doctorate from U.C. Berkeley, and that she received them in near record time. Her specialties are in nuclear physics, nuclear engineering, and computer science; and she is an acknowledged expert." He nodded at Afsoon. "We say this not to flatter, but to state facts that are pertinent. More importantly, to us, is that she has converted to our faith and that appears to be wholly genuine. We do not wish to offend, but we presume that her family are *Ahl al-Kitāb* and follow the religion of the prophet Abraham in the Hebrew way."

It was a question. "Brother" nodded.

"May I speak to Afsoon?"

"*Belah*," "Brother" answered and nodded his acquiescence to Afsoon.

She lifted her eyes and turned them to Ali and Ibriham.

"Afsoon, we take note that you do not dress or talk or act as do the Western women who dishonor their womanhood. From your comments at Berkeley, we take it that you reject many of the corruptions of Western society while still having a highly sophisticated Western education. Am I correct in these assumptions?"

"I believe that is pretty much correct. I have taken years to come to the moment of conversion, to say with genuine conviction, '*Allahu akbar*'! As you seem to know, I have spent many years and many hard hours of study to learn the science of providing energy to the people—to my people."

Ali and Ibrahim both smiled at that declaration.

"We realize that you have grown up in a country that considers itself to be a friend of our enemy, Israel, and that you have, no doubt, been exposed to much negative commentary about our native and beloved Persia. Does that preclude you from using your talents to help our mutual ancestral home in its quest for legitimate use of power sources that are readily available in the West?"

"I am not good at doing what the Westerners call, 'beating about the bush.' I will be direct, Ali and Ibriham. I have no problem with helping Iran develop its nuclear power, if I were to be so honored as to be given employment in Iran. In fact, I have been trying to decide whether to take a break from America for a while. Some Persian friends have invited me to join them in Sweden for a year to study some advanced technical aspects of nuclear manufacturing. It is a chance I don't have here in the United States, because the U.S. Atomic Energy Commission, the Departments of State and Defense all say that the Swedish studies may have implications about weapons.

"I am inclined to take up the invitation by my Swedish friends, what do you think?"

"We are products of Islam, Sister; and—as you know—Allah's religion grants free will and choice to all Muslims. We do not see any reason why you should not follow the desires of your heart."

Afsoon kept a soda cracker expression on her face, determined not to demonstrate her deep-seated conviction that the two VEVAK agents were practiced hypocrites with the tongues of serpents.

"And what do you think, Brothers?"

The two large men knitted their eyebrows and whispered to each other.

"Judaism and Our own personal convictions accept the sovereignty of the individual to make his or her own choices. Afsoon can do as she pleases with the blessing of her orthodox family. While we as Americans would not condone an attack on Israel or America, we have no real problem with Iran making prudent preparations to defend itself from attack. We are friends of the Haredi sect, Neturei Karta; as good muslims and like our haredi friends, we do not recognize the State of Israel, but we are arabs who do not wish to see Jews die just because they follow their religion, different as it is from our own."

"That is certainly our belief. You could not have stated it better."

Afsoon echoed the sentiments, "I have come to that conclusion myself. I am glad we were able to talk. I believe you have clarified things for me. I am a cautious person, and I take things one at a time. I will give serious consideration to the idea of going to Sweden and then see what the future holds from there."

The VEVAK agents had gotten more than they had hoped for; so, they left it at that.

"It has been most pleasurable to meet with you members of the Mouradipour family and to learn of your ideas. Perhaps we will meet again."

"Perhaps we will. Thank you for making this meeting possible, Mullah Omar. You have been most helpful," Afsoon said and stood up.

The men shook hands, and they went their separate ways.

The next day, Afsoon called Uncle Neal and the Mouradipours again, and brought Gideon up to date about all that had transpired. Neal told her to sit tight, and he would get back to her.

CHAPTER SEVENTEEN

Interactive Sweden-America Festival, Austin, Texas, March 9, 2006

The weather was gorgeous—bright sun in a lapis lazuli sky, spring grasses, not a hint of wind. It was 82° and balmy, a perfect day for the SXSW-Texas Bicycle Racing Association annual race. The venue was perfect; Liberty Hill Ranch had plenty of room and acres of parking. There was an easygoing Texas atmosphere, perfect for the race. The agenda of the day before in the festival featured presentations, seminars, and events related to the emerging technology field, as well as showcases of new digital works, video games and innovative ideas. It was one of the most important opportunities of the year to showcase everything that was good about Sweden and how closely entwined the Swedes were with their American cousins.

The governor of Texas, Darryl Junior Strait, gave a speech; and the mayor of Austin, Hank Lovell—in his iconic ten-gallon straw cowboy hat—introduced the dignitaries. The senator, congressman, and the attorney general of the United States—who was a native born son of the city—were all there along with the Swedish ambassador, Jonas Zillacus, Ivor Swensen, the honorary consul general of Sweden in New York, Ali Nylander, the consular agent in charge of trade and economic affairs, Dr. Arvid Bergström, counselor for Swedish defense, Counselor Ms. Sanna Kullberg, special advisor, Homeland Security Affairs, Magnus Bielvenstram, minister-counselor, Trade and Economic Affairs, Gabriella Andraesson, Public Diplomacy, Press and Communication counselor at Embassy of Sweden, and Johannes Hjerdstadt, the undersecretary for embassy affairs. Also present on the platform were representatives from the U.S. Department of State, the British Embassy, and the Consul General of Switzerland in New York

Mayor Sanderson was very complimentary about Ms. Andraesson's speech the previous evening that dealt with digital diplomacy among Sweden, Switzerland, the U.K., and the U.S. She had deftly described the interwoven work by all of the countries to leverage social media to represent each of their countries to the world and for their welcoming spirit of friendship and cooperation in the digital age. It did not hurt that she was a statuesque true blond with a robust and athletic Nordic physique. Not mentioned was the presence of Adm. Neal Daastrup, the DDDIA, who made himself a shade of obscurity under a small copse of live oaks.

The excitement of the day—and, if truth be known, for whole festival—was the fourth annual bicycle race from Austin 75 miles ENE to San Antonio through the beautiful rolling hills and straightaways of the Texas Hill Country. A casual straw vote would have determined that Ms. Andraesson was the odds-on favorite. Some of the men who would make that vote might also have thought she could even win the race, but not many of them cared.

After the starting gun signaled the beginning of the race, and the cyclists sped away at a feverish pace, 3D made his way through the crowd of spectators and sidled up to Ali.

"Hello, Ali," he said quietly without looking directly at the Swedish diplomat.

Ali started slightly, although he had been expecting Neal's approach.

"Hello, Neal. I presume this is not just a coincidental encounter between two bike racing enthusiasts."

"Very perceptive of you, my Norse friend. I won't keep you. There's been a breakthrough, and our young friend and I think it's time for your friends to meet with us again."

"I'll arrange it. When?"

"How about on the nineteenth? Is that enough time?"

"No problem. Same place?"

"Yes, please."

"See you then. Keep safe, Neal."

"Thanks; you, too, Ali."

Neal was gone, and Ali was leaving when he passed Hank Lovell.

"Great day, Hank. Thanks for all the support."

"Our pleasure. See you at the Georgetown Grand on ... let's see ... what day is it?"

"May nineteenth."

113

CHAPTER EIGHTEEN

Chancery of the Embassy of Sweden, 2900 K St NW, Washington, D.C., May 19, 2006

Gideon handled all of the arrangements for what became an emergency meeting because 3D was involved in a DIA problem that took him to Kabul, Afghanistan, and the time was very short. He could not delegate any of the work to his secretaries because of the classified nature of the information. He was harried and frustrated by the time the day arrived. Even then, he was unsure that everyone would be able to make it. He could only give scanty details by telephone; so, he hoped that the stress he put on the need for the meeting would suffice.

As on the previous occasion when the members of the Iran Nuclear Interdiction Project met at the Swedish chancery in Georgetown, they all entered by arrangement through the rear entrance. Gideon was relieved and heaved a deep sigh of relaxation when he was greeted at the door by Ali Nylander and Neal Daastrup, who had flown in at literally the last minute. He looked haggard, but was his usual ebullient self, nonetheless.

"Hi, Neal. Am I ever glad to see you. I have my fingers crossed about whether or not everyone else will get here. It has been a close thing."

"You can't even imagine how glad I am to be here. I still have sand in my teeth. Come on in. Other than me, you are the first of the group to arrive. You and I can go to the conference room, and Ali can play the host."

The two men were able to make their way unescorted to the conference room in the private corporate offices in the section of the chancery that housed the Embassy of Iceland. They chatted about the projected roles they each would play as Afsoon left for Sweden and the project began to ratchet up on the human level.

By fifteen minutes later, everyone was assembled around the handsome conference table. From the Swedes, the members again included: Ali Nylander, the consular agent in charge of trade and economic affairs, Dr. Arvid Bergström, counselor for Swedish defense, Counselor Ms. Sanna Kullberg, special advisor, Homeland Security Affairs, Magnus Bielvenstram, minister-counselor, Trade and Economic Affairs, Gabriella Andraesson—beautiful winner of the SW/SX bike race in Austin—Public Diplomacy, Press and Communication counselor at the Embassy of Sweden, and Johannes Hjerdstadt, the undersecretary for embassy affairs and some extracurricular activities that 3D was more aware of than any of the other members. From the American side, the members were all present: Afsoon Daastrup, Gideon Emmanuel Rothsberger IV, Levi and Aaron Schmuel, Gideon Emmanuel Rothsberger III, Daniel and Abraham Mouradipour representing the *Sayanim*, Randall Caruthers from the Department of State, Annette Redstone from the CIA, and Lincoln Magalini, the president's national security advisor. From Israel: Gen. Zwi Rosenstein, second in command in the Mossad, and Moises Levinsky, representative of the Tel Aviv Kosher Nostra. Carter Miller-Partridge from the SAS represented the U.K.

Ali said, "We should get right to it. Neal can bring us up to date from where we left off the last time we met."

Neal was brief but complete. The meeting at the CIA "Farm," the subsequent progress of getting the computer attack details completed, Afsoon's real education and the manufactured one at Berkeley, the in-depth cover story—now completed—and her transition from Persian Jewish girl in a privileged family to her conversion to Islam at a radicalized Shi'i mosque in Los Angeles.

"The news that brought us here is best told by Afsoon. She has played her role perfectly, and that plus all the work done that is adjunctive to her personal performance appears to be paying off. Afsoon?"

"I'll spare you a lot of detail. The Mouradipour family has been superb. They overcame their shock and misapprehensions about using the name of their daughter to supply us with the Afsoon Mouradipour cover. The DIA and CIA have created unimpeachable documents that verify every possible aspect of the cover character's life from birth certificate to grade school diploma to graduation from Beverly Hills High to a masters and doctorate from U.C. Berkeley. Some arm twisting was necessary by the Rothsbergers and Mrs. Hershowitz to convince the liberal Berkeley president to get on board; but when he did, the process could not have gone more smoothly. Again, the

Mouradipours arranged a crucial education in Persian Judaism and then an entrée into the world of extremist Shi'i Muslims. They very smoothly found a way for me to appear to be genuinely interested in Islam, then in the Iranian Shi'i version of Islam, then to go through the conversion education process and actual conversion. I have been an active and obedient Shi'i woman for two years, and all of the effort put out by everyone here apparently paid off on March second."

Afsoon then presented the story of what happened when she was approached by what she presumed were VEVAK agents at the mosque on Venice Boulevard. She was effusive with her thanks for all that the Mouradipours did to carry off the charade.

"I know it had to be a bitter pill for them to swallow. The very idea that their own privileged daughter would consider leaving the religion of her ancestors, let alone flirting with conversion to Islam, had to be repulsive. To extend that bit of theater to the enth degree where that wayward daughter actually converts to a brand of radical Islam that comes from and has corrupted their beloved homeland and drove them out is nothing less than losing a child to a foreign war. And there is more to come for them and for me. If I believed in luck, I would say that we are all most lucky to have them aboard."

She gave an appreciative nod to Daniel Mouradipour, who put two fingers to his lips and brushed them towards her in a gesture of affection.

Neal waited until he was sure she was finished, then said, "All right, we can pretty much see what has to be done in the near term. Most of that will be up to our Swedish cohorts, and Ali can explain in a second. The Rothsbergers, Schmuels, the Mossad, the CIA with all their devious hackers and corrupters, and the Kosher Nostra will continue to work on the long-term aspects of the Iran Nuclear Interdiction Project. Brenda and Daniel will continue to bite their nails and be the home that Afsoon needs and will always need here in Georgetown. My friends, it does take a village; and we are Afsoon's and our country's—our Western civilization's—village. Okay, Ali?"

Mr. Nylander stood to give his presentation formally.

"I warn all of you again that the nation of Sweden and the ambassador here in Georgetown does not know about this project, and would disapprove it and prevent it if they did. Those of us Swedes in this room stand to lose our careers—maybe even our freedom—if we are exposed. Let me emphasize how crucial to us is secrecy. Nobody must ever speak or write a thing about what we do or say to further this ambitious project. That

116

said, I will let Johannes Hjerdstadt with his connections to the shadowy *FMUndSäkC*, and Dr. Arvid Bergström from the defense department, handle the details."

Hjersdstadt was the spokesman.

"Ladies and gentlemen. We have been prepared for quite some time for this contingency. Afsoon Mouradipour's papers are all in order—awaiting only the placement of appropriate dates—for her to emigrate to Sweden. It is our best judgment that the plan will proceed most successfully if we start low and go slow as the doctors like to say. She can be an expatriate living in Sweden and attending Stockholm University there for a year or two; then she can become completely radicalized when the time is right and renounce her U.S. citizenship or be more cautious and apply for dual Swedish and American citizenship. We have the papers ready for either choice, including a well-worn Swedish passport that has eight years left on it before it expires. The skids are greased to extend it whenever she needs to have that done.

"She has long-time friends—male and female—who are bona fide students at the university, and her room in their apartment is ready for her arrival. Never mind that Afsoon Daastrup has never met any of them. If there are any further suggestions, comments, or questions, I would be glad to entertain them now."

He looked at every face, and no one had anything to say.

"All right, thanks for your attention and help."

Ali and Neal stood to signal the end of the conference. The members of the Iran Nuclear Interdiction Project filed out without talking. Dr. Bergström and Johannes Hjerdstadt diverted Neal, Levi, Aaron, Zwi, and Moises before they left the chancery.

Dr. Bergström said, "Look, from here on out, there is likely to be some ugliness; and we have to protect that little girl who can be regarded as an irreplaceable asset or a profoundly useful agent, or just as a deserving human being. The project—for all of its fancy electronic aspects—boils down to making her look good, for her to be able to infiltrate into the very heart of the monster, and keeping her as safe as if she were our own daughter. She will need all the help we have in our armamentaria. Please keep in touch. We can't have mistakes, certainly not mistakes of miscommunication or failure to communicate. We are going to see and do things that can never be divulged, and we must cover each others' backs. We cannot be judgmental. I predict there will be kidnappings, torture, betrayal of friends and enemies, and murder most foul before we are done. We all believe in the cause. We must believe in the cause *and* each other and always protect our members no matter what. I commit myself. Do you?"

It was a sober moment, and Dr. Bergström had put it well.

Every right hand reached to the center of the group of hard men and made a knot of fists. Not a word was spoken. Nothing needed to be said among this band of brothers.

CHAPTER NINETEEN

Home of Daniel and Brenda Daastrup, 1210 Potomac St. NW, Georgetown, Washington, D.C., September 3, 2006

The entire Daastrup family—Daniel and Brenda and their children, Neal and Ruth, and their children—gathered for a farewell party for Afsoon. Gideon and Aaron Schmuel were there to wish her godspeed.

Daniel spoke for the family, "This is the first of our brood to fly away from the nest, and I—for one—will miss her deeply. It is true that Afsoon has been away a great deal of the time since she came to us when she was sixteen, but she has been here every year for her birthday when we have the annual family photograph done. Afsoon, you have grown up to be a beautiful young woman, and we consider you to be a family treasure. Bon voyage!"

Afsoon nodded her gratitude and shed a tear. Brenda and Daniel gave her a hug. All six children—Daniel Jr., who was twenty-seven—a year older than Afsoon—and Abigail, Mary, Ruth, Evan, and Michael, who were younger ranging in age from nine years to twenty-one years that festive day—crowded Afsoon and smothered her with affectionate hugs. Then Afsoon really cried, but just for a moment.

Ruth took the next opportunity, "Afsoon, what a pleasure it has been to have you as part of our big family. You are fun and funny, and I don't even have to comment on how bright you are. You will knock 'em dead in Sweden, but don't forget where you live."

Afsoon gave her a hug.

Aaron took his turn, "Little sister, I plan to get to Stockholm from time to time, and will look you up in your dump at the university. Don't do anything I wouldn't do."

Afsoon stuck her tongue out at him.

Gideon was next. His voice was a little shaky.

"Afsoon, we will all watch over you. I am going to do more business in Stockholm than I need to just to get to see how you are doing. We'll all try not to bother you too much, but we probably will anyway. I wish you every success. Come back in safety, little sister."

He hugged Afsoon and held her a bit longer than a brother might. She enjoyed the contact, but it made her uncomfortable.

They had a birthday cake—six months before Afsoon's putative birthday—and the children teased her with candles that could not be extinguished by blowing on them to make a wish. Afsoon was amused by that bit of Americana with which she was not familiar, for all of her efforts at acculturation. She was charmed by Abigail, Mary, Ruth, who giggled uncontrollably at the success of their prank, and gave them each another exuberant embrace. Small evidences of her acceptance into the family confirmed again her place as part of the family, and she was always touched by them and never blasé.

Neal and Ruth's youngest—nine-year-old Dietrich, named after one of Neal's shadowy German contacts—picked the longest straw and was thereby elected to be the distributor of the presents. All of the children lined up in descending order of size to present their gifts, all heartfelt and extravagant because of the importance of the occasion. Afsoon's cousins—Stephen, age eleven, the twins—Martha and Elizabeth, and Dietrich—lined up with Daniel Jr., Abigail, Mary, Ruth, Evan, and Michael to give her something from their hearts to show her how much she really meant to them all. Then, Afsoon really cried.

"It is the best birthday I ever had," was all she could manage to say.

Brenda took her aside into her office as the party began to break up.

"Afsoon, my dear, I hope you know how much we love you. We are always your family. Don't you dare forget that. I will worry every minute you are away. I know all this wretched Iran Project business will keep you from communicating with us, but think of us. We all love you. This will pass sometime; and you will be back here; so, we can spoil you; and you and I and the girls can have some quality girl time together."

She blinked back tears. Afsoon embraced her with all the fervor she had.

"Oh, Mom, you cannot know how much you mean to me. You made me part of a family. I never had one before except for my sort-of brother, Nassir. I don't know if I could ever find him again, so being part of the Daastrup family means everything to me. I want to go on long road trips, go camping, climb mountains, have parties, and do everything that you do in a family

120

with you. But first, you know there is something I have to do. I know the big picture is more important than my own feelings, but I have to do something in my life to help the defenseless little girls and women in Iran. I wish I was a thousand women, and I could help all of the tormented women in Islam. I make every effort to love them more than I hate the religion and the monsters who are at the head of it, but I am not a good enough person to get to that point. I could never be a Christian; it would just be too hard."

"Whatever else you may be, my dear, you are regarded as a saint by the Daastrup family. Remember that and take our love with you wherever you go."

They held each other in a final embrace, then Brenda went up to bed.

Gideon lingered after everyone else went home or to bed.

"Afsoon, can we go for a little walk?," he asked.

"Sure, I'm too excited to sleep. Thank you for coming out here all the way from San Francisco."

"It is nothing. Besides, I have something I want to say; and I have had to get my courage up to say it. I managed to do that on the plane ride."

Afsoon gave him a querying look, but waited to let him tell her what was on his mind in his own way. They walked around the block along well-lit streets. The evening was warm and still. There was a full moon misted with sea air.

"Afsoon, there is something I have to say to you. I have debated too long to find the right time, and both of us have been so busy and so involved with other stuff that it never seemed appropriate. I'll just come out with it. I am twenty-six and a lot of people think I am a cold fish. I have grown up as an Orthodox Jew, and that makes one a bit of a cold fish, I think. Oh, crap, I'm dithering. Afsoon … I love you. I have loved you ever since we met. I know that we come from different ends of the earth, different cultures, different life's experiences; but I don't care about any of that. I love you. I want us to have a courting relationship—to use a quaint old Victorian term—so you might come to feel the same way about me. Please think about it. I will come and see you in Sweden all the time if you want. I want to be a part of your life. It's stupid and premature, I know; but I can't see life without you."

"Oh, Gideon. I don't know what to say. I care for you very much. You know that. It is true—too true—that we come from the ends of the earth both figuratively and literally. I have dreaded the coming of this day, because I know that you have feelings for me. I don't want to be abrupt, but it is just not possible for me to have such a relationship with you or any other man."

She started to cry and hated herself for being unable to hold back the surging tide of her pent-up feelings.

"I'm sorry I upset you, Afsoon. I wouldn't do that for the world."

121

"Gideon, you dear man, it isn't you. It is what happened to me. I have never really talked about it to anyone before, but it is only fair for you to be able to understand. I have love for you, I really do; but I cannot love you in that way. I mean that literally."

He held her hand and waited.

"Oh, Gideon, it hurts even to think about it but here goes. You cannot imagine how much I hate the Iranians, the Muslims—the ones who robbed me of my childhood and ruined my womanhood. I think you have heard about what they did. You haven't seen my scars; and even if you did, you would not be looking at the worst scars—the ones on my soul, if I believed in souls. My genitalia are nothing but rigid scars. A man of religion—damn him—cut all of what matters to a woman away. I am left without libido or desire. To have sex would be excruciating. Even if you thought we could have a loving but celibate marriage, I could never be happy knowing that sexual pleasure is something I cannot give.

"It must be given—not taken—and I have known what it is to have it forced upon me.

Somewhere in the deepest recesses of my being is a demon that says, 'Never again.' You are the only one who will ever know this, and I tell you because I trust you to keep my secret. I killed a man who tried to rape me again. To have you touch me in any kind of man-to-woman way would excite that bestial anger in me. I could not bear to inflict that on you. Please love me in another way. I want to have you in my life. To have you reject me would be unbearable. I cherish you, but I am so damaged that I cannot give you the love you deserve."

The dam broke. For the first time in her entire life, the constraints that held back her emotions gave way. She sobbed, and he held her in his arms unable to give her anything else. They stood in the street in a desperate embrace until the hurricane passed.

"I will always love you and respect you more than I do anyone else, my dear Afsoon. I think I understand how you feel; I can't possibly even imagine what you have been through. No matter what else happens in our lives, I will always be there for you. I will protect you with my life if needs be. Don't cut me out."

He was crying now, almost as bitterly as she was.

"I won't."

He let her go at the door to the Dastrups' home. He was in no shape to face anybody else that night. She slipped up to her room to put a cold wet cloth on her swollen face.

122

§§§§§

Home of Daniel and Esther Mouradipour, 375 Trousdale Place, Beverly Hills, California, September 7, 2006

The second farewell party—this time for Afsoon Mouradipour—was less dramatic but no less heartfelt. Every member of the large Mouradipour clan who could come to the family mansion was there to see their family hero off to the next battle in the war in which they were all engaged. As soon as Afsoon walked in the door—which she did without knocking, a privilege she cherished because it was tangible evidence that this was another family to which she belonged—Ruth, the effervescent social butterfly of the family, swept her up in her arms.

"Let me tell you about all the social media stuff I've been doing for you," she said as soon as Afsoon could catch her breath.

With a little trepidation about the possibility of accidental divulging of secret information, Afsoon said, "Tell me while we take a look."

Ruth beamed. Even though Afsoon was getting older, she seemed to be tuning in to the social media that every one of Ruth's age considered to have transplanted handwriting, phones, e-mail, and face-to-face encounters that were so stressful. They went to Ruth's computer.

"See, there's your picture when you made captain of the girl's soccer team, when you graduated from Beverly Hills High, when you got the math prize at Berkeley, when you won the engineering scholarship for nuclear engineering, when you graduated with your B.A.—those are the oldies. This is latest one of you doing something great. This is your graduation with a masters. You were top in your class, and I can prove it. This little thing I scanned in is your letter of commendation from President Tate-Waring."

"Those are great. Are there any family things or personal things?"

"You betcha. In your bio, I put a whole bunch of things from the family albums—vacations, birthday dinners, crazy days at the beach where we all had to wear old-lady 1920s 'bathing wear.' The whole schmear is in there. You have put out a Facebook share item at least once a week for the last ten years, and a couple of tweets a day. I have to say you aren't up to par in the tweeting department."

Afsoon scrolled through the work Ruth had done. It was as if she were viewing the life of someone else—which, of course—she was. It was so well done that VEVAK would not have the tiniest suspicion.

"Ruth, you are fabulous. I am sure our friends over in Iran will get a look at this stuff, and I will be in like Flynn. You are a genius."

"I have to confess that I had a lot of help. The photoshopping was done by spooky people not from here and not like us. The records at Beverly Hills elementary, middle school, junior high, and high school are incredible. If I didn't know better, I would believe in all of the records and photographs myself. It kind of tickles me to have an older sister, one that I never knew."

"You all did a great job, and I know it was lots of work, Ruth. Way to go."

"Afsoon ... I'm glad you're my sister. I really mean it."

"Oh, Ruth. That's wonderful of you to say. I love you, too. You know from the little that anyone can share about the real me is that I didn't have much of a childhood. I had no real family; and, except for one person, the family I had was awful. You guys are great, and I will always hold you in my heart as family."

"Me, too you. You be careful, you hear. I don't really know what you are up to, but I am afraid it is not all that safe. Come back to us. Don't take chances you don't have to. I couldn't stand it if ... well, something happened."

"I'm very careful, and I have lots of help. You stay in there for me, please."

"You know I will."

Ruth had had her turn. The rest of the children swarmed her. She hugged each of them and said their names more than once.

"Abraham, big brother, little brother Eli, sweet little sister Kelsey, and big sister Rivka, how much I love you; how much you mean to me!"

Daniel and Esther joined in, and everyone assured Afsoon how much she was loved and that they would always deem her to be a Mouradipour. For Afsoon—who never really had a family—having two was a surfeit of riches beyond her imagination before she came to America. It was one more reason for her to treasure her citizenship.

When the emotions died down, Abraham spoke for everyone, "Enough of this gushy stuff, I'm starved. Let's go eat."

It took four cars to get the family plus two rabbis and their wives and children to the *Habayit* [Hebrew—Home]—the most expensive Persian restaurant in Westwood—and a popular landmark on West Pico Boulevard in Tehrangeles. It was a clean, tiny joint in the corner of a strip mall, with just eight tables. The celebrating Mouradipour family reserved the entire restaurant. It was an expensive choice; and the rabbis' wives, Bathseba and Sarah, put up a faint effort to protest such an extravagance. Rabbi Elijah Shofet and Rabbi Ya'akov ben Yitzchak IV were not at all averse to getting the occasional

124

freebie—kosher, of course; and they downed more than their share of the fine wines Daniel Mouradipour provided.

The glatt kosher Mediterranean dinner was nothing short of a potentate's feast: Israeli salads, shawarma, parsley falafel, hummous, babaganoush, and chicken shishlik, grilled chicken pita smothered in spicy green sauce, matzo ball soup, large portions of meatballs served with rice, fresh heated pita and crunchy cucumber-tomato salad, and Schnitzel Ashkenazi.

The overfull family watched soccer on the big screen until it was time for Afsoon to leave.

CHAPTER TWENTY

Stockholms Universitet [Stockholm University], Campus Roslagen Student Housing, Room 302, September 9, 2006

The United Airlines flight from LAX was comfortable and on time. The only worrisome aspect of Afsoon's trip to Stockholm to begin her study abroad was that she recognized the Iranian man—the one who had introduced himself as Ali ibn Massoud—from the Ali and the Twelve Imams Shi'i mosque in Los Angeles covertly watching her in the boarding area of her flight. That could not have been a coincidence. On the way to security check-in, she had thought she saw the other Iranian—Ibriham—from the mosque; but she was not entirely sure then. Seeing Ali in the boarding area—especially after he had told her about being aware of her during her graduate work at Berkeley—was a dead giveaway that the two men were VEVAK agents. Afsoon cleared customs and immigration without a second glance from the immigration agents. Thanks to her DIA handlers, her passport, residence permit—visa—and university student papers were perfect—in fact, they were genuine, except for her.

DIA agents Nick Staphanakis and Michael Grodmore—assigned to watch over Afsoon on that leg of her trip—came to the same immediate conclusion as Afsoon that she was under surveillance by VEVAK. They informed 3D of the fact.

Adm. Daastrup smiled into the phone and said, "Hooked."

Afsoon was met at ARN [Stockholm Arlanda International Airport] by two vivacious, smiling, round-faced blond girls who held up a sign with her name: "Afsoon Mouradipour." It was hot that fall day, and the two girls were dressed to show a considerable amount of skin.

126

"Welcome to Sweden," Ingrid Hakkensdatter said and introduced herself. "This is Marta, Marta Olson."

"Hi," Afsoon said and shook their hands.

Marta took Afsoon's bags, and Ingrid took her hand and led her towards the Arlanda Express Train station.

"Don't look around, Afsoon, but you have two admirers," Ingrid said in a quiet conversational tone without looking around herself. "Two Iranian male admirers. They have been focused on nothing but you since your plane landed. Not to worry, our people are here, too. Marta and I are with *Säpo*. That's short for *Säkerhetspolisen*, literally "the Security Police—really, the Swedish Security Service." We have a mutual friend, we understand—Johannes Hjerdstadt."

Afsoon shook her head slightly, and her facial expression indicated that the name did not register.

"How about, Ali Nylander?"

"Oh, yes," Afsoon answered in the same conversational tone.

"Johannes told us that 3D—somebody you are supposed to know—thinks it is okay that the VEVAK officers are on your tail. In fact, he thinks it is a good thing because your cover seems to be holding up well. That's all we get to know about you and your business."

The Swedish girls already had tickets; so, the three of them boarded the Arlanda Express Train for the 25-mile ride from Märsta south to the Stockholm central train station. From there, they took a taxi to the student union building of the university.

"We thought you would like to walk and enjoy the day. It's a beauty, don't you think?" Ingrid said.

Afsoon noticed that the stroll to the housing area was slow, punctuated by brief stops while the girls took turns looking around, and was circuitous. It took at least half an hour longer than a straight path would have taken. Marta carried a hand mirror and frequently looked behind them.

They stopped at the third apartment block of the Campus Roslagen Student Housing units.

"No young men taking our fancy, I'm afraid," Ingrid said with a broad toothsome smile. "Guess we don't rate. Sad. But this is where we live. Third floor, room 302."

As they settled Afsoon in, the two Swedish agents filled her in on the apartment. It was simple—almost new—and attractive with good quality Ikea furniture. 302, like most of the apartments in the building, had been refurbished inside. The apartments in the building were modern and equipped with their own bathrooms, shared kitchenettes; and Afsoon's was fitted out with a microwave, a cooker, and a fridge/freezer.

"You are one lucky girl, Afsoon. Accomodations are hard to find in Stockholm, especially at this time of year when the semester is just about to start. Apartments here are almost impossible to get. You are important, we figure; and you have friends with a lot of pull. Great thing for us. We get to live in the lap or luxury until you decide to move on. Hope it's not too soon. Difficult to find accomodations in Stockholm. There are lots of frauds out there looking to take advantage of people like us. They scam students by collecting money up front for an apartment that doesn't even belong to them. The brochures at the U all tell you to check out the rooms and ownership first before you sign a contract and not to pay until you have a legal contract. You got to avoid all of that with big brother's help."

"Thanks for all the help, Ingrid. You too, Marta," Afsoon said noncommittally.

The agents took the hint and were more careful not to appear to be prying.

As Afsoon unpacked, Marta saw her hijab and could not help but comment.

"Afsoon, you should know that head coverings are not really illegal, but they are frowned upon. You won't make many friends wearing a scarf."

"With respect, Marta, I am not here to make friends. I have a purpose. Don't get me wrong, I really do want to be friends with you over and above all of us doing what we must. And I need your help."

"Name it."

"I need to find the nearest Shi'i mosque; so, I can get started there. The only one I could find on the internet was in Trollhättan. How far away is that, and how do I get there?"

"There are lots of mosques right here in Stockholm. Do you have to go to a Shi'i one?"

"I do."

"Well, that is a bit tough."

She was already checking her iPhone.

"It's a $126 round trip flight on Golden Air from ARN to BMA [Stockholm Arlanda to Trollhättan Bromma] and it takes three hours and a quarter. You could take the train from Stockholm Central then change trains and go Göteborg Central and switch again and go to Trollhättan. That would cost you almost $175 round trip and would take four and a half hours one way. Or, you could rent a car for $95 one way. It'll take you about five and three-quarters hours. It seems like a pretty big project. Hope it's worth it."

"That's really tough. I need something better. Any ideas?"

"I don't bother using my brain at all. I have an iPhone. Let's see what my peripheral brain can find out."

She made a few deft thumb movements, then said, "Well, there is something. I surfed a site and found out that most Muslims in Sweden find it too difficult to get to a mosque and usually don't like the ones available to them anyway, especially the Shi'ites. They usually practice their faith in so-called 'Basement mosques.' My handy extra brain warns that those 'Basement mosques' tend to be more radical. The Shi'ite ones are under a lot of scrutiny by the security services and the police because of some trouble with young people who have been radicalized, even a couple of bombings. The imam of one of them was briefly arrested on suspicion of harboring extremist fugitives, but not much came of it. Seems the Iranian government made a big stink saying that Sweden was prejudiced against Muslims, and it was an insult and highly disrespectful to detain an Iranian cleric. He was let go; but he appears in street rallies and demonstrations pretty frequently ranting against Sweden, the U.S., and Israel."

"Anymore information … like an address or telephone number for the imam?"

"No phone, but here's the address." Afsoon read from Ingrid's mobile phone: Jennifer Gustafsson's home, 6066 Arne Beurlings Torg, number 78. "It is a dead end just southwest of Torsansgatan Street. There's a comment that it is a pretty run-down area that has not yet been included in the plan to make 700 new student flats by 2008."

"Can you tell me how to get there?"

"Stockholm is a great place. You can get anywhere by the city bus line. We'll map out the bus routes and numbers and the changes you need to make. Kista is located between the centre of Stockholm and the international airport Arlanda. The address is something like six miles from the Kista city center. It will be easy to get there by bus. That's not the issue. It is primarily a working class area, seems to have a lot of Muslims in the area—poor people. It doesn't sound like too good of an area. Maybe you ought to take a friend or two with you if you go."

"I won't want to draw attention to myself; so, I will probably go alone. Thanks for the offer. I will keep you in the loop whenever I go there or probably anywhere else for that matter."

"Good idea. That way, Marga and I and the powers in the security service won't have to fret."

Afsoon discovered that the ever efficient DIA—working with Johannes Hjerdstadt and his *Säpo* officer—had unobtrusively registered her in the

129

university as a post-grad student in Islamic studies and some lab classes in advanced computer science and nuclear engineering. In fact, Stockholm University was just experimenting with the idea of having a nuclear engineering class; and the intelligence services had offered Afsoon's expertise to the faculty to teach the introductory class for engineers. That efficiency left her with nothing to do for two days; so, she decided to make her first foray into the world of Shi'ite Muslims in Sweden and even possibly to announce her presence among some radicals as an added plus. She studied the information the *Säpo* girls provided and boarded the number 9 bus, hoping to get to the "Basement mosque" before *Dhuhr* [the noonday prayer].

She was careful to wear very modest clothing and to forego any makeup. She stuffed a plain grey hijab into her purse for the trip to avoid drawing unnecessary attention to herself. Nevertheless, she was aware of an Iranian man who glanced her way throughout the trip to Kista. She decided not to pay any attention to him, but kept her old friend—the straight razor—within easy reach all of the time. The trip was long enough that she calmed down and enjoyed the scenery.

Stockholm is a beautiful compact city—enchanting green in summer, a kaliedescope of color in the fall, and a dazzling white in winter. It is a city of striking and memorable contrasts—water and islands, history and innovation, small town and big city, short winter days and long, light summer nights—with a dazzling array of impressions for a young girl on her own in a sophisticated European city. Stockholm has history—visible everywhere— but Afsoon also could look out of any window and see the latest in fashion worn by beautiful people. All around her sat earnest people working with the latest in IT [Information technology].

The trendy Stockholmers are often used as a test market by international companies because they are quick to pick up on the latest trends.

If Afsoon were to take an interest, she would shortly learn that the city is a hotbed of fashion, youth culture, and entertainment of every description. Stockholm is the cultural hub and economic center of Sweden—the home of the Nobel Prize. The capital city has many set-aside green areas and is surrounded by water. Stockholm is one third water, one third greenbelt, and one third city. Just outside the city, there is an archipelago of 24,000 islands. Stockholm—the Royal Capital of Sweden—is a city built on fourteen islands; so, throughout her stay in Sweden, Afsoon was never far from the water. She looked out the sparklingly clean bus windows at an assortment of well-preserved medieval buildings standing alongside modern architecture.

130

Her starting place, Stockholm University—first established in 1878—is located in the center of the world's first national city park, close to city center; and—like the surrounding city—is an eye-soothing island of green. Kista is a nice city for the most part—if a bit sterile—located northwest of central Stockholm. It is divided by the Stockholm Metro blue line into a western part that is primarily a working class and middle class residential area—where Afsoon was headed—and an eastern part occupied by commercial ventures. She was struck by her short view of that commercial section and could not help but think that the Iranian spies she knew were there would be making full use of the IT facilities she was seeing: Kista hosts departments of both the Royal Institute of Technology and Stockholm University. At one time, the two were jointly known as "the IT University." In the 1980s, when Afsoon was living her life as an abused little girl, Kista was referred to as Chipsta or as Sweden's Silicon Valley. In 2006—as Afsoon passed through it for the first time—Kista Science City was a vibrant cluster of ICT industries with more than 20,000 people involved in developing next generation of mobile tele-communications and information and communications solutions—right up Afsoon's alley.

Kista is named after an old farm, still located in the area of apartment buildings adjacent to Afsoon's destination. The construction of the modern parts was started in the 1970s and was continuing to the middle years of the twenty-first century. The city was originally planned in accordance with a long tradition in the City of Stockholm, aimed at creating *boende* [homes] in local neighbourhoods—served by the subway—which provided a public transport link to Stockholm City and the rest of the region. However—where Afsoon was going—the construction of *boende* and apartments outstripped the capacity of the county to provide inexpensive transportation to the areas that far out. Most of the streets in Kista are named after towns and places in Denmark, Iceland, Greenland and Faroe Islands, or after locally famous people like Arne Buerlings.

Afsoon was let off the city bus on the corner of Torsnasgatan and Arne Buerlings Torg streets—which, convenient for her—was a regular city bus stop. In contrast to the green beauty, cleanliness, and orderliness of her campus and Stockholm city proper, the area where she alighted from the bus was seedy and over-the-hill, overdue for a renovation. Walls of buildings were covered in Arabic and Farsi graffiti, and trash covered the margins of the streets and empty lots. Abandoned vehicles were evident, and new cars were nowhere to be seen.

She opened her purse, took out the hijab, and turned left. She walked to the cul-de-sac of the dead end street and paused to try and determine which was 6066. She had voluntarily walked away from the love, peace, and comfort of her mother—her mothers, and her two families. Afsoon felt like she had been resurrected; and now, she felt like she was standing on the edge of a precipice, and there was no going back.

It was eleven forty-five. Her reverie was interrupted by the approach of two vehicles—a rusted old Volvo, which once might have been blue—and a small white Toyota pickup truck. She had to move quickly to get out of the way. The vehicles stopped, and five men got out of them and walked briskly towards the large apartment building on her left. They took frequent glances at their wristwatches. The men all wore heavy black beards, heavy dark clothing, and knitted *taqiyahs* [skull caps; also known as kufis or topis] to emulate Muhammad. There was little doubt who the men were or their destination. It was nearly time for the *Dhuhr*. She screwed up her courage and followed them into the building.

Afsoon waited until the last man entered the apartment—number 78. She hesitantly knocked but knew that she had to be early enough not to disturb the men as they began their prayers. A woman in a heavy black chador opened the door just enough to see Afsoon standing there.

"What do you want?" she asked curtly in Swedish with a strong Iranian accent.

"Sorry, I don't speak Swedish yet. I'm just learning."

The woman shifted to English with which she seemed more comfortable than with Swedish. She repeated her question.

I was told this was a Shi'i mosque. I am new at the university, and I wanted to pray at a mosque of believers."

"Who told you about us?"

"Some friends at the university. I mean no harm."

"Are you a cop or a reporter? You look like one. At least your head is covered."

"No, I am from Iran—Tehran. I was studying in America before I came here."

"What's your name?"

"Afsoon. Afsoon Mouradipour."

"Hurry up. Come in before prayers start. The men are in the other room. My sister and I pray together in the kitchen. I'm Jennifer Gustafsson, my sister's Annika. We share the apartment with a believer from Isfahan because housing is so expensive. He has the two back rooms. We cook for him. No improprieties, you understand. He is strict. If we did anything wrong of that kind, he and the other men would kill us; and they would be right to do so,

132

of course. After prayers, you will meet the men. Be careful; keep your eyes down; and don't show your ankles or hands any more than you have to. Hurry, it's time."

Annika acknowledged Afsoon only with her eyes, then the three women knelt on the prayer rug in the middle of the kitchen floor.

When the *Dhuhr* was completed, Afsoon said, "That is a beautiful carpet, where was it made?"

Annika told her that it was made in Iranian Azerbiajani by their mother. It was the only thing of value they were able to bring to Sweden when their family moved to Stockholm to find work.

Jennifer boiled water for tea, and Annika scurried about to set out biscuits and to serve tea to the men. The women waited until the men had had their fill.

"Brothers, this is Afsoon. She comes from Allah's country—from Tehran. She wanted to attend prayers with us because she had no place else to go."

"She is not properly dressed," said the oldest of the men.

He was austerely dressed, even by Iranian standards. Unlike the other men, his beard was flecked with strands of grey.

Afsoon kept her eyes down.

"I have not yet had time to get proper clothing. I will need instruction on how things are done here. That is part of why I am here today, Sirs."

"The women will help you, Sister. We welcome you," said one of the young men.

Afsoon was aware that the young men were tall, strong, and fit—very martial in appearance. She was sure that she had come to the right place and hoped she was making a good start with them. Idle chatter was not the custom among these people; and shortly, the men nodded to the women and left.

"I must go also. Thank you for your Islamic hospitality. May I come again sometime? It is difficult for me to get away from the university, but I can come sometimes."

"You will always be welcome, Sister. Here, I have written down an address where you can get proper clothing for an Islamic woman. You will feel more comfortable wearing a chador when you come here. And, I think it would be better for you to come for *Asr* [night prayers] to keep the neighbors from becoming too curious. Go with God."

Afsoon left. She had not been able to determine what the two sisters looked like, but presumed that they were Swedes who had converted. For the life of her, she could not imagine why.

The men stopped by their car and the truck. They spoke rapidly in Farsi because they did not like to be seen over long in the street.

The young man who had spoken to Afsoon said to the others, "I'm sure that is the woman that the one we call Ali ibn Massoud told us to expect. We will have to cultivate her. I am sure it will be no problem to run into her at the U. If she is the one, she should be pretty obvious. There are not too many Iranian computer scientists or nuclear engineers at Stockholm University. I am not even sure if there is a department of nuclear engineering. I will check her out and work to make contact. Don't mention anything to the two girls. They have their uses, but they can't be trusted."

CHAPTER TWENTY-ONE

Office of the Senior Vice-President, Rothsberger Family Bankers, 423 Montgomery Street, the Financial District, San Francisco, California, September 12, 2006

The office intercom flashed.

Gideon pressed the button. "What is it, Kelsey?" he asked his executive secretary.

"Mrs. Hershowitz is here. Did you remember your appointment with her?"

"No. You are my memory. If you say I have an appointment, then I do. Show her in; as if anyone could stop her."

Rebecca Hershowitz—Gideon's maternal grandmother—swept into the room. A grand entry and exit was her forte. She was dressed to the nines as always.

Gideon had moved quickly to the front of his desk and gave her a hug and a triple cheek kiss.

"Hi, Grandmom. What brings you to our humble workplace —out slumming?"

"No, my boy; I like to get down to the Wall Street of the west and the FiDi from time to time. And I can't help it, I still think of you as a boy despite all of your accomplishments and your present important position. I do have important business, though. Are we secure in here? I have something to tell you about our mutual project."

"The whole bank building is swept for bugs daily, and my office twice a day."

"You're busy; so, I'll get right to it. I have a source from the Dayan side— my maternal people—that should be valuable for you. You may not have heard of her, but you have a sort-of second cousin or auntie once removed or something like that who lives outside of Tehran—has done for more than forty years."

Gideon raised a quizzical eyebrow but did not interrupt.

"She is an interesting sort: she's a reformed Jew; she is an American citizen; she is a widow who operates a fantastically successful horse breeding business by herself—well, with hired hands—and she lets on to the Jewish community and to Rahimi's thugs that she is one of the Haredi sect of the Neturei Karta. However, it is important for you—and you alone—to know that she is a dedicated *Sayanim* who works with the Mossad upon occasion. She is rich, and they let her travel at will. She is an outspoken defender of Iran and an even louder opponent of America's treatment of Iran in public. As you can guess without stretching credulity too far, her private thoughts and life are a different matter."

"Wow, at least I have one true eccentric in my family."

"Two, Gideon; you are forgetting me."

"I would never do that, Grandmom. You are the greatly loved black sheep of the family."

"And I come bearing a gift for the Iran Nuclear Interdiction Project. First, her name: Elizabeth Dayan. She took back her maiden name when her husband died. She thought she would fit in with the Jewish community better if she had a Persian Jewish name. Nichols wasn't going to work. Second, her Mossad handler is none other than your old friend, Zwi Rosenstein. Third, she is disgusted with the hate Israel program of the Iranian leadership since the revolution; and she has declared a personal vendetta against their policies of hurting women and of blowing Israel to kingdom come. She is more than ripe for recruitment.

In fact, she has offered to invest in the nuclear energy program and wants to meet with the other investing bankers when you go to Tehran next. She has made it entirely public that she will insist on having free access to the sites where her money will be invested. The most incredible thing about her whole story is that the Supreme Leader and Moqtada al-Benizir, the head of the Atomic Energy Organization of Iran—the AEOI—are actively courting her money and have not refused her anything. She is a perfect agent for you and ready to help. You will need to make sure to meet her."

"How did you get all of this information?"

"I have my ways."

"Sort of spy ways?"

"Sort of family spy ways."

136

"I go to Tehran next week for a banking and Iran business conference. Will she be there? Is she expecting me?"

"Yes and yes."

She gave him an affectionate grandmotherly smile. She was a beautiful mature woman who did not look grandmotherly, and no one in the family would ever be so disrespectful as to suggest that she did.

"Have to go. See you after you get back, my dear. Bon voyage. Now, I have to get over to Union Square and some serious shopping."

"See you Grandmom, and thanks a million."

§§§§§

Fourth Floor Conference Room, Bank Melli [BMI], Ferdowsi Building, Tehran, Iran, September 18, 2006

Gideon and Aaron flew into Tehran on separate flights and a day apart from one another. Gideon was met by his limousine driver at the front entry hall of Mehrebad Airport, west of the city. The chauffeur took him swiftly over the Mohammed Baqer-e Sadr Highway—the entrance to Tehran—and then to Azadi Square while Gideon read *The Tehran Times, Iran's Leading International Daily*—from front to back. He went to his reserved room on the third floor of the Five Star Azadi Grand Hotel in Cross Chamran, Evin, and rested well from his flight in order to be at his best at the Iran Economic Summit meetings the following week. For two decades, the meetings were held in the hotel; but during the previous month, the Supreme Leader and Finance Minister Arash Behdad changed the venue to BMI—the largest bank in Iran and across the Islamic world—without explanation.

Aaron caught a taxi from Mehrebad that took him to the Arya Hotel on Hoseyn Marvi St., Azadi Square, a considerably less ostentatious place than the one chosen by Gideon. And—unlike Gideon—he left the hotel around midnight and did not return until six in the morning while he attended to business.

Gideon left his room on the third floor of Azadi Grand Hotel with more than enough time to avoid being late to the summit meeting and had his chauffeur let him off at Ferdowsi Square at Enghelab Street and Ferdowsi Avenue to walk the rest of the way on the intensely busy main thoroughfare. The chauffeur drove to the bank building's parking lot to endure the long wait for his rich client.

Gideon took in the embassies of Germany, Great Britain, and Turkey, and the buildings of the National Bank of Iran and Bank Sepah. He had transacted nuclear energy plant building business with both of them as he set up his network of investors in Iran's peaceful nuclear energy building program. There were several museums he wanted to visit—the National Jewels Museum and Bank Sepah's Coin Museum primarily—but there had never been time, and today was no exception. From the square and stretching down Ferdowsi Avenue, Gideon saw the results of the high inflation brought on by U.S. and European unilateral sanctions. Money changing booths and men on the street were doing a brisk business changing yellow 50,000 and pink 100,000-rial notes bearing Khomeini's face for U.S. currency. The inflation rate was 30 percent on that September day. Gideon estimated that there were 200 people waiting impatiently in the broiling sun in queues in front of the official exchange kiosks in the square—which is the center of the legal trade; and another 300—perhaps more—waiting to deal with the dubious street vendors stretching up the avenue.

All around him were semi-desperate people trying to get the attention of a half-dozen men standing on a raised platform clutching small calculators and large stacks of cash working feverishly taking orders from the public. Most of the people pleading to make the money changes knew that they would quite possibly be the victims of counterfeiters, overchargers, and men whose math was faulty. The hawkers of money held large stacks of American money in one hand and a calculator in the other, briskly relieving the citizens of Tehran of their increasingly worthless savings. The same people would probably be back in a week or two to repeat the same process as the value of their life's savings continue to decline as the interest rates continued to soar. Each transaction took less than thirty seconds from start to finish.

On a side street, the pace of money changing was even more frenetic. There was an even larger and more restless crowd formed around the entrance to a dark passageway. Older and more discouraged men sat on parked motorbikes—having lost their automobiles—watching younger men clap together bundles of crisp new 500-euro and $100 USD notes above their heads. The young men—not yet defeated by the Western world sanctions and mismanagement of the Iranian economy by the country's inept religious leader or the approaching hyperflation—were dressed in tight black jeans and flashy European tee shirts. They leaned nonchalantly against the alley walls, yelling out prices to the crowd that was now barging its way through the narrow passage. Their prices were heavily inflated—even compared to those being offered on Ferdowsi Avenue itself—which were already inflaming the soaring market rate of foreign currency. Nonetheless, business was thick and fast. There seemed to Gideon to be a scenario reminiscent of what he had read about the German Weimar Republic as the pre-WWII inflation destroyed the financial lives of millions of hapless citizens.

Gideon heard an old woman in a worn chador shouting at one of the cocky young men, "Please, Brother, take pity on an old mother. I have waited much of the day to change my money into Euros. Tomorrow, my rials will be worthless; and I will be on the street."

She pulled a large stack of 50,000 yellow rial bank notes from her handbag and waved them at him. She was ignored, and Gideon worried for her safety waving such a bundle of cash for everyone to see.

"Be kind," she shouted in her hoarse voice that was growing weaker, "that your mother may go to heaven with a full belly!"

As he approached the Bank Melli building, Gideon caught snippets of conversation from men on the street. A man selling fresh walnuts out of a large glass vat of water to the passing panic traders gesticulated to a fellow vendor, a man with an ice cream cart. The day was scorching hot, and both men were doing a brisk business.

The walnut seller shook his finger at the scene and spoke intemperately to the ice cream vendor, "Our donkey of a president is responsible for all of this. Our money is worthless; our people beg in the street. It is shameful in Iran that this should be taking place. We never have good management here, not even when the Shah ran things. Maybe we can get a new bunch of thieves in the government in the next election. They can't be worse than this one," he exclaimed, raising his voice.

Gideon was aware that people were beginning to move away from the critic of the regime. It was not altogether smart to be around such a man. Who knew where VEVAK was when someone told the truth?

Not that Gideon Emmanuel Rothsberger IV was an especially greedy man, but he could not help but enjoy watching the painful human drama unfolding around him. Rothsberger & Company Bankers—under the direction of its shrewd senior vice president—reluctantly had had to insist on all of its investments in the Iranian nuclear energy building program being backed by gold. Despite the value of the Iran rial falling week to week, the bottom line of the investment did not change. The nation of Iran had agreed to a rock-solid contract with G.R. IV's banking consortium, and he was in Tehran to collect the now overdue installment. He had a huge lever against the nuclear production program—failure to pay the ever-mounting interest and the amortized portion of the principal that had come due would kick into motion an automatic increase of the interest rate to 28 percent. Failure to make good on even this installment would trigger an automatic cancellation of all funding for Project *Jahannam Adur* [Hell's Fire], which would set back the completion for years, even decades.

The arrogant banker—Ali Mohamed Mustaffen, director of the Central Bank of the Islamic Republic of Iran—would lose great face and probably his career. The life's work of Moqtada al-Benizir, head of the Atomic Energy Organization Iran [AEOI], would be set back so long that he, too, would probably be looking for work in an increasingly difficult economy and without a letter of recommendation from his employers, the Supreme Leader and the president of the Islamic Republic. Even making the payment would deplete the gold reserves available for the Hell Fire project and result in a trickle-down effect that would slow the process. Above and beyond the financial impact, both of the senior officials in the nuclear project knew that the Supreme Leader, Grand Ayatollah Ali ibn Abi Rahimi, and Mohsen Shahamatdoost, president of the Islamic Republic of Iran, were not forgiving men.

CHAPTER TWENTY-TWO

Gideon was smiling as he walked up the stone stairs of the Ferdowsi Building, past the four tall slender columns and into the government owned BMI bank. The building was an imposing stark set of block stone cubes four stories tall. It was a serious place; and—while not quite foreboding—it was hardly an inviting one. The only architectural design that gave a nod to ascetic concerns was the entrance that had a slight graceful concave curve of the façade above the impressive front doors. The elevators were crowded; so, he took the stairs. His self-enforced running and workout schedule was paying off; he was not even breathing hard when he reached the fourth floor conference room.

He was an early arrival to the fourth ECO Ministerial meeting of the Economic Cooperation Organization (ECO) combined with the Islamic Republic of Iran and Eurasian Cooperation Conference. He took his reserved seat next to a quiet middle-aged man who was bearded and dressed in a black suit and white shirt buttoned to the top like all bankers in the country. The sign in front of him read PRESIDENT, BANK SEPAH, HORMOZ MOHAMMAD-BAGHER.

"You are very young. I have studied your history and find it quite remarkable, Mr. Rothsberger. I also applaud your chutzpah—Gideon from the Tanakh narrative—the young man from the tribe of Manasseh, the feller of trees—who perhaps has come to free the people of Israel in the name of his God, Adonai Elohim."

Gideon laughed, "You are obviously a scholar of the Tanakh, Mr. Mohammad-Bagher. I commend you. However, I am nothing of a destroyer. Rather, I come to build, if that is permitted for me. I don't have any lofty or heroic motives; I am here to make money."

141

"You certainly would not be here if the Supreme Leader perceived the least threat from you. You are a prime example that we Persians do not hate our Semitic brethren—just the Occupiers in Israel. Perhaps you and I will work together to see to it that my beloved Persia has a source of energy until the *Yawm al-Qiyāmah* or *Yawm ad-Din* [Day of Judgment] is upon us. The Prophet told us that it would be 50,000 years; so, perhaps I should not concern myself overmuch."

"Mr. Mohammad-Bagher, you are probably a better scholar of the Hebrew Bible than I. I am familiar with my namesake, of course; but I would certainly not arrogate his qualities to me. In fact, I am very glad to be able to have these few minutes to learn from you. May I ask you a few questions, Sir?"

"Nothing personal or treasonous, I hope," Mohammad-Bagher said with a twinkle in his eyes and a broad smile.

Gideon laughed.

"And I promise not to discuss religion or politics."

"So, young man, how can I enlighten you?"

"I admit to a concern, one my colleagues share. We have heard rumors that the BMI is nearly insolvent and may be on the verge of bankruptcy with the Western sanctions, the drought, and the level of debt incurred by the bank. What can you tell me?"

"You cut right to the heart of things. I like that in a man. I am, of course, a private banker and not privy to the financial bottom line of the government's bank. So far as I know, Bank Melli Iran is the largest in Iran and probably in the entire Islamic world. It is second richest to the Central Bank of Iran, and I am informed that both are doing well, although they are under a strain. I have to tell you that you pose a threat. You made a most difficult contract with the government of the Islamic Republic and the Central Bank. They will have to struggle some to come up with sufficient gold to meet your contractual demands. Perhaps, you should accept a less difficult medium of collateral."

"Iran rials?"

"That would be most helpful and would ensure the success of my bank's investment in the nuclear energy program; and—I dare say—that of most of the banks in the country. You would certainly build friends here if you did. However, it would be naïve of me to expect a debt of this size to be backed by our currency that cannot even be traded on international markets. Perhaps you could accept a somewhat discounted trade in Euros or even U.S. dollars."

"My consortium has discussed discounts and has rejected them. We must be practical; the rial has lost 60 percent of its value against the dollar just in the past two months. We came as businessmen—not as Jews or nationals of our various countries, or ideologues. We have tens of thousands of investors whom we cannot fail. It would be considered improper to do so, if not outright criminal. I am afraid, Sir, that we will have to stick to our contract and hope that the unfortunate chain of events that would occur should a failure of the Persian government to honor its debts take place could be weathered by Iran."

"When all is said and done, I am sure the Supreme Leader and the president will honor the debts; it is the Islamic way of honor to be honest traders. It is comforting to see Mr. Sağlam coming to the dais."

"I have every confidence that that is so, and that is a large part of why I came personally to be sure that there is no miscommunication. I also came to learn and am looking forward to this seminar. Looks like they are ready to start," Gideon said and nodded towards the head table on the dais.

Hojatollah Mazandarani, the president of BMI, Ali Mohamed Mustaffen, director of the Central Bank, retired Gen. Hooman Mirza-Zelli, from the Majlis [Iranian Parliament], and Oğuz Ülkü Paşazade Sağlam—the billionaire CEO of the Turkish government's *Türkiye Petrolleri Anonim Ortaklığı* [*TPAO*-Turkish Petroleum Corporation]—assumed their seats.

Mr. Mazandarani lightly tapped his gavel on the hardwood table.

"Welcome, gentlemen. The annual financial summit of Iran is declared to be in session. We have the honor of hearing from Mr. Ali Mohamed Mustaffen, the esteemed director of the Central Bank, as our keynote speaker. Mr. Mustaffen."

Mustaffen looked tired and not nearly as arrogant as when Gideon first met him.

"Thank you for attending. Many of you have come from great distances and have taken time away from your pressing business. There is much to be discussed here today, and most of that will be done in committee. However, I will address rumors and will correct them with facts. First, and most important, is the rumor that the sanctions imposed by the Great Satan and its European lapdogs have crippled the economy of the Islamic Republic of Iran. I state categorically that that is not so. But I do admit that the sanctions have placed a strain on our efforts to move forward.

"The Great Satan—acting without cause—imposed unilateral sanctions against our beloved country. They have trumped up the notion that we are making nuclear weapons, that we intend to start a war. All we are doing is trying to create clean, efficient energy while they reject peaceful uses of such energy in their own country. What hypocrites they are; they have thousands of nuclear weapons and yet they accuse us of making weapons to defend ourselves. Last October, Great Satan placed heavy restrictive measures to reduce

143

Iran's ability to conduct financial transactions between the state-owned banks of Iran—the Central Bank and BMI, among others—and United States and European citizens, and private organizations. Bank Melli was included in these sanctions, on the specious grounds that the bank provides financial services to Iran's so-called nuclear weapons and ballistic missile programs. I have here a fabricated fact sheet released by the U.S. Treasury Department," he waved a thick stack of papers, "which spreads the lies that between 2002 and 2006, our Bank Melli sent at least $100 million to Hamas—the Palestinian Islamic Jihad—and other groups they call terrorists, via the Quds Force, a branch of the Iranian Revolutionary Guard.

"That is a wicked lie. Our financial transactions are entirely above board. We do not finance terrorism; it would be counterproductive to our national aims and contrary to our mandate from God to care for and to protect our people. Let me come to the bottom line. Our banks are sound; our economy is in good condition; and your investments are safe.

"Yes, it is true that the sanctions—those acts of war—perpetrated against us have had an effect. We are experiencing some inflation. We are having difficulty in carrying out financial dealings with the rest of the world. I am sad to report that our Sunni brethren have decided to cave into the Great Satan and to aid the U.S. in its unwarranted attacks. There is a notable exception; our noble friends in Syria still stand with us. I tell you here and now that we shall overcome this temporary setback, because Allah, may all glory be to His name, is our God; and He will bring us victory.

"There is market volatility, and it has become too risky to trade—so much so that we have had to take some extraordinary measures. Beginning tomorrow, we will shut down currency listing websites and clear Ferdowsi Square and the avenue of traders. Unscrupulous black marketeers are dragging down the value of the rial; and we must; and we will, regain control. President Shahamatdoost will make the announcement on state television this evening. Thank you for your attention."

It was worse than Gideon had thought. Iran had been bellicose in its denial that the U.S.-led sanctions were effective, but Mustaffen's unusually candid outburst was enough for Gideon.

He kept a bland expression, but inwardly he was shouting, "*It's working. The project to hamper the progress of weapons production is showing results, and nothing overt has been done by our people yet!*"

The next speaker was Hojatollah Mazandarani, the president of BMI. Evidently, this first day of the summit was going to be a level of candor unheard of since the revolution.

144

"We are taking immediate measures to shore up our currency. The rial has lost 15 percent of its value against the Great Satan's almighty dollar in recent days and has lost almost 50 percent of its value in the past two months."

Gideon knew that the figure was more like 60 percent or even 65 percent, but he held his peace and maintained his facial control.

"In December, the rial was 12,790 to the dollar."

Gideon had just walked in off the trading street where the rate had gone from 13,000 rials to 37,780 to the dollar in the past ten days. At this rate, the Republic would have to begin printing larger denomination bills or to have functionaries cross out the printed value and to fill in numbers that were larger by logarithmic quantities. He was waiting to see if a critic of the regime would be allowed to speak. He had seen several prominent members of the political opposition sitting near the dais, and found the prospects that some real complaints would surface fascinating.

When the BMI president finished his hardline speech, Gideon was surpised to see the man with whom he had been speaking stand up and walk to the podium. His name was not on the printed agenda. More surprising, the recent candidate for the presidency, Hassan Shambayati—who had protested the election results as rigged—accompanied Mr. Mohammad-Bagher, president of Bank Sepah, to the dais.

"Gentlemen," Mohammad-Bagher said, "I have little more to offer here, but I will head a committee that will discuss the economy in depth this afternoon. I hope you will be able to attend. Now—with the permission of Chairman Mustaffen, I will introduce a man who needs no introduction—to speak to you briefly on the state of the economy."

He gestured to the well-known opposition candidate.

"Mr. Shambayati."

"At the beginning of 2006, Iran reacted to what can only be described as a currency crash by setting an official foreign exchange rate of 12,260 rials per dollar, a reasonable measure considering the circumstances we face. That rate is offered to selected importers of prioritized goods like food and medicine, also a noble idea. But in our political system beset by patronage for the wealthy bazaaris and nepotism that favors the friends of the leaders of the revolution, Iran's cheap, official-rate petrodollars end up in the hands of the well-connected, who take advantage of vast opportunities to make money though arbitrage, at the expense of the man on the street, the widow, and the orphan.

"Our growing number of poor people lives on subsidies that drain the life-blood of our nation's financial well-being, and the rich with friends in government make millions of rials on their cheap dollars. The common people suffer the most in this critical time. My wife and I have a daughter studying art history at the Sorbonne in Paris, and a son studying economics in London. It has been difficult to nearly impossible to send them money because banks do not do business with Iran anymore—with the exception of the consortium headed by Mr. Gideon Rothsberger, who is attending the seminar today. I am deeply concerned personally and for the nation because now—even if we could send money—it would not be worth enough to allow our children to have their educations abroad.

"There are many theories being touted around Tehran about the cause of our economy's crash. Some speculate that President Shahamatdoost's political enemies want to cause him problems. Let me tell you without reservation that the political opposition—which I head—is not involved. We are genuinely fearful for our country and will not allow politics from ourside to add to the state of alarm. There are certainly enough problems in the country already without politicians needing to manufacture more. Other theories blame a well-intentioned but ill-conceived government effort a month ago to set up an auction for licensed importers and exporters to trade currencies; the volume of transactions quickly jumped almost twentyfold and diverted cash away from the black market. Instead of helping, the effect was temporary; and the black market is flourishing. The government unwittingly gave a massive shot in the arms of the speculators.

"Whatever the cause may be, the consequences are abundantly evident. Panic buying is eroding the value of the rial and flooding our Iranian economy with cheap rials, adding to Iran's already cripplingly high inflation. These confiscatory exchange rates deprive Iran's middle class of their savings and their very livelihoods. The biggest drain on our citizens is inflation, not the actions of the Great Satan—although the West certainly has a share of the blame. Officially, the rate of inflation this week is listed by the government as 20 percent, but it is very significantly higher in reality.

"A perfect storm of President Shahamatdoost's subsidy cuts and the unprecedented and unconscionable flooding of our already floundering economy with massive oil revenues for populist political purposes have put even the most basic of staple commodities out of the reach of many Iranians. Prices of chicken, lamb, goat, and even vegetables, to say nothing of the diverse array of imported foods and other goods—which have been one of the mainstays of Iran's markets over the years since the revolution—have more than doubled since 2003. I fear for panic, malnutrition—even starvation in the rural areas—and political unrest.

"I beg President Shahamatdoost and our Supreme Leader Agha Rahimi to attend to these problems. I pledge our party's cooperation so that we can all work together to bring an end to the current crisis. Peaceful nuclear energy is a solution for Iran's problems sometime in the future; but the expense is a major drain on the economy,; and we should back away from it for now. In the name of Allah, the merciful, do not allow a waste of the people's precious money to be expended on any more weaponry."

Gideon would not have been surprised if Sahamatdoost's VEVAK police marched down the aisle and arrested the heedlessly outspoken perpetual opposition candidate, but it did not happen. The level of unease was palpable, however, and the chairman of the fourth ECO Ministerial meeting, Hojatollah Mazandarani, president of BMI, announced a brief intermission.

The room cleared for cigarette breaks and visits to the bathrooms. Gideon, two security guards, and the lone woman attending the seminar, were left in the conference room. As casually as possible, Gideon made his way across the room to meet the woman.

"Mrs. Dayan," I presume," he said, and extended his hand.

The singular woman was approaching seventy years of age, but had the strength and bearing of a vigorous fifty-year-old. She was appropriately covered with a deep maroon hijab and a beautiful patterned silk dress that covered her from her neck to her wrists and ankles. A few unruly wisps of white hair peaked out from under the edges of the hijab and accented her deeply tanned face, which was lined with topographical wrinkles from her long hours in the saddle.

"Indeed," the formidable matron answered and took his hand in a grip that rivaled that of a strong man. "And you are the prodigy Gideon Rothsberger I hear so much about."

"Flattery will get you everywhere," Gideon smiled. "It is good to meet you, Mrs. Dayan. My grandmother, Rebecca, speaks very highly of you—her relative."

"We must have a talk, but not here, and not today, my boy. The walls have ears, as we Americans say. In a month or so, we will have our annual horse auction at the ranch. You might consider attending and making an investment. Horses are valuable and also wonderful. You will be quite taken with our stock, I am sure."

"And, we can talk."

She nodded, then turned and left the room before the suspicious ears in the walls and the eyes of the guards in the room became attentive to the only two Jews allowed to attend the ECO meetings.

The five-minute intermission concluded, and the attendees resumed their seats. The seminar continued without incident. The next speaker was the invited foreign guest, Oğuz Ülkü Paşazade Sağlam, the CEO of the Turkish government's *Türkiye Petrolleri Anonim Ortaklığı* [*TPAO*-Turkish Petroleum Corporation].

"Thank you, President Mustaffen, President Mohammad-Bagher, Gen. Hooman Mirza-Zelli, and honored guests," Mr. Sağlam began. "I am sure none of you underestimate the value of your petroleum industry; and I hope you regard Turkey as your ally, especially in these difficult economic times. I am empowered to speak for the Turkish government on these issues, and I want to assure you that we are still able to communicate with the governments and financial institutions of the United States and Europe on your behalf.

"Allow me to refresh your memories about Turkey's central position in the production and transportation of petroleum. Our country is key to the success of the producers, the refiners, and the buyers. We sit in the middle between Russia, the Caspian Sea, oil rich former Soviet Union countries, the thriving Middle-East, and the massive demand centers of Europe as the most important energy transit hub in the world. Nearly three million barrels of crude oil pass through our facilities every day, and we are a major market for oil and natural gas supplies ourselves.

"We are Iran's and Russia's best customer. Turkey is a major transit point for seaborne traded oil and is becoming ever more important for pipeline-traded oil and natural gas. We struggle to build enough tankers to serve the ever growing volumes of Russian and Caspian oil being sent by tanker via the Turkish Straits to Western markets. We have a terminal on our Mediterranean coast at Ceyhan that serves as an outlet for oil exports from northern Iraq, Azerbaijan, and Iran. Because of the fact that our role is so crucial, the government of Turkey has rolled almost all production and transportation into one company—TPAO—of which I am the CEO. TPAO produced almost 75 percent of the domestic petroleum used by Turkey, but Iran provides 45 percent of our needs. Our pipelines, tankers, and terminals are crucial and could be vulnerable to attack by our Kurdish minority rebels. They have become increasingly sophisticated in the past several years.

"We are actively exploring our southeast region and have proved oil reserves there approaching 300 million barrels—most in the Hakkari basin. We believe that we will eventually be able to extract 8-10 or maybe even 12 billion barrels of crude from the Black Sea. We are in a territorial dispute with Greece or Aegean Sea sources, so that is not presently a viable source for us. None of that will be enough. Our oil production varies between 40 and 90 thousand barrels per day, and that is far short of what our burgeoning economy needs. Turkey is on the fastest growing economies in the world. Every year our population grows; our oil consumption grows; and our need for more and more oil grows. We are now consuming over 706,000 barrels per day. So, the fact is that we import well over 90 percent of the liquid fuels—diesel fuel, refined oils, jet fuel, and LPG [liquified petroleum gas]—Turkey uses. We expect that need to double in the next ten years.

"There are several conclusions to be drawn from what I have told you. First, we have great need for Iran's oil; 45 percent of our crude oil imports come from Iran at this point in time. Any decrease in that flow would require us to buy more and more from Iraq. Second, Russia's production is decreasing and is not expected to increase in the future. It may come as no surprise, but Russia is not always a reliable business partner."

Most of the men in the room nodded in agreement.

"Second, rumors of war and sanctions imposed by the West are most troubling to us. We would have to make radical changes in where we get oil should the Israelis or the Americans decide that Iran is making a thermonuclear device and the missile systems to deliver a payload. We would presume that Iran—in that case, would be undependable—and we would increase our input from Iraq, even to the point of subsidizing their production and to form joint ventures with ExxonMobil, Petrobras, and others.

An attack by the Americans or the Israelis or both could wreck our pipelines, transit stations, and tankers. Their navies could mount a blockade that would prevent us getting supplies, shipping supplies, and would ruin Turkey. It goes without saying that such a war must not happen. We are your friends; but in our own national interests, we cannot allow you to produce nuclear weapons. Please do not place us in the position of having to defend ourselves."

It was music to Gideon's ears, and the finely tuned gears of his mind ran a number of pernicious options past his reasoning centers. The Iran Nuclear Interdiction Project looked to be more feasible than ever and more complicated and full of risks. He determined to run his ideas past Adm. Daastrup before he broached the subject with anyone else.

The morning session closed for lunch. Gideon sat alone at a table in the back of the cafeteria style lunch room. He was alone by choice and because virtually none of the men attending the meeting—other than his German banking colleagues—would sit with a Jew. He read a little of *Gozaresh*—the Persian language national newspaper—more to practice his developing fluency with Farsi than to glean actual news. The paper was notoriously biased towards Islamic topics and the government's take on issues. He was reading

149

the *Tehran Times, Iran's Leading International Daily* with some interest when he felt a tap on his shoulder.

It was Gerhardt Lowenstein, Gideon's opposite number in the Bonn DeutscheBank branch—and, known only to Gideon—he was a closet Jew.

"Gideon, may I join you for a moment?"

"Sure. Sorry, I've finished lunch."

"So have I. I have a message from Mustaffen and Mohammad-Bagher. They want to meet us day after tomorrow before we fly back to Europe."

"That has to be a good sign. When and where?"

§§§§§

Tower of Bank Markazi, Mirdamad Building, 144 Mirdamad Boulevard, Tehran, Iran, September 20, 2006.

All participants in the meeting were seated in Ali Mohamed Mustaffen's ante-room at ten o'clock sharp waiting expectantly. Mustaffen and Mohammad-Bagher walked into the anteroom from the Central Bank president's office, which was not a surprise. There was a surprise when Gideon and his banking colleagues walked into the conference room. Four other men were seated at the handsome table. Gideon knew three of them, but one he did not know and would never have expected to see in this room—an Orthodox rabbi.

The other three men were Mohsen Shahamatdoost, president of the Republic of Iran, Moqtada al-Benizir, head of the Atomic Energy Organization Iran (AEOI), Ali Muhummad Sharifi, Iranian foreign minister, and Hormoz Mohammad-Bagher, president of Bank Sepah—all of whom Gideon had met and was on at least a nodding acquaintance basis. The man who interested Gideon most was Rabbi Ya'akov ben Avraham, ha-Rav—a rabbi and a son of a rabbi, a Jew and an Iranian. Knowing that there were fewer than 9,000 Jews left in Iran, the rabbi was a considerable anomaly in the gathering.

After limited pleasantries, thick Turkish coffee, and some excessively sweet pulpy Iranian fruit juices, Mustaffen got down to business.

"Gentlemen, we have received what amounts to a bill from your banking consortium. You realize that we consider it rude at best to be considered as common debtors. Surely, you don't question our intention to pay your usurious demands since we have a contract. And more surely, you cannot possibly question our ability to pay. What have you to say for yourself, Mr. Rothsberger? You made it clear during our last meeting that you were the

150

spokesman for the financial consortium that is providing funding for our peaceful nuclear program."

"That is correct, Sir. To be both clear and necessarily blunt—but without intending disrespect—we are here because our several requests for the installment payment for this quarter have not been answered. The "bill"—a perfectly reasonable term for a perfectly reasonable request—is now more than two months past due. Our agreement was that payment would be in gold—physical gold. President Mustaffen, would you please share your intentions regarding our business arrangement?"

"We intend to pay you."

There was a several minute pause—an awkward silence.

"When?" Gideon asked tersely.

"When the government of Iran sees fit."

"We cannot work with such an indefinite timetable. We are here today to collect. If we leave Tehran without seeing that a transfer of gold from you to us has been ordered, our contract will be considered null and void. We will be obliged to freeze all Iranian assets in our many banks until we have collected sufficiently from the accounts to meet the obligation. That will be a substantial drain on your foreign hard currency, and will result in a loss of any further funding for your nuclear energy project from what amounts to the only banks in the West with whom you can do business. Even if I were inclined to do so, Rothsberger Family Bank in the United States is bound not to do business with you in accordance with the sanctions imposed by the American government. It is your decision, Sir. We are serious about money despite not being particularly concerned by ideology, prestige, politics, or power."

There was another pregnant pause.

"We have an alternative proposal for you. The government of Iran will guarantee the rial at 13,000 rials to one U.S. dollar and make a wire transfer by the close of business today. We will not have to reduce our stores of gold that form the foundation of our monetary system, and you will have your money."

"There is a reason why we insisted on payment in physical gold. You are experiencing double digit inflation, and the infrastructure, even the food, durable goods, and replacement parts for your military, nuclear ambitions, and transportation systems are feeling the serious inroads imposed by the American sanctions. We are all men whose eyes are open in this room—practical men. Governmental propaganda aside, that is why we insisted on physical gold, and that is why we put it to you directly, President, that is what we must have today; or we will no longer be in business together. As we see it, you have serious decisions to make."

For the first time, Mohsen Shahamatdoost, president of the Republic of Iran, spoke up, "We will not be bullied or threatened, young man. You are among your betters—serious men with an unstoppable agenda. It is your privilege to be a part of our grand plan to provide our people with clean, safe energy for as long as any of us can imagine. You will lose the investment of a lifetime. I demand that you reconsider your obstinate position, you greedy Jew."

"I did not come here to be insulted, and I did not come here to be paid with an empty promise. I gather that we are at an impasse. Therefore, the consortium hereby cancels its contract with the Islamic Republic of Islam and will not return in the future. Good day, gentlemen."

He rose from his chair, and all of the rest of the bankers stood with him.

Rabbi ben Avraham held up his hand.

"Gideon, I understand that you come from an Orthodox family and are a practicing member of the *Kashim* [Persian-Jewish people] yourself. Let us reason together. We Jews here have learned to be careful to negotiate in good faith. In return, our Islamic friends ask only that we be good Iranians and that we not support Israel. Neither of those requirements is burdensome to us. We Jews, as part of the Iranian people, request of you, our brother, to consider a plan that would benefit us all. As a gesture of good faith, the Supreme Leader has communicated with me that—if you remain hard-hearted—and must have the gold—the physical gold, as you put it—then we will tighten our belts once more and let some of the human needs of our people slide for a time. You will have your gold this time but; in return, we ask that a more liberal interpretation of the payment schedule be agreed upon. A handshake will be sufficient among us men of the Book. We ask that the contract be extended for three more years with payments at six month intervals, and with a 1 percent increase in the interest rate. This would be compounded over the life of the loan. I understand that would be a rather significant windfall for your consortium. Can we agree?"

Gideon knew that he and the hard bargaining Iranians had been looking eye to eye, and this meant that they were the first to blink. He nodded to his consortium members, and they made small positive hand gestures.

"We agree. The deal will be as you have presented it, Rabbi; but it is contingent on a cargo of gold being received by us before the close of business one week from today."

The Iranians stood. All of the men—Western and Eastern—spat on the palms of their right hands and shook hands with every member of the opposing side.

152

CHAPTER TWENTY-THREE

Stockholms Universitet [Stockholm University], *Studenthuset* [Student Union Building], September 28, 2006

Afsoon was aware all day that she was seeing the same Middle-Easterner man in various different places and times. There were too many coincidences, and Afsoon was rapidly becoming a nonbeliever in coincidences. Furthermore, the young man was none to adept at surveilling her. She was able to get a good enough look at him on several occasions that she recognized him as the young man who had spoken kindly when she went to the "Basement mosque" the first time.

On her own, she decided to put her suspicions of being surveilled to the test. The island of Djurgården is only a short walk from the pulse of the inner city, and Stockholmers and visitors alike go there to relax in the leafy shade and to feast their eyes on a green landscape comparable to what is found in Ireland. She ambled her way around the small island, stopping frequently to enjoy an elaborate interest in a flower garden, an out-of-the-way statue, or a fountain. The Middle-Easterner was always nearby, although he was making a serious effort to be unobtrusive. He wore different hats, took glasses and sunglasses on and off, and changed shirts and his jacket several times. He was carrying a supermarket bag where he presumably kept his impromptu disguise materials. Whatever the man's elaborate and distracting attentions, Afsoon's sightings of him were well above anything that could be passed off as coincidence.

Her uncle, 3D, had warned her that he was almost certainly a VEVAK agent the evening she had first seen him on Arne Beurlings Torg. She had called the secure line at the DDDIA's office at noon when she had seen the man for the third time—when she was on Djurgården Island—and was certain beyond reasonable doubt that this was the same man. The Iranian was not menacing, nor did he approach her. He seemed content to watch her. It was a bit creepy, but Afsoon went about her regular routine without reacting to him.

The VEVAK agent was seated in the back of the auditorium when Afsoon presented her inaugural lecture on the practical issues of nuclear engineering. When Afsoon glanced his way, he had a bewildered look on his face, as if he had happened into a lecture hall where the instructor was speaking Klingon—not that he would have any idea what Klingon was.

Afsoon had to admit that for anyone but the completely initiated, a lecture on nuclear engineering was dull stuff.

"Fossil fuel-based electricity is projected to account for more than 40 percent of global greenhouse gas emissions by 2020," she said. "In the U.S.—one of the world's worst polluters—90 percent of the carbon emissions from the generation of electricity come from burning coal, even though this accounts for only half of the electricity produced. Putting nuclear power on the table as a viable alternative to the smoke and ash of coal will allow the global community—including Sweden—to achieve very long-term gains in the control of carbon dioxide emissions, as well as providing very efficient energy.

"We have to be practical and frugal. Almost no city, state, or country is willing to spend a great deal of money for long-term benefits that antagonize the voters in the short-run. The prospects for nuclear energy as an option in the developed world are limited and, in the nondeveloped world, are nonexistent. The issue of getting nuclear power available to the people on a wide scale is difficult because of four confounding problems: 1. high initial costs and relatively high maintenance costs compared to coal and—to a lesser degree—to burning petroleum products, 2. perceived adverse safety, environmental, and health effects. This is not supported by empirical evidence, especially in comparison to other fuel sources. 3. possible potential security risks stemming from proliferation. This is a highly unlikely scenario owing to excellent security measures at nuclear plants and the difficulty of converting peaceful purpose materials into weapons grade materials, and 4. unresolved challenges in long-term management of nuclear wastes.

This a real problem, mostly due to the general hysteria over even the word "nuclear." It is true that no one can guarantee that any waste product container can be 100 percent secure over a vast amount of time. We humans are clever and resourceful. We will find methods to mitigate the higher initial costs of nuclear energy production and, I predict, will make this clean source of energy competitive over the next seventy-five years or even less. The value of protecting against CO_2 increases in the atmosphere is incalculable.

"If the United States were to progress from its 360 GWe [GigaWats of energy] to 1000 GWe by 2050, nuclear energy's share of nuclear capacity would be a constant percentage—the same as currently. Despite the growth scenario, studies indicate that nuclear power would make a significant beneficial contribution to reducing CO2 emissions.

"Recommendations by a Harvard/Georgetown study group to make the production and use of nuclear energy viable include the following:

1. Place increased emphasis on the once-through fuel cycle afforded by nuclear energy as best meeting the criteria of low costs and proliferation resistance.

2. Governments can offer a limited production tax-credit to private sector investors who successfully build new nuclear plants. This tax credit is extendable to other carbon-free electricity technologies and is not paid unless and until the new plant becomes operational.

3. Governments should more fully analyze life-cycle health and safety impacts of fuel cycle facilities and educate their citizens to the facts in contrast to the superstitions that now exist.

4. The U.S. should create a model Department of Energy [DOE] long-term waste management research and develop program and make it available without a patent and gratis to public and private entities around the world without discrimination.

5. The DOE should establish a Nuclear System Modeling project that would collect all of the engineering data and perform the analysis necessary to evaluate alternative reactor concepts and fuel cycles from all sources using the criteria of cost, safety, waste, and proliferation resistance. Expensive development projects should be delayed pending the outcome of this multi-year effort.

6. The United States and other developed countries that forego proliferation--i.e., risky enrichment and reprocessing activities--would be granted a preferred position to receive nuclear fuel and waste management services from nations that operate the entire fuel cycle. Sanctions involving all areas described in this list should be the negative incentive exacted from companies and nations to bring them into line.

7. Nuclear power should be considered just one of several alternative non-carbon energy sources, and all such sources should be studied

to find which, if any, meet the same base requirements demanded of nuclear energy.

"Thank you, ladies and gentlemen, fellow students. In our next lecture, we will begin to understand what the engineering requirements, regulations, and safeguards that must be part of a widespread increase in building and bringing on-line new nuclear energy production facilities are."

Afsoon watched the putative VEVAK agent slip out of the lecture hall. She was sure she had not seen the last of him. She packed up her laptop and notes and headed for the *Studenthuset* [Student Union Building] to relax and unwind.

She found a comfortable overstuffed chair in a corner of the large open hall of the first floor, draped her legs over the arms of the chair, and began to catch up on the local newspapers—*Dagens Nyheter* and *Svenska Dagbladet*. The Student Union Building is an open, simple building with straight lines and sharp corners. The walls are more glass than support structure that provides a nearly panoramic view of the outside grounds. That portion of the walls which is not glass is a facade of granite and wood. The building is L-shaped, with three main floors and a narrow fourth floor in the section that adjoins the A-building. The ground floor has a granite facade; the middle section has a glass wall that makes one wonder what holds the building up; while the top floor has a strong Swedish timber facade. On the south side of the building is an attractive open garden, under which a geothermal heating and cooling system plant has been constructed. In keeping with the overall green character of the ultramodern building, the roof is covered in Sedum, which contributes to the greenery of the surrounding area and reduces runoff of water from the building to the stormwater system.

Afsoon had been in her chair for just short of an hour when she saw the first of two men who seemed rather out of place. The first was the VEVAK agent who was casually sauntering around the area where Afsoon was sitting, obviously trying not to appear obvious. He seemed rather nervous and took a full fifteen minutes to make it to the chair across from her.

"Is this chair taken?" he asked.

It was a silly approach, since there were dozens of unoccupied chairs. It could easily have been a more-or-less awkward and cautious approach of a shy boy to a beautiful and sophisticated young woman. It did not shout of spycraft.

He broke the ice with, "Are you Dr. Mouradipour?"

"I am."

"I was very impressed with your lecture on nuclear energy. I have to confess that I am an arts major and am only spending a year in Sweden."

He laughed.

"My real confession is that I didn't understand a word of what you said, but I was impressed anyway."

"Didn't I meet you at the mosque on Arne Beurlings Torg recently?" Afsoon asked, already knowing the answer and waiting to see if he would lie.

"We did. I am surprised that you would remember such an unimportant student as me."

"I did not see an unimportant student. I saw a brother. How is your stay in Sweden going?"

"Not so good really. It has been terrible getting a room. My friends and I can't afford a good apartment; and, even if we could, we still can't seem to find one. Landlords won't rent to people from the Middle-East because they think we will pack several families in a couple of rooms and will trash the place. We're all bachelors, and I guess they're not too far wrong."

"So what do you do?"

"Me and my friends couch-surf."

"What is couch-surfing, pray tell.... Sorry, I didn't catch your name."

"I don't have any manners. It's Salar Sabeti. Anyway, me and my friends come to Sweden pretty irregularly and stay a few days to a few months. We learned that, if you are in desperate need for an accommodation, you can find a temporarily place to stay for some time and make friends in the new city through what everybody calls couch-surfing."

"How do you find a place?"

"There are bulletin boards all over the campus at the U and at bus and train stations. After a while, we can get places through a kind of network of poor people who have to keep moving around all of the time to be able to have a roof over their heads."

"Sounds difficult."

"It is. Where do you live, if I may ask?"

That question raised a prickle of fear in Afsoon.

"On campus."

Since she did not offer more, he let it drop.

It was then that Afsoon saw the second man who seemed out of place in the Student Union Building. He was a big, muscular man with a short-cropped shock of red hair. His clothes were old Swedish military fatigues, and he was carrying an uncomfortable appearing old ruck-sack. None of that was particularly out-of-place; many Swedes have red hair; many men are strong and virile; but none of them was Aaron Schmuel. Aaron scarcely glanced at her, but he took a seat fifty feet away and developed a rapt interest in a discarded copy of *Svenska Dagbladet*. Sabeti did not seem to notice him.

"Will I see you at prayers this Friday, Dr. Mouradipour?"

"I plan to come, if I can get away."

"It would be better if you wore a chador. The older men are pretty old-fashioned about women being covered up."

"Thank you. I realized that the first time I came for prayers. I have proper clothing now. Jennifer Gustafsson told me where to find used ones."

"She's a good sister. She's been a big help for ... us guys from Iran."

Afsoon's fine-tuned ear heard something a little different in Sabeti's accent. It was not the typical Tehrani accent—the most widely-used accent of the Persian language. To Afsoon, it had more of the Esfahani quality.

She decided to try something a little more forward. She spoke to him in Farsi, knowing that her accent would not be typical of Tehran.

"Brother, where in Iran do you come from?"

He did not act surprised when she switched to Farsi.

"A village near Esfahan."

"I like your accent."

"Yours sounds more educated—like you grew up near Tehran University. I guess that's natural since you are so educated. As I said when I first sat down, I am impressed."

"Thank you."

"Well," Sabar said, "I shouldn't keep you any longer. I hope we can get to talk after prayers on Friday. There are some people I would like you to meet. They are kind of important people."

"Sounds interesting. I'll see you then."

Sabar left and again took a circuitous route through the large open area of the Student Union and disappeared into the throng of debaters gathered on the commons.

Afsoon collected her things and walked casually in the direction of where Aaron was sitting. He did not glance up until she passed next to his chair. She pretended to drop her keys.

"Fancy meeting you here," she said. "Anything up?"

"Not really. Let's meet in the garden. It's a little more private."

Afsoon went out the front, and Aaron left by the rear entry where the garden was. He was sitting on a stone bench when Afsoon found him. She sat on the grass near his bench.

158

"We shouldn't be seen together for very long, Afsoon," he said. "I think the place is full of VEVAK agents. That one was younger than most and might as well have been wearing a sandwich board advertising VEVAK."

Afsoon had not heard the term "sandwich board," but she got the drift.

"Seems so."

"Does he seem safe? I mean, any negative vibes, like he could be suspicious of you?"

"I don't think so. I really think he is just a homesick boy from Isfahan who is on his first assignment. He was probably chosen because he is not threatening. Some of the men in the mosque on Arne Beurlings Torg were more like what I remember of VEVAK agents. I'm supposed to meet with them this Friday."

"Be on your guard, Afsoon. I'll have guys watching you all the way. Give your best scream if you get into trouble. We'll be with you in less than a minute, I guarantee. Don't get in over your head."

"I won't."

"Watch for a guy in a bright blue university tee shirt and white shorts when you leave your apartment. He's one of mine. You won't see me again for a while. Stay safe."

"You, too, Aaron. It made me feel better seeing you in the Student Union. I am very glad you have my back."

"And I always will."

With that, he got up and walked away without looking back.

CHAPTER TWENTY-FOUR

28314 Terrace Drive, Saint Francis Wood nabe, San Francisco, California, September 28, 2006

Gideon sat in his home office in the Rothsberger mansion and waited for the conference call to connect. Events in the Iran Nuclear Interdiction Project had been escalating for the past two weeks, and the principals needed to be made aware of the changes.

The phone rang and an operator asked, "Is this a secure line?"

"Yes."

The secure line had been installed by DIA and NSA technicians more than two years previously.

"Is this G.R. IV?"

"Yes, Ma'am."

"I will check the availability of the conferees and then return to you."

Two minutes passed.

"Everyone is present for the conference call. All persons have security clearance for the information."

Adm. Daastrup's voice came on next, "Hello, everyone. Let's do a quick check-in: Gideon III? Gideon IV? Zwi? Moises? Max? Aaron? Levi? Afsoon? Ali? Arvid? Sanna? Magnus? Johannes? Daniel? Abraham? Randall? Annette? Carter? Lincoln? Elizabeth Dayan?"

All twenty voices gave quick "Yes" replies as their name was mentioned.

Levi's harsh voice said, "Sounds like roll call for a pirate ship."

A little polite laughter greeted his attempt at humor.

160

Adm. Daastrup said, "For the record, all information is for those of you on this conference call and no one else. Everyone on the line has been vetted and has Ultra Top-Secret clearance and need-to-know status...."

CIA agent Annette Redstone interrupted the rear admiral, "I have no idea who Elizabeth Dayan is. I—for one—need to know before we start passing top-secret information."

3D answered.

"She has been thoroughly vetted. Let's have the Rothsbergers tell us about her. Sorry to be talking about you, Elizabeth, as if you weren't on the line."

"That's all right. Gideon—either one of them—can fill you in."

Her voice had a peculiar metallic ring to it as if she were talking inside a metal cylinder. 3D knew she was on an encrypted sat phone somewhere outside a building in Iran.

G.R. III said, "G.R. IV has had the most to do with her. They met at the fourth ECO Ministerial meeting of the Economic Cooperation Organization (ECO) in Tehran ten days ago. Let him tell you about that meeting."

G.R. IV's voice came on the line, "Hello everyone. I first learned about Mrs. Dayan from my grandmother who has family connections with Dayans and personally with Elizabeth. To be brief, Mrs. Dayan is an American citizen and has an American passport. She has lived just outside Tehran for more than forty years—since before the revolution. She and Farah Pahlavi—the late Shah's wife—were fast friends. In fact, Elizabeth and Farah were best friends before she married the Shah—before she was the princess consort, the queen consort, or the Empress of Iran; she was Farah Diba then. My grandmother is a Dayan and is related to Elizabeth through an aunt. Elizabeth has never renounced her American citizenship, has never opposed the current regime— at least openly—and—because she has considerable money that she invests in government projects—she is tolerated by President Shahamatdoost and the Supreme Leader. She is doubly cursed: she is an American in a country that hates Americans, and she is an unrepentant Jew in a nation that despises the whole Jewish race.

"Mrs. Dayan runs a highly successful horse breeding ranch that is hard work and keeps her out of trouble and out of the limelight. She is accepted because of her money and because she is known to Jews and Muslims alike to be a member of the Haredi sect Neturei Karta, which is opposed to the State of Israel. Of interest to us, she has a long clandestine involvement with the CIA and the DIA and has lately been working with Aaron Schmuel. Mrs. Dayan and I met briefly at the recent ECO conference. Her son, Elias, has had some direct work for us as recently as last week. Aaron can tell you more.

Suffice it, to say, Elizabeth Dayan is more than a casual friend of the United States; she is a highly valued American agent who is considered by the top officials of the country to be a reliable and important part of our intelligence community who risks her life and livelihood for us in Iran. Aaron and I will meet with her and her family at the Dayan ranch when the family holds their annual stock auction."

He let it go at that.

"Anybody else have questions?"

There were none.

"So, Gideon, since you have been telling us about Mrs. Dayan, why don't you go on and tell us about what you've been up to," Adm. Daastrup said.

"I presume that all of you read the newspapers and watch CNN. You are aware that a financial crisis occurred in Iran that has been rumoured to have set back the timetable for nuclear R&D. That occurred because the consortium of non-American banks took a tough line and required gold from the government as payment on the first installment of their loan. Three things came from that: first, there was anger directed at me—but in the end—they gave in. Our consortium was accepted as hard and unbending, but honest. We have come to be regarded as having hearts of flint interested only in money. I see no indication that the Iranians are suspicious of our intentions at this point.

"Second, the government had to react to the American and European sanctions and to the necessity to pay us with gold by delaying its nuclear R&D and especially by holding off on further purchase of uranium ore. The press of the country's demands for infrastructure maintenance, food, transportation, and to stave off the demands and restiveness of the poor—which have been fomented by the political opposition—was imperative.

"We have set back their progress on the development of nuclear weapons by more than a year—perhaps as much as three. Third, their suppliers are not as trusting as they once were because of failures by the Iranians to pay their bills in a timely fashion. Future dealings will be more cautious and expensive. Compounding that for the Iranian regime, Ali Mohamed Mustaffen, the director of Iran's central bank, has declared in public that BMI has no current debt to the central bank and has had no delay in repaying its international commitments. Both of those statements are bald face lies, and ones that are making Mustaffen a more cautious man. The Supreme Leader and President Shahamatdoost don't buy a word of it, which makes Mustaffen's position tenuous. We will see nuclear progress move a good deal more slowly until they can bring in more hard money."

162

Chapter Twenty-Four

It was Aaron's turn next.

"I will be as brief as possible. You have read or seen on television only a part of our activities—those of my team and highly vetted and untraceable DIA, Kosher Nostra, and Mossad agents. By agreement with them, I will be the spokesman for all of my team members.

"We have been busy. During the week of the ECO conference—while Gideon was having tea with the snootin' groupers of Iranian society—we got our hands dirty. During our active week, two major Iranian nuclear scientists met untimely ends. Professor Mostafa Rafsanjani—a nuclear physics professor at Tehran University—who is considered to be the best of their best nuclear energy minds—suffered a most unfortunate accident. He is—or was—an avid rock climber and a risk taker. He and two friends attended a nuclear physics seminar put on by Jundi-Shapur University of Technology in Dezful. Shevi waterfall is located a bit north of Dezful and is considered one of the most beautiful waterfalls in Iran with a height of about 85 meters. Professor Rafsanjani and his two friends rappelled down from the top of the very powerful waterfall and somehow got their lines entangled. The lines snared their legs, tipping them upside down. In what had to be a terrible death, all three men held out against the torrent of water washing over them like a firehose for several hours but finally became exhausted and drowned. The university held a prayer vigil for the men and their families.

"Ali Ahmadi Mowzoon, director of the Natanz nuclear enrichment facility, was killed in their very modern laboratory when a detonator device for their latest nuclear weapon device accidently exploded, killing seventy-two scientists, technicians and staff. That unfortunate occurrence did not make the news. There is not a scintilla of evidence implicating the Iran Nuclear Interdiction Project.

"Needless to say, Moqtada al-Benizir, head of the Atomic Energy Organization Iran (AEOI), and Behrouz Omidi, director of the Ministry of Intelligence and National Security of the Islamic Republic of Iran (MISIRI)—VEVAK—are desperately searching for replacement experts all around the world. They have not been successful as yet in Iran or the rest of the Muslim world. There are signs that our Afsoon is being secretly courted in Sweden.

"The Associated Press reported that two of Iran's major pipelines—the Odessa-Brody pipeline in Ukraine, which currently transports crude oil into Odessa and then on to Iran, and the 350-mile long Turkish Samsun-Ceyhan pipeline that carries a million barrels of crude oil per day to the Mediterranean coast—much of which originated in northern Iran—were sabotaged and will be out of commission for two years, it is estimated. There is some evidence to implicate Kurdish rebels in the attacks, but not enough to stand up in a United Nations court. As usual, the Iranian regime has hinted that the CIA, the Mossad, and even the recent candidate for the presidency, Hassan Shambayati, and his party members mounted the attacks. In private meetings with the Supreme Leader—according to our Agent Ex—it has been admitted that there is no evidence for any of the usual suspects being the culprits involved. Thus far, there is no indication that the Iranian powers-that-be even suspect the existence of our Iran Nuclear Interdiction Project.

"Finally, our informants at the Zirconium Production Plant (ZPP)—located 280 kilometers south of Tehran that produces the necessary ingredients and alloys for nuclear reactors—tell us that the plant was hit by a computer virus that caused their gas supercentrifuges to behave erratically. Some sped up and some slowed down, which interfered with the achievement of the precision needed for the uranium enrichment process. Finally, some 2,000 of the centrifuges sped up to the point that they froze and were destroyed. This alone—it is estimated—will set back the production program at least a year. It could well be more if their suppliers are not able to replace the centrifuges in that period.

The U.S. and Israel are prime suspects, of course; and even though they can't prove it, our governments and businesses will have to be very vigilant for retaliatory cyber attacks."

The final report to the teleconference group came from Ali Nylander, consular agent in charge of trade and economic affairs for the Swedish embassy in Washington, D.C. In the interest of efficiency, he was the spokesman for Sweden and for Afsoon Mouradipour.

"Our report is brief as well. Afsoon has successfully emigrated to Sweden and is in the process of applying for dual U.S. and Swedish citizenship. That is a long process that we cannot change. She is settling in as a student at Stockholm University, but she has a few hurdles to get over. The university requires that she be proficient in the Swedish language before she can officially matriculate. They were willing to bend the rules somewhat because of her value as an adjunct professor of physics—to be their only nuclear energy/nuclear engineering instructor. She has been given temporary permission to take classes with the awarding of credit depending on her successfully passing the entrance examination in the Swedish language. We are all aware of Afsoon's remarkable linguistic abilities and do not see this as an impediment to any part of her stay in Stockholm.

"Our remarkable young agent has a very rigorous academic schedule lined out for her—which will result in her obtaining a second Ph.D.—if she can handle it all. This year she is taking classes in parallel computations for large-scale problems, advanced computer science courses including administration of relational databases, algorithms and data structures, and decision and risk analysis. The following year, she is tentatively set up to take computational methods for stochastics, differential equation mathematics models, analysis and simulation. All of those are felt by the higher ups in our Iran Nuclear Interdiction Project to be enticements for the Iranian recruiters. What we are shooting for is to have Afsoon be recruited for one of the top positions in the AEOI and placement in a senior administrative job in one of the big operations.

"Afsoon is protected by two of our best Swedish agents, Marta Olson and Ingrid Hakkensdatter, as well as DIA agents Nick Staphanakis and Michael Grodmore. She has been approached by several VEVAK agents who operate out of a so-called 'Basement mosque' in Stockholm that has all of the characteristics of a front for an Iranian Shi'ite terrorist cell. That cell has been loud about its disapproval of everything Western, but they have not caused any recent terrorist acts. They seem to be concentrating on their recruitment of our Afsoon. This far, it all seems positive. Afsoon does not seem to be threatened in any way and, in fact, appears to have entered into a careful courtship with the Iranian spies. We are monitoring the entire process very carefully."

"And we are deeply appreciative of what the Swedish security services are doing for Afsoon and our project, Ari," said Adm. Daastrup. "To wrap this all up, let's hear from Afsoon herself."

Afsoon's soft voice came through clearly on the secure conference call lines.

"I have met with a couple of agents who seem to be pretty obviously VEVAK. I am expected to attend prayers this Friday, and I think they are going to be more overt about trying to get me to help their nuclear energy production cause. I presume that will mean going to Iran, but I can't be sure about that yet. By the way, I am making progress in my Swedish language classes. I think I will be good enough to pass the university test in two weeks and will have enough facility with Swedish that I will be able to work with Swedish code language in a few months. That would give us all one more avenue of secrecy with which we can work."

"If that's all from the group, we will conclude our conference call with that," said 3D. "We should do this again in a month or so, depending on how much activity we are having. Thank all of you for your dedication and work. I know the risks you are taking, and I am prepared to do anything I possibly can to preserve the secrecy of our project and the safety of all of our agents in whatever capacity they are working.

CHAPTER TWENTY-FIVE

6066 Arne Beurlings Torg, number 78, Jennifer Gustafsson's home and location of the "basement Shi'ite mosque," October 6, 2006

Afsoon suspected that she was followed from her apartment on campus to the makeshift mosque on Arne Beurlings Torg, and was convinced that she was being shadowed when she saw the same Middle-Eastern man board the bus and ride almost all the way with her. He got off two stops before the Arne Beurlings Torg stop where Afsoon left the bus.

She was ten minutes early and was greeted with a fresh cup of tea by the Gustafsson sisters, Jennifer and Annika. Five minutes before the *Maghrib* [sunset prayer] was to begin, six men walked in—including the man who had walked behind her from her apartment to the bus and the second man who had ridden the bus with her to the suburbs. That removed any lingering doubt Afsoon might have had about coincidences. The older man who had been present in the mosque when she first attended prayers there—that time it was the noon prayer, the *Dhuhr*—was with them, and two men she had not seen before.

All of the men nodded a taciturn greeting to the women, then retired to the apartment room that had been modified to serve as a proper mosque. The three women attended to their prayers in Annika's bedroom.

Afsoon had taken care to change into a chador for this visit to the apartment, and the older man did not offer any criticism about her modesty.

The young man who had ridden on the same bus greeted her, "Welcome, Sister. We were told that we might expect you. We hope you feel at home here with us."

"I do, thank you."

166

"I believe we have a mutual friend—two, in fact. Perhaps you remember Ali ibn Massoud from America. You met him in the Ali and the Twelve Imams Mosque in downtown Los Angeles, and Salar Sabeti, who talked with you in the student union building at the university."

Afsoon's antennae were up. Way up. Her "chance" meetings with the fit young men removed all doubt about the degree of surveillance she had been undergoing. There was also no doubt in her mind that she was among VEVAK agents—probably everyone in the apartment that day. It was something of a stretch for her to act surprised. However, her training with the DIA and the Mossad stood her in good stead. She was ready for the direction this conversation was taking.

"I do recall. Pleasant young gentlemen."

"They are more than that, Sister. They are on special missions here in the decadent west—including Sweden, and the Great Satan. Both of the young men—like the rest of us here—are acting in the service of Allah to achieve His ends. Does that surprise you or shock you?"

"No. But then, all men and women should be ever on the alert to recognize opportunities to serve Allah."

"Well spoken, Daughter," said the older man.

Afsoon noted that he wore a clean suit and shirt, and his shoes were polished, unlike the first time she saw him. It was obvious that he had taken considerable care with his grooming—was it for her? She waited demurely for him to continue.

"My dear, I am Ayatollah Mammad Qazwini. I serve his holiness, the Supreme Leader, Grand Ayatollah Ali ibn Abi Rahimi. I presume you know who he is."

"Certainly. It is an honor to meet you, Ayatollah."

"We are informed that you are a recent convert to the one true religion."

"That is true, *Agha*."

"We are also informed that you are most gifted with intelligence from Allah, the beneficent one, and that you have received a superior education in the sciences."

"You give me too much honor, *Agha*."

"I think not. While your modesty commends you, I would rather learn more about your accomplishments and talents. Perhaps, then, I can suggest ways you might serve Allah."

"What is it that you wish to know about me, Ayatollah?"

"Please—if it does not seem that I am prying—tell me about your education."

Afsoon paused for a modest moment then told him about her education and her degrees, taking great care to differentiate in the telling between her real-life experiences in Georgetown, and her cover-life "experiences" in Beverly Hills and Berkeley.

She concluded with a brief summary of her credits, "I have been awarded a B.A. in physics with a major in nuclear physics, a masters in computer science emphasizing the use of computers in nuclear engineering, and a Ph.D. in nuclear engineering from the University of California in Berkeley."

"And what brings you to Sweden?"

"I felt a degree of discrimination and prejudice against my chosen religion, especially that I had chosen to follow the path of the Twelvers. I wanted to pursue Islamic studies at Stockholm University, and perhaps to further my scientific education in the field of nuclear physics and nuclear engineering. Unfortunately, there is no definite Islamic studies department and apparently no interest in the Islamic student per se. I could take the odd class here and there, but they are all very basic and slanted towards Christians learning a few basics about our great religion rather than granting me access to the great thinkers of our glorious history.

"Frankly, the nuclear science studies available here at Stockholm University are woefully lacking. In fact, I have become a teacher rather than a student here. I was mistaken about the opportunites to become more immersed in Islamic studies or nuclear science. I am not much inclined toward the Sunni; so, I am trying to further my immersion as a Muslim in our humble mosque here where the doctrine of the Shi'i is available in its pure form. As for the science, I am able to pursue an education in computer science, which will help since it is not limited just to things I already know."

"And after Sweden?"

"I don't know. I am somewhat reluctant to go back to America because of the fact that the interest in having nuclear power plants is so ... so, backwards. The Christian religious right and scientific conservatives have prevented any real opportunities in my field there. Besides, I am a committed Muslim—a Shi'ite—and proud of it. That is difficult in America—and here in Sweden—for that matter. For example, on Monday evening, I am going to be part of a panel that is going to discuss halal slaughter of animals. I am sure you know that our way is illegal in Sweden. I will be arguing in favor of the freedom to practice our religious dietary rules just as the Jews are free to be kosher or not. The perennial argument about the prejudice against wearing the hijab will undoubtedly surface again, and I will have to defend our faith against its misinformed detractors.

"Although I originally planned to spend two or even three years in Sweden, I am a bit disappointed. I am going to finish out at least one year here, then I shall have to look for employment. You would, of course, have no reason to know it; but my family is unwilling to support my life as a Muslim, although they have not rejected me altogether. Because of my conversion to Islam, they will not provide financial support for me until I can get a job in my chosen academic field. It is a difficult marketplace for graduates right now. But I am going on too much. I apologize."

"No apology is necessary, Daughter. There are other places that would welcome your talents, educational achievements, and expertise than Europe and the United States. For example, the government of Iran—in its wisdom—has scheduled an international symposium on nuclear energy, especially for peaceful purposes. Since you are Iranian by birth, and a recognized expert, perhaps you might want to be a part of it."

"Oh, Ayatollah, that would be exciting. It has been a very long time since I was in Iran, and I would love to visit. I believe I could make a contribution to the symposium, if that is not immodest of me. I have some new material in computer science as it relates to nuclear energy and especially to nuclear engineering that might be of interest. But ... the agenda for the meetings is probably already established. I would love to attend, anyway."

The ayatollah studied her for a moment. It was decision time, and he did not want to tip his hand if the girl was not truly ready.

"Let me see if there is interest in the AEOI. I have a personal relationship with Moqtada al-Benizir, head of the Atomic Energy Organization of Iran, and his family. I am going back to Tehran tomorrow and will contact him then. How can I contact you?"

It was Afsoon's turn to have a decision time. She was reluctant to seem to be too enthusiastic, but she recognized that this could be the entering wedge to get her back to Iran in a potential position of influence within the budding Iranian nuclear engineering industry. She kept her face free of emotion and ran the decision algorithm very rapidly through her mind. She realized that by giving this Iranian cleric—who undoubtedly had a hand-in-glove relationship with the VEVAK—her telephone number, she could be putting herself in danger. If she behaved coyly or appeared to be reticent, she might be causing irreparable damage to her chances to return to Iran as a Trojan horse.

The silence was becoming awkward.

"Are you concerned that a modest and proper young lady should not give out her personal information, Afsoon?"

"Yes, Ayatollah. I am concerned that you would think that I am not entirely correct in my obedience to the requirements of Allah's dictates for women."

"Let me assure you that my intentions and those of the young men here are entirely above board. In fact, all of us are prepared to offer you significant protection. We are all too well aware of the risks a pure young Shi'i woman faces. You and your information are safe with us."

Afsoon made her decision—one of those crossing-the-Rubicon moments.

"Here is the telephone number in my apartment."

She handed the ayatollah a notebook sheet with her contact information.

"I live in Campus Roslagen Student Housing with two roommates—two Christian women. It would be better that they not know the details of any communications between the Muslim community and me."

"Of course. Do you know this place, Hassan?" he asked on the young man who had ridden on the bus with her from campus.

"I do, Ayatollah. I have not been polite enough. Afsoon ... may I call you Afsoon?"

"Please do. Dr. Mouradipour is so stuffy."

"My name is Hassan Tajbakhsh. I hope you will not be alarmed if you see me walking near you. I wish to be of service. My friend, Mohammad ... Mohammad Ali Nikookar, and I will see to it that you are safe."

The young man who had shadowed her from her apartment to the bus nodded his head.

Hassan continued, "Here is a telephone number for Mohammad and me. If you have difficulty or need help and cannot reach us, you already have the number for Jennifer and Annika. As you might imagine, all of our numbers are for mobiles. Landline phones are much too expensive for the likes of us."

He handed Afsoon a set of telephone numbers for himself and Mohammad, and for the ayatollah and the two sisters in whose apartment they were standing.

Afsoon wore her chador as far as the corner of Arne Beurlings Torg and Torsansgatan Street before she got to the municipal bus stop. She hurriedly dropped her chador and stuffed it into her carry bag, being careful to be sure she was not being observed. She put on a hijab; so, she would be less conspicuous on the bus.

As soon as she walked into her apartment, she met Ingrid and Marta and told them what had transpired at the "basement mosque" and had them make a copy of the handwritten note with all of the names and telephone numbers of the people whom she presumed were the VEVAK agents assigned to recruit her.

"I can't use my cell phone or even a throwaway because they might be able to trace it somehow. You guys get hold of Admiral Daastrup and the rest, please."

"Consider it done."

The agents in the apartment on Arne Beurlings Torg compared notes.

Ali Hossein—one of the men who had not introduced himself—put it succinctly, "That girl is either the greatest find we have ever seen, or she is the cleverest spy we have ever seen. My opinion is that although she is highly intelligent, she is not cunning and clever like a spy—I think she is just what she appears to be: earnest, pure, highly educated, and naïve. If she is even half of the nuclear scientist we have evidence that she is, Afsoon Mouradipour is the discovery of the age for the nuclear energy—even the nuclear weapons program—of Iran."

"Anyone disagree with Ali?" the ayatollah asked, looking directly at each of his VEVAK agents in turn.

No one did.

"Then we will make her our number one target. As of now, you are to stop all those recruitment efforts that are going nowhere and concentrate on Afsoon. We will begin a background check that will be as thorough as anything the department has ever done. I will call Tehran as soon as I get back to my place. Be of joy, my friends. I believe that Allah has smiled on us and will use this scientist—even though she is a mere girl—to make our dreams of Project *Jahannam Adur* [Hell's Fire] into a reality."

§§§§§

Hôtel de Crillon, 10, Place de la Concorde, Paris, October 28, 2006.

It was early evening. The Rothsbergers had spent the previous two days on a whirlwind tour of all the tourist haunts of Paris, which included the venerable old hotel in which they were now sitting. The hôtel is located at the foot of the Champs-Élysées and is one of two identical stone palaces on the Place de la Concorde separated by the rue Royale. The hôtel's majestic and ornate eighteenth century architecture enthralled generations of visitors and guests and served as the host accommodation for some of history's greatest French and international events.

Over the past 300 years, the most famous hôtel in Paris was witness to the reign of two French kings, the French Revolution, the Napoleonic Empire, and the birth of the League of Nations. In February 1778, the building served

171

as the venue for the official signing of the first treaties between the newly-founded United States and France. That treaty recognized the Declaration of Independence of the United States and a trade agreement with France as a generous trading partner. King Louis XVI went to the guillotine in the Place de la Concorde directly in front of the building in 1793.

The three Gideon Emmanuel Rothsbergers sat at the kitchen table of their suite sipping from their cups of coffee from among the thirty Euro coffees offered in the Hôtel. Tahmineh and Leila WERE SITTING ACROSS FROM EACH OTHER AT A SMALL WRITING TABLE viewing the same spreadsheet on each of their laptops.

G.R. II, Gideon's grandfather, asked the core questions, "My son and grandson, we are losing money at an increasing rate with this project the two of you have gotten us involved in to stop those Philistines in Iran from making an atomic bomb. Is our expense and risk worth the potential benefit? Is there an end to the drain? We are here in the City of Lights to sign another contract with the devil to fund their murderous plan. Are you sure that you can control them? Will you be able to answer to your family and your country if they outmaneuver you and use our money to make their bomb? You know they despise us even though they need us."

G.R. III answered, "Dad, you asked a lot of questions there. Your grandson and I have been very careful on all fronts to protect our money, our lives, and our reputations. So far—until the beginning of this October—we have not only been safe, but we have been making 14 percent interest on a Vast amount of money we have loaned. Although we have not gotten our shipment of gold thus far this month, we have been paid in the hardest of hard currency every month since we got into bed with the devil and his minions. If we lost our current outlay entirely, we would still be ahead financially. You know how terrible the regime has made life for those pathetic few Persian Jews left in Iran and how terrible it would be for those maniacs to be able to blackmail the whole civilized world, to say nothing of the threat they would pose for the Jews of Israel if they were to get a functional WMD.

"So consider the plus column: we are out $100 million as of yesterday, but they need us more than we need them. All Gideon needs to do is to send Bank Markazi a notice of default ten days from now, and all of their legitimate funding sources will disappear in less than a month. Along with that, they will be forced to stop all nuclear production—whether peaceful or for weapons. At best—if they remain overdrawn—their interest rate automatically goes up. They will have to cut their infrastructure, transportation, and healthcare funding drastically. With elections coming up, Shahamatdoost's chances will lessen drastically if his people have to experience an even greater austerity program. They will come up with the gold, and I don't think it will take them a month. They certainly love their WMD project more than they love their people. They may have to put it on hold until after the elections in January, which will put them behind more than a full year while they retool and do all of the security and start-up procedures again. This worked once before, and it set them back. This time will be no better for them."

Playing the Devil's Advocate, G.R. II said, "They still have their illegal sources."

"Let me answer that, Grandfather," G.R. IV said. "They depend on their Afghanistan heroin and marijuana trade, their trafficking in untaxed cigarettes—most of which was stolen by the mafia and resold at a highly reduced price to the terrorists, and to their out-and-out armed robbery and burglary crime syndicate. Taken in toto, all of those sources do not bring in enough to maintain the WMD program by themselves. Furthermore, all of those sources are vulnerable. The CIA can twist a few arms in the Afghan government, and they will make a raid that will decimate this year's opium poppy crop. Granted, the Afghans won't wreck any more than this one year's worth, but they are amenable to Uncle Sam providing funding to cover the losses for another season or two if the need arises.

The cigarette trafficking is lucrative, I will grant you that. However, the FBI could swoop in anytime they wanted and make wholesale arrests of the Mafia dons and their soldiers if our people were to apply the right kind and degree of pressure. The Kosher Nostra and some of our friends in Israel and in the dark alleys of Crown Heights, Brooklyn could easily mount a spectacular heist that NEITHER the Iranians NOR their suppliers could complain to the cops about. Our people are just biding their time until we give them the word. That would shut the bomb makers down for a couple of years."

"You have it all figured out have you, my overly bright grandson?"

"Maybe not everything, but a lot of careful work has gone into this project. We may have a Trojan Horse to add to the mix, and will be able to work from the inside out like a bunch of termites. That's classified and not quite ready, but I just want you to rest at ease that your money appears to be pretty safe. I have that much figured out, Grandfather."

Then G.R. II threw G.R. IV a curve ball from way out in left field.

"If you've got it all so well figured out, how come you aren't married? How come you don't even have a girl friend, a big strapping rich boy like you? There has to be a football stadium full of eligible young Jewish girls who would jump at the chance to share a coffee with you."

"I'm too busy for the time being. I'll get to it in due time, Grandfather."

"And maybe the grown-ups will come up with a little help, who knows?" G.R. II said with an enigmatic smile.

G.R. IV just smiled indulgently at the grandfather who had spoiled him rotten when he was a child.

"Hey, you two, it's time to clean up and get to the vocal soloist program we promised your mother and her mother that we would go see when they get back from shopping. We'll have to get a move on; so, we don't keep them waiting," said G.R. III.

He had a slight twinkle in his eye that did not escape G.R. IV, even though he was unsure what his father's amusement was about. The women and Gideon's younger brother and sister arrived shortly after that conversation. While they freshened up, Gideon's maternal grandmother, Rebecca Hershowitz, commented.

"I love this old place, but I have to admit that it now looks more than a bit long in the tooth. It's BECOMING frayed around its edges; the rooms are old-fashioned and ill adapted to the modern world. If you look closely at them, you can't help but notice that they are fairly dirty. The service is still superb—five stars—and location second to none, that no one can deny; and the location is incomparable. I learned from my business people here that it is slated to be closed down in a couple of years for a major renovation. That's kind of sad, I think, but I'll be back for the reopening."

The family were all surprised and a little depressed by Rebecca's revelation, but nothing was going to spoil the magic of the evening that G.R. II and III and Rebecca and Chava had planned for the unsuspecting G.R. IV.

The Rothsberger family traveled by two limousines from the Hôtel de Crillon to the Place de la Bastille. It was a beautiful crisp fall evening. The Place de la Bastille was bathed in light from the newly installed streetlight system. The Rothsberger women were enchanted by the marvelous building whose first concert was held on July 13, 1989 to celebrate the bicentennial of the French Revolution. The interior of the remarkable building was almost as ornate as the original Palais Garnier that it supplanted. Upstairs was a 2,700-seat auditorium for the performance of major operas and symphonies.

The three Gideon Emmanuel Rothsbergers, Chava, twin sisters Tahmineh and Leila, age twenty-one, and Grandmaman Rebecca Hershowitz were escorted to their front row center seats in the 500-seat amphitheater under the main hall of the Opéra Bastille. They were on time to the Parisian debut of a Persian Jewish soprano, Miriam Shahnameh, who was taking the country by storm.

The somewhat more intimate venue beneath that auditorium was the setting for a life-changing experience for Gideon.

174

CHAPTER TWENTY-SIX

Opéra Bastille, Place de la Bastille, Paris, October 28, 2006

Gideon enjoyed the ambience of the beautiful venue, but was fairly sure that he was going to have to endure a very boring evening. Despite his broad and deep education in the classics, he preferred popular music, and found symphonies and concerts tedious. The stage was bare to the point of being stark. A black lacquered grand piano stood on the right. Aside from the piano bench, there were two folding chairs a little to the left and behind the piano. There was no microphone. The lights dimmed and the director of the Opéra Bastille entered from stage left to introduce the featured soloist, Miriam Shahnameh. It was an overblown introduction—standard Parisian hyperbole—in Gideon's opinion. Before she came onto the stage, he envisioned a portly and homely but remarkably talented young woman with a lifetime of classical operatic training and little in the way of appeal for him or the other younger members of the audience. He chaffed in his tuxedo.

The hall became dark, and the spotlight shifted to stage right, bathing the piano in brilliant focus while the director exited to the left unseen. The audience grew quiet. A middle-aged woman dressed in a long black gown entered, and Gideon presumed that his worst fears for the evening were being realized. However—after a slight bow—she took her seat on the piano bench. Next, a young man carrying a violin entered and took his seat on one of the folding chairs. A minute of anticipation passed, then the violinists began playing softly, an arrangement of Handel's *Oh, Had I Jubal's Lyre*, from *Joshua*. The piece was beautiful, but so gentle and soothing that Gideon began to grow sleepy.

175

Any drowsiness or lack of interest evaporated when the most beautiful woman Gideon had ever seen quietly walked onto the stage and took her place dead center. The spotlight shifted to her, and soft secondary stage lights held the first two performers in a glow. The featured soloist of the evening introduced herself and gave a small synopsis of her first number.

"I will first sing for you the beautiful music that my accompaniest, Geraldine Duvalier, and my friend and violinist from the Paris symphony, Anthony de Viau, has been playing. George Fredric Handel began the score for his oratorio on July 19, 1747 and; incredibly, he completed the entire work only one month later. This master work focuses on the battle of Jericho fought by my ancestors, the Israelites. Caleb—one of the princes of the tribe of Judah and one of Judaism's greatest heroes—was the military leader at the time. His daughter, Achsah, sang *Oh, Had I Jubal's Lyre* in honor of her betrothed Othniel's valor in the battle. In this hauntingly beautiful song, Achsah praises the God of Israel for keeping her beloved safe during the conflict. I hope you like it."

She had Gideon's attention, if for no other reason than her almost unearthly beauty. She was slight, had jet-black long hair, creamy white skin, and a perfectly proportioned face and figure. She exhibited every aspect of feminine beauty that Gideon had learned during his education in mathematics. For some arcane reason, the mathematics of human beauty—as first described by Leonardo of Pisa or (Filius Bonacci), alias Leonardo Fibonacci, born in 1175. He gave the world the Fibonacci Sequence defined by Phi, the Golden Ratio or description of the divine—and the modern Marquardt Beauty Analysis came to the awestruck young man's now overheated psyche.

The vision of loveliness was singing directly to him:

> *Oh, had I Jubal's lyre,*
> *Or Miriam's tuneful voice!*
> *To sounds like his I would aspire,*
> *In songs like hers rejoice.*
> *My humble strains but faintly show,*
> *How much to Heav'n and thee I owe.*

Watching her lissome body enclosed in all modesty and her face that seemed to be lit up with the fervor of the music coming from her perfectly trained voice, he expected nothing less than perfection; and she delivered. She hit and held her high Cs and controlled her triple octave capacity without a single quaver or break in the melody. He was enchanted. If ever any boy

176

had been struck by an arrow from Cupid's bow, it was Gideon Emmanuel Rothsberger IV.

Miriam's repertoire included Henry Purcell and Colonel Henry Heveningham's *If Music Be the Food of Love, Version III* from the seventeenth century. The message was for him: "Sure I must perish by your charms, unless you save me in your arms." She moved smoothly into Mozart's *Deh Vieni, Non Tardar from Le Nozze di Figaro*—"Oh, it seems that earth, heaven and the comfort of this place, answer my heart's amorous fire, as the night supports my ruse," then into Reyanold Hahn's nineteenth century *To Chloris*—"If it's true, Chloris, that you love me, and I understand that you love me well, I do not believe that even the kings could have a happiness equal to mine."

She ended the first half of her program with Hugo Wolf's *Er Ist's* [It's spring!], a lighter number speaking to the three main senses—seeing, smelling, and hearing. The song and the girl seemed to promise the rejuvenating qualities of spring and a quality promising renewal. Gideon was hooked by intermission.

"She's lovely, isn't she, Son?" Chava said as she took his arm.

"More than that, Mother. I lack the vocabulary."

Chava smiled.

"There's Dad. I would like to have a word with him."

G.R. III was standing a little away from the main crowd. The crowd was noisy and smiling. Everywhere he walked, Gideon heard the rich Frenchmen and their elegant wives singing Miriam's praises. G.R. III was talking to an unapologetically Orthodox late middle-aged man. Gideon waited politely to be invited into the conversation.

"Ah, Gideon, how timely. Allow me to introduce you to Elijah Shahnameh. He is Miriam's father."

For all of Gideon's worldly experience, he suddenly became shy.

"It is a pleasure to meet you, Gideon. Your father and grandfather have told me so much about you. Did you enjoy my daughter's performance, young man?"

"Immensely, Sir. Pardon me if I ask an impertinent question, but is she as nice as she is beautiful and talented?"

G.R. III and Mr. Shahnameh exchanged a brief smile.

"She most certainly is. Miriam is our only child and is our pride and joy. She is virtuous and honors her father and mother. A father could not ask for more."

Gideon's grandfather, G.R. II, joined the men.

"Elijah," he said, "your daughter is exquisite. I remember her as a charming child, and now she has grown into a magnificent young woman. I am sure the entire Shahnameh clan is proud tonight. I have been talking to old friends I haven't seen in decades—some whom I last saw when we were getting out of Tehran just before the revolution was heating up. It has been a great experience. I'm sorry, though, I have become overtired for some reason and will have to get back to the hotel."

"Nothing serious, I hope."

"No, probably the strain of business. Before I leave, might I suggest that you introduce your daughter to my grandson here. He has become a fine young man and a strong hand in our business."

"It would give me great pleasure," said Mr. Shahnameh.

Another of those small smiles passed among the three older men.

They returned to the last half of Miriam's performance. This time, she shared the stage with her two accompanists—each of which presented a solo—virtuoso piano and violin numbers, and a duet—Nikolai Rimsky-Korsakov's, *The Flight of the Bumblebee.* Miriam's last number was a departure from her heavy classical repertoire. She was all animation and smiles as she concluded with Leonard Bernstein's *A Little Bit in Love* from *Wonderful Town*—"When he looks at me, everything's hazy and all out of focus. When he touches me, I'm in a spell of a strange hocus-pocus."

Even though it was dark in the auditorium, she was singing to Gideon.

Chava squeezed her husband G.R. III's hand and said, "Well done, my love."

§§§§§

Faculty of Social Sciences of the University of Tehran, outside the main University Campus, January 7, 2007.

Afsoon Mouradipour was the third speaker on the first day of the Tehran Nuclear Energy Symposium. It was a day of firsts: the symposium was the first ever hosted by Iran, and Afsoon was the first woman ever to deliver a major scientific lecture at the university. She was dressed in a new chador that allowed only the central portion of her face to be seen. She delivered her highly technical speech to a well-educated international audience. The quality of the speech and the fact that it was given by a woman in a nation known for its maltreatment of women rated Afsoon with a standing ovation initiated by the foreign scientists who occupied the 100-seat lecture hall. Iranian nuclear scientists joined in soon after the foreigners stood; and, finally, and with some reluctance, the entire audience was on its feet. It was a singular experience for Afsoon, and a moment of minor revelation for some important members of the audience.

178

Afsoon was driven back to her hotel—the Five-Star Azadi Grand Hotel in Cross Chamran—accompanied by a severe-faced female chaperon and three VEVAK officers—the driver and two very martial-appearing bodyguards. Afsoon was unsure whether they were afraid that she would escape and foment a new Iranian revolution, or if—as was more likely—she was too valuable to allow any harm to befall her.

The following morning, she received a message from the reservation desk asking that she be ready to travel to the president's office for a meeting. Her blood pressure and heart rate climbed, but she remained outwardly calm. She had been prepared for this opportunity for more than a year.

A black Sil limousine flying the flags of the president of the Islamic Republic of Iran arrived at the entryway of Afsoon's hotel, and they flew across the city with a motorcycle escort making a parting of the ways on the otherwise chaotic and overcrowded city streets. The small motorcade flashed past the Brazilian embassy and to the presidential palace, located adjacent to the Sa'abad Palace complex in the Shemiran area of Tehran. There the young woman—perhaps the first woman in postrevolutionary history other than a char woman to enter the presidential offices—was escorted to President Shahamatdoost's private office. There, besides President Mohsen Shahamatdoost, she was introduced to Moqtada al-Benizir, head of the Atomic Energy Organization Iran (AEOI), and his two deputies, Esfandiari Razizadeh and Razmara Tassoudji, and the chief engineer for research and development at the Bushehr nuclear plant, Amir Vehrahrami. Afsoon concentrated to be able to remember the names of all of the men, knowing that the sweetest thing any man can hear is the sound of his own name.

Amir Vehrahrami greeted her, "Dr. Mouradipour, we are appreciative that you have found time to talk with us. Because I am the most informed on your work and achievements, the other gentlemen have elected me to be the spokesman."

Afsoon nodded. She knew that it was more likely that the other important men could not bring themselves to have a business negotiation with a woman unless forced by circumstances to do so. She waited for the chief engineer to continue.

"We all realize that you are currently doing postdoctoral work at the University of Stockholm, that you are a highly accomplished computer scientist, nuclear physicist, a nuclear engineer, and that you have fairly recently converted to the one true religion."

"That is all true. I hope you don't think badly about me ... like I have been boastful about my accomplishments. That would not be good for a proper girl to do."

"No, Dr. Mouradipour. Instead, we wonder if you would like to work for the government of Iran in our nuclear research and engineering efforts. You, no doubt, are wondering why such important men are here to meet with you. They do not have time to waste; and they, like me, think you have something very worthwhile to contribute to the revolution. If you feel that such a career is not for you, then we can have a cup of tea, congratulate you for your accomplishments, and part on good terms. If you have further interest, then please let us know and we can begin a process to bring you in with us. I have to warn you that we have to be very security conscious; and we have to be sure that you, indeed, have the qualifications. That will take some time to determine, I'm sure you realize."

"I am so flattered that you think so well of me. I gave the possibility of working with you considerable thought during my stay in Tehran. We should probably get to know each other better and then each of us can make a decision. I believe my education and experience could prove valuable to you. I am willing to be tested, if you would like that. I will have some requirements of my own, as well. I will tell you one thing. I am not any good at business, like how much I should get paid. I trust that your offer will be reasonable. I think we should meet again—perhaps in Stockholm and again in Iran—before either of us makes a final decision. What do you think about that?"

"That is exactly what we had in mind. Do any of you gentlemen have any questions for Dr. Mouradipour before we take her back to her hotel?"

Dr. al-Benizir said, "For now, I have just one. Can you keep secrets? Our enemies—including those in the country where you are an official citizen—are most desirous to learn our most critical national secrets. Can we be assured that you are willing to give your full allegiance to us?

"Yes, provided I am treated with respect and am not shunted off to meaningless paperwork or anything demeaning like that just because I am not currently an Iranian citizen. I was born in Tehran; my birth certificate attests to my authenticity. Its number is three digits—address [892], Fifth District, Residence of Tehran."

That was a lie, but the Iranian birth certificate was as real as the world's best forgers in the CIA could make it and would withstand almost any scrutiny.

Dr. al-Benizir turned to the president.

President Shahamatdoost posed his one question, "You are new to the faith. Can we be certain that your faith in Allah is genuine and will be lasting? I ask you that because before you are permitted to work with us in our nuclear energy programs, you will have to have an audience with the Supreme Leader. You cannot lie to him. He is one of Allah's chosen men, and he can see into your very soul."

"I am a true and believing convert—a Muslim, one who submits to Allah. I have given up a great deal to say that. If I come to Iran to work, I am sure my family will have nothing to do with me. It is one thing to become a believer in Islam and to turn my back on my family's strong belief in Judaism, and quite another to work for a government that they believe has corrupted Persia. I am not sure that they could accept me if I did that."

"Are you ready to commit to such a future, Dr. Mouradipour?" the president asked more gently than before.

"I am not yet fully ready to do so. As I said to Dr. Vehrahrami, we all should give this a great deal of thought before we commit to each other. I will tell you this, however: I can make up my mind in less than a month if we can meet and agree to certain terms and arrangements. If and when I do come to a decision, I will not back away from it. If I come with you, your goals and desires will be my goals and desires. Your secrets will be my secrets. That I swear. As I said, I ask little in return other than a decent livelihood—nothing extravagant—and good treatment."

"I appreciate your candor. I suggest that you and Dr. Vehrahrami get together in ten days or less. I see no reason why that first meeting cannot be held in Stockholm. As you might imagine, even the fact that an Iranian nuclear scientist is in Sweden must be considered to be an Iranian state secret. He will contact you, and he and our agents will determine a meeting place."

"I agree. I will give your suggestions careful consideration in the mean time."

"Good. Now, I think it is time for Dr. Razizadeh and Dr. Tassoudji to escort you home. You will have full security while you are here. We wish you safe travel. I hope that we can work together."

Back at the hotel, Afsoon was aware of the presence of VEVAK agents all around her. She was certain that all telephones and computers were being monitored; so, she made no attempt to contact anyone in the Iran Nuclear Interdiction Project. She would leave that until she was safely back in Stockholm and could be certain that her communications were secure. Afsoon knew she was taking the first steps to become a spy, and she did not have to be told that the consequences of being discovered would be worse than anything else she had suffered at the hands of the Iranian Islamic regime thus far in her life.

CHAPTER TWENTY-SEVEN

Opéra Bastille, Place de la Bastille, Paris, October 28, 2006, late in the evening

Gideon's introduction to the greatly loved daughter of Elijah and Ruth Shahnameh seemed to be much more easily accomplished than he had anticipated. She had to be one of the most sought after young women in all of the Orthodox world—beautiful, talented, rich, and the only child of a very influential family. Gideon wondered how he would ever even get to talk to her—especially one-on-one—let alone have the right setting to express his feelings towards her. What where his feelings, exactly? He was a confused and humble young man as the vision of a woman floated to where he and her father were standing.

Mr. Shahnameh embraced Miriam exuberantly, lifting her off her feet.

"You were marvelous, my dear, as always. I think you outdid yourself tonight. Mother and I are so proud of you that we could burst."

"Daddy, you are embarrassing me," she protested halfheartedly.

"Miriam, my child, may I present an admirer of yours."

Gideon blushed and felt like a bumbling boy.

"Miriam, this is Gideon Rothsberger. I know you have met his grandfather who controls their global enterprises from Paris. His father is president of the family bank in San Francisco. Gideon, this is my beloved daughter in whom I am well pleased. Miriam is a recent graduate of the Conservatoire de Paris where she studied music from all over the world and the history of music and the Berklee College of Music in Boston."

"Daddy, please," Miriam pleaded, blushing profusely.

Her father laughed, "Sorry, my dear, I let my fatherly bias get the better of me."

Gideon extended his hand, "It is an honor to meet you, Miss Shahnameh. Your performance was ... absolutely enchanting. I have to admit that until tonight, I was not really a fan of high opera."

Miriam laughed an easy and inclusive laugh.

"Thank you, Gideon. I have heard something about your accomplishments as well. You should be glad that neither your father nor your mother is here to embarrass you."

In a few moments, Gideon noticed that all four parents had found other people to chat with, and he and Miriam were alone in the crowd. In short order, they were talking like old friends.

Elijah Shahnameh and G.R. II and III found a private place to talk, and their wives found another. The substance of their conversations was the same.

"What a successful night. All of our planning was worthwhile. We can sign the preliminary papers tonight. I think we will be watching the breaking of the glass under the *chupah* [the wedding canopy] very soon. *Mazel Tov*! [Congratulations!]"

AN OVERVIEW OF ISLAM

"When I was midway down the mountain, I heard a voice from Heaven saying, 'O Muhammad! Thou art the Apostle of God and I am Gabriel.' I raised my head towards heaven to see, and lo! Gabriel in the form of a man, with feet astride the horizon saying, 'O Muhammad! Thou art the Apostle of God and saying, 'I am Gabriel.' I stood gazing at him, moving neither forward nor backward; then I began to turn my face away from him; but towards whatever region of the sky I looked, I saw him as before."
                                                        -The Hadith

Human beings have demonstrated a need to believe in the supernatural since they first began to gather in groups. The fertility goddess Mother Earth religion is the world's oldest religion, probably dating as far back as 15,000 to 12,000 B.C.E. and is now only a historical footnote. The religion that considered another fertility goddess, Artemis, flourished from about 8,000 B.C.E for nearly 4,000 years—years full of upheavals so dramatic that twice the knowledge of writing appeared and disappeared. Hinduism had no specific time or origin, nor did it have a clearly known founder. It has continually evolved over the millennia. The best scholarship dates the origin of the Hindu religion to about 2,000 B.C.E. Judaism—with its own tribal god Yahweh—originated sometime shortly before the time of Moses, at about the same time as Hinduism—about 2,000 B.C.E. It originated as the beliefs and practices of the people known as "Israel." The form of the religion known to the modern world—classical, or rabbinic, Judaism—did not emerge until the 1st century C.E. Buddhism entered the world in a well verified time

184

and place and with a clearly known historical founder, Siddhartha Gautama. Most scholars consider that date to be about 500 B.C.E.

Christianity had a founder—Joshua [or transliterated to the Greek form Jason [Jesus] of Nazareth who had a brief ministry—about three years, from approximately 28 to 31 C.E. The historicity of Jesus has been debated by scholars since that time. The religion started as an offshoot of Judaism, and it is not definite that Jesus and his earliest followers saw it as anything more than that. The most dynamic—and perhaps the rightful founder of the worldwide religion that was inclusive of people beyond the Jews—was Saul [or Paul] of Tarsus—born about 2 C.E. and died sometime shortly after 46 C.E. He has a less doubted historicity. He championed the cause of Christianity being for Jews and Gentiles alike sometime in the middle part of the first century C.E.

Modern Christianity with all of its Roman pomp and Protestant defiance got its start with the intercession of Roman Emperor Constantine—born about 285 C.E, and died about 337 C.E. Constantine defeated the numerically stronger army of Maxentius at the Battle at the Milvian Bridge in October 312 C.E. and claimed that he saw a vision that caused him to convert to Christianity. He gathered the disparate elements of the Christian hierarchy in the Council of Nicaea in 325 C.E. and forced them to establish a unified set of dogmas, procedures, and rituals, and made Christianity the state church of Rome—the most powerful nation in the world. Effectively, the Christian church—as it is now recognized—came into being that year.

Islam is the latest of the great world religions to make its appearance and did so with a definite historical founder at a historically verified time and place. Muhammad—born 570 C.E. and died 632 C.E.—started Islam in the deserts of Arabia shortly after he claimed to have a vision and to receive holy writings from his God, Allah, in 610 C.E. Of all of the founders of the world's great religions, Muhammad stands out as having had the most direct and unchanged influence on his followers—and therefore, the world—of any leader. The religion brought into being by Muhammad is the most aggressive, feared, and defended system of belief in the world of the twenty-first century. Until the advent of widespread Islamic individual and state-sponsored terrorism during the latter half of the 1900s, most westerners knew little of and cared less about the religion that dominated the Middle-East.

Muhammad was born in Mecca and was a descendant of the noble Hashim family of Mecca on his father's side and a major tribe of Medina—the Yathrib—on his mother's. He married a wealthy widow named Khadijah—fifteen years his senior—and became financially independent as a result of that successful marriage. They had six children, and Muhammad remained monogamous until after Khadijah's death fifteen years after their marriage. From the age of twenty-five onward, he became highly interested in spiritual matters; and—at the age of forty—he lived for a time in a cave on Mount Hira. There he spent his time in contemplation and went through what was apparently a profound religious experience. He emerged from that period of isolation convinced that he had been given a unique prophetic mission to the Arabic peoples by Allah—a generic name for any number of gods in the Arabian polytheistic society.

In addition to his personal spiritual awakening, Muhammad became the Prophet and Messenger of God, an implacable social reformer, a crusader against the entrenched evils of Arabic society, and eventually a warrior bent on converting all the world to the religion of his monotheistic god—by the sword if and when necessary. His religion was inclusive so long as absolute submission to Allah, to the Prophet, and to the tenets of Islam was accepted and practiced. Unbelievers were discriminated against; those who resisted were attacked and often annihilated. With such aggressive proselytization, the religion spread throughout the Middle-East until today there are over a billion adherents in twenty-two Muslim nations of the Middle-East and significant majorities in forty-four other countries. It is one of the—if not, the—fastest growing of all the major religions.

After Muhammad refused a bribe to halt his proselyting efforts, he was driven out of Mecca. The Prophet and his few follower families escaped to Yathrib—where he and his religion flourished. The arrival date, September 14, 622—called the Hegira—became thereafter the first day of the Muslim calendar. A series of battles ensued that ended with Muhammad and his Muslims taking Mecca. Shortly thereafter, he and his followers made a pilgrimage to Mecca. The inhabitants were allowed or forced by the followers of the Prophet to accept Islam, and the Prophet gained full control of the city and the region. He personally destroyed the idols in the ancient Ka'bah and established the old pagan shrine as the most holy place for Allah. The holy pilgrimage for Muslims—*the Hajj*—commemorates the pilgrimages of the Prophet and persists today as one of the five pillars of Islam.

History provides the origin of the Muslims' continuing systemic hatred of their Semite cousins, the Jews. Muhammad was incensed that the Jews did not accept him as a prophet. He made a truce with the Jewish Banu Qaynuqa tribe and resolved to deal with them for their rejection of him as a prophet. The Muslim army laid siege to the tribe's city and defeated them. In a compromise move to avoid a mass slaughter of the defeated, the Jews were forced to agree to leave with their lives but to turn over all their earthly possessions to Muhammad. A second Jewish tribe—the Banu Nadir—was expelled from their city when one of their members planned to kill Muhammad. The Muslims learned of the assassination plot and attacked. After a two-week seige, the Jews were forced into exile; and muhammad took possession of their property.

A third tribe—the Banu Qurayza—was massacred after the battle of the Trench. The Jews had agreed to fight for Muhammad against the Meccans then treacherously changed sides. After the Muslim fighters finally defeated the Meccans, the Jewish tribal home was laid siege. After twenty-five days, the Banu Qurayza surrendered. In an act of unbridled barbarity, the Muslims beheaded all the men—some 600-900 of them—and the women and children were taken by the Muslims and sold into slavery. After a period of time when the Muslims exacted confiscatory taxes on the remaining Jews, as many of the Jews as could be located were banished to Syria.

Muhammad's vengeful god, Allah, vented his anger in the scripture he revealed verbatim to his Prophet: "Say [O Muhammad to the people of the Book]: "Shall I inform you of something worse than that, regarding the recompense from Allah: those [Jews] who incurred the Curse of Allah and His Wrath, those of whom—some—He transformed into monkeys and swines, those who worshipped Taghut [false deities; such are worse in rank (on the Day of Resurrection in the Hellfire)], and far more astray from the Right Path," *Sura* 5:60. There are hadiths—exact quotes from Muhammad—that also convey the hatred and violent intentions that have persisted to the present day. This is one example: "Allah's Apostle said, The Hour will not be established until you fight with the Jews, and the stone behind which a Jew will be hiding will say: 'O Muslim! There is a Jew hiding behind me, so kill him,'" *Sahih Bukhari* 4.52.177.

In 2013, a scientifically constructed and conducted survey was taken of 1010 Palestinians in the West Bank, Gaza, on the question of who was in agreement with the hadith in the Hamas Charter "about the need to kill Jews hiding behind stones or trees." 73 percent of the 1010 Palestinians agreed with the hadith. Also in 2013, a popular and influential Pakistani religious leader, Pirzada Muhammad Raza Saqib Mustafai, said: "When the Jews are wiped out ... the sun of peace [will] begin to rise on the entire world." It is not the ranting of mentally disturbed people or of fringe lunatics, it is the opinion of a significant majority of the *umma*—the Muslim community at large.

The basic doctrine, beliefs, and practices of Islam—aside from the accretions gathered over 1500 years of practice—are quite simple. Islam means belief in and submission to Allah, the One God. A Muslim is one who submits. There are five main pillars of the religion. The pillars are:

1. Expression of belief in full honesty and in public in Allah—the *shahadah*—"There is no God but God." The companion pronouncement is "and Muhammad is the Messenger of Allah."
2. *Salah*—the requirement to pray five times a day—precisely timed.
3. *Zakat*—to share wealth with Muslims—almsgiving.
4. *Sawm*—fasting and other sacrifices during the month of Ramadan to further the Muslim's reflection on his religion and life and to achieve self-discipline. Fasting means to refrain from having all kinds of food, drink, and sexual intercourse from dawn to sunset.
5. The *Hajj*—the requirement for a faithful Muslim to make the pilgrimage to Mecca at least once in his/her lifetime if health, conditions, and finances permit. The *Hajj* is considered to be both a physical and spiritual journey. Muslims by the hundreds of thousands travel to the holy city of Mecca to perform the required rites of the pilgrimage. They are expected to spend their days in complete devotion to worship and to ask God for forgiveness and for anything else they wish to ask for. They also perform specific rituals, including walking seven times around the *Kaaba*, touching the Black Stone, traveling seven times between Mount Safa and Mount Marwah, and symbolically stoning the Devil in Mina.

Of lesser importance and not spelled out with the same clarity and simplicity in the only book of scripture in Islam—the holy *Qur'an*—are the Commandments. They are:

1. Acknowledge the unitary character of God.
2. Study the holy scripture requirements to respect the people of the *umma*—the Muslim community. But that injunction does not necessarily pertain to the unbelievers.
3. Respect the rights of other people—largely an admonition for Muslim/Muslim interaction to comply with the *Qur'an*, but the requirement is not set forward in any clarity or specificity.
4. Be generous but not a squanderer, again to the *umma*, not the unbelievers.
5. Avoid killing except for justifiable cause.

6. Do not commit adultery. Chastity, restraint, and modesty are required of women. Men are only required specifically to be kind to their wives and to treat them with justice and consideration. This seeming inequity is considered a powerful method of keeping balance in the community.

7. Safeguard the possessions of orphans.

8. Deal justly and equitably with Muslims.

9. Be pure of heart and mind.

10. Be humble and unpretentious—follow the example of the Prophet.

Comparatively speaking, rite and ritual practices occupy a significantly lesser part of Islam compared to paganism, the polytheistic religions, and Christianity, but the outward practices of the religion are crucial for the believers—the Muslims. Outward expressions of Islam include prayers, ritual fasting, prohibition of alcohol and pork, requirement for women to dress modestly—in some countries and sects, severely so. It is, however, the reality that Islam is meant to be a complete way of life for its followers. It includes an extensive and deeply studied set of beliefs and a moral code that covers every action that Muslims take in their lives. Penalties for deviation—especially apostasy or defaming the Prophet—may result in most draconian punishments, even death; and, in some Muslim areas, perceived immodesty or immorality by women can result in the same drastic consequences.

Freedom, democracy, and innovation [in Islam, innovation is any act done without a previous pattern—a willful intention to make change or activities that are considered progressive or are alterations of established ideas and practices, especially in the religion—usually taken to mean that the person seeks to change Islam or to start a new sect with differing views or practices.] are all major taboos. Many fundamentalists take that to mean anything that did not exist during the Prophet's time. *Bid'ah* [innovation in Islam] is roundly condemned. Consider: *"Wa sharrul Umoori Muhdathaatuhaa, Wa kulla Bid'atin dhaialah, wa kulla dhalatin fin-naar."* [Sahih Hadith, translated from the Arabic: "Every innovation is a misguidance and every misguidance goes to Hell fire."

There is considerable similarity between the *Old* and *New Testaments* and the *Qur'anic* beliefs. The *Qur'an* is considered to be the culmination of a series of divine messages that started—according to Islamic belief—with the messages revealed to Adam—regarded in Islam as the first prophet—and continued with the *Suhuf Ibrahim*—scrolls of Abraham, the *Tawrat* (Torah or Pentateuch) of Moses, the *Zabur* (*Tehillim* or Book of Psalms) of David, and the *Injil* (Gospel) of Jesus. The *Qur'an* assumes familiarity with major narratives recounted in Jewish and Christian scriptures, summarizing some, dwelling at length on others, and in some cases presenting alternative accounts and interpretations of events.

The practices of Islam occupy a third place position in the religion, but have evolved to a dominant importance in the life of Muslims and in the interactions of Muslims vis-à-vis other Muslims, and Muslims vis-à-vis non-Muslims. The level of intolerance for perceived deviators or nonbelievers has escalated dramatically in the last three decades, especially since the intifada.

The life of a Muslim is dictated by social practices that have developed into an iron rigidity in some areas and among some subsets of Muslims, from marriage to the slaughter of sheep and the dietary laws. Muslim tradition forbids the consumption of alcohol or foods that are not *halal* such as pork. [Arabic: lawful or legal, designating any object or an action that is permissible to use or engage in, according to Islamic law.] The term is used to designate food seen as permissible according to Sharia, and the opposite of halal is haraam. *Halal* is fairly similar to Jewish kosher, and it is highly likely that the Islamic tradition evolved from the Jewish one. Although Islamic law does not present a comprehensive list of pure foods and drinks that are permissible, it does prohibit:

- Pork, blood and blood products
- The meat of dead animals except fish and locusts
- Beasts having sharp canine teeth
- Birds having claws and talons in their feet
- Animals whose meat carries a stink in it because they feed on filth
- Tamed donkeys
- Hyena meat
- Any piece cut from a living animal
- Animals slaughtered in the name of someone other than God.
- Slaughtering an animal in any other way except the prescribed manner—*Dhabihah*—and of [*tazkiyah*]—cleansing] by taking God's name every time an animal is killed for food, which involves cutting the throat of the animal, hanging it upside down, and draining the blood. The animal must be slaughtered by a Muslim or by one of the People of the Book—generally speaking, a Christian or a Jew—while mentioning the name of God.
- Slaughtering with a blunt blade.
- Physically ripping out the esophagus is strictly forbidden.

- Modern methods of slaughter such as captive bolt stunning and electrocuting.
- Causing the animal excessive pain during slaughter,.
- Animals for food may not be killed by being boiled or electrocuted, and the carcass should be hung upside down for long enough to be blood-free.
- Hunting on land while a Muslim is in the state of pilgrimage. Fishing is permitted, even for travelers, anytime. Organizations have emerged around the world certifying that food products and ingredients met *dhabiha* standards. However, Muslims must ensure that all foods, particularly processed foods, pharmaceuticals, and nonfood items like cosmetics are also *halal*. Often, these products contain animal by-products or other ingredients that are not permissible for Muslim consumption. Some animals and manners of death or preparation can make certain things *haram* to eat. These include what are regarded as unclean animals such as pork in any form—such as gelatin, from which 50 percent of the world's gelatin is made—and "dead animals," i.e., those that died naturally.
- Intoxicants of any kind
- It is forbidden in Islamic religion to make graven images or statues or other representations of God, or Allah. Over the centuries, the practice has evolved to the point that no real animal or person may be depicted.

A major debate among the four schools of Islamic law relates to whether or not women can be voluntary martyrs like men, even though the *Qur'an* forbids suicide and there is a prohibition against elective suicide to achieve martyrdom. Slavery and polygamy have never been formally banned; but in the modern era, neither practice is widespread.

Purification—*wudu* [ablution] is required before performing certain rituals, most importantly before prayers. Mosques maintain communal washing facilities for the purpose of washing the hands, face, arms and feet with clean water. Since Muslims are required to pray at least five times every day at various times throughout the day from dawn until the night, this ensures that Muslims maintain a high level of hygiene.

Circumcision is an important religious duty in Islam and required by believers to perform on their newborn sons. The practice was probably adopted from the Jewish practice that antedated the advent of Islam. It is also done to imitate Muhammad, who was circumcised. The controversial prac-

191

tice of female circumcision that is present in many parts of the world does not have any religious authority as does male circumcision, and the practice is all too often a horrific torture for young girls performed under filthy condition and amounts to genital mutilation [FGM] without anesthesia. Female circumcision robs the girl of sexual pleasure and often of her life, and adds a dramatically horrific level to the pain of giving birth. Defenders of the practice cite religious tradition as if it were scriptural as evidence that FGM is required in Islam—for some, it is religion.

Recitation of the *Shadada* [There is no god but God; Muhammad is the messenger of God.] in public marks a young Muslim's formal entry into Islam. There is no set age for this rite, though it is most commonly celebrated during the teenage years.

Birth, marriage, and death have significant rituals attached. Birth and marriage are not so different from the Judeo-Christian traditions to merit discussion here; but death rituals are fairly adamantly fixed throughout the Muslim world. Death is considered by Muslims to be the most important event in a person's path to God, and the dying person is surrounded and supported by family and friends. Prayers and other passages from the *Qur'an* are read for the dying person, who repents of sins and—when possible—performs rituals of purification. At the time of death, those present at the deathbed whisper the *shahadah* in the dying person's ear. When possible, the dying person recites it as well. When death appears near, family members recite *surah* 36 from the *Qur'an*, which describes God's raising of the dead on the Day of Judgment.

The body of the deceased person must be buried as promptly as possible, preferably by sunset on the day of the death. The family of the deceased person is responsible for preparing the body for burial and for saying *janazah* [the funeral prayers/prayers for the dead], which are not typically said in the mosque. The body is buried in a plain white shroud. If the person went on pilgrimage to Mecca, then he or she is buried in the pilgrimage garments. Male relatives climb into the grave to arrange the body on its right side in a hollow niche in the wall of the grave. They turn the deceased's face toward Mecca, supporting the cheek with a stone. The last person in the grave with the body again whispers the *shahadah* in the deceased's ear. Each member of the assembled party throws soil into the grave, and a member of the party recites a blessing that summarizes the key beliefs of Muslims. Shi'i Muslims also recite the names of the twelve imams. Graves are marked with simple stone markers, to emphasize the equality of all people in death.

Violence, voluntary martyrdom, and terrorism are now such common occurrences in the life of Muslims and their neighbors that it would be inaccurate to omit such actions as practices or traditions comparable to polygamy, avoidance of pork, and circumcision. Children in Islamic schools are taught to hate; they learn chants such as "Kill Great Satan," "Kill little Satan," "Hate kaffirs," etc. Violence, kidnapping, theft, and harsh insults are an unavoidable part of life of a modern Muslim and have been acceptable for hundreds of years. Such behavior is at least quasi-approved, and in many congregations almost obligatory. Money is provided for the families of young martyrs; charitable foundations use their money to further terrorist causes. Islamic fundamentalism is diverse, extensive, and disorganized. Even mainstream Islam has no central governing body, no true or clear-cut hierarchy—with Iran being a partial exception with the dictatorial control by the clergy.

Violent fundamentalism within Islam arises from the vast poverty-stricken and largely ignorant, even illiterate set of Muslims who consider themselves dependent on the whims of a self-appointed mullah or a self-serving charismatic figure bent on avarice, an agenda of violent jihadism, and recruitment of martyrs for his cause. These self-appointed Islamic leaders encourage ignorance—especially among women—and prey on young people who are desperate enough to sacrifice their lives in order that their families can receive financial rewards. Recently deceased Usama bin Laden—considered to be a *mujtahid*, one who has been certified as capable of interpreting religious law—comes quickly to mind since he provided funding for many impoverished martyrs' families.

Fundamentalists—by the majority accepted meaning of the term throughout mainstream Islam—have as a long-standing goal the reintroduction of Sharia. It amounts to an obsession for Islamist movements in some Muslim countries. Small Muslim minorities in Asia (e.g. in India) have been granted institutional recognition of Sharia to adjudicate their personal and community affairs.

In western countries—where Muslim immigration is more recent—Muslim minorities have introduced Sharia family law, for use in their own disputes, with varying degrees of success (e.g. Britain's Muslim Arbitration Tribunal). Attempts to impose Sharia have been accompanied by controversy, violence, and even warfare (e.g., the Second Sudanese Civil War). There is a strenuous effort by fundamentalists to have Sharia law—applied only to Muslims for the time being—introduced as part of the legal systems of the Eurozone and the Americas. There have been experiments—especially in the area of Muslim family law—in several Western countries, but most of them have not been allowed to persist because of the antidemocratic aspects of Sharia, the Western view that Sharia is abusive to women, and Sharia causes

193

erosion in acceptance of the long-standing national and local legal authority and principles of democracy in jurisprudence so widely accepted and even cherished in the West.

A more accurate term than "fundamentalist" for use in today's world, and one preferred by moderate and observant Muslims and nonMuslim students of Islam is "Radical Islam," which quickly brings to mind Usama bin Laden and his al Qaeda cadres and mujahedin, Egypt's Muslim Brotherhood, the Palestinian Hamas, Iranian/Palestinian Hezbollah, and the host of other frankly murderous terroristic fringe groups acting on their own in the name of Islam throughout the Muslim and even the nonMuslim world.

It is forbidden in Islamic religion to make graven images or statues or other representations of God, or Allah. Over the centuries, the practice has evolved to the point that no real animal or person may be depicted. Islamic tile work is superb and depicts only geometric designs or letters or saying from the *Qur'an*. Islamic architecture—whether of temples or other buildings—are major works of religious and cultural artistic splendor. Such art forms are well represented throughout most of the Muslim world.

An important responsibility for a Muslim and largely misunderstood by nonMuslims is the concept of jihad. Westerners equate jihad with Muslim religiously based terroristic murders. The word as generally used historically and within the older mainstream *umma* indicates a struggle of the self, communicating about one's faith, obedience to God, and the effort to live a religiously holy and personally and socially righteous life—a holy crusade of self-improvement. Jihad as holy war—the jihad of the sword—is to be fought only when the faith is being attacked or when Muslims are prevented from practicing their faith. The *Qur'an* unequivocally forbids suicide, even voluntarily giving one's life as a martyr. Death in battle—not an elected choice—is the definition of martyr. The concept of jihad and the practice of wanton homicidal and suicidal terrorism is not historical Islam. The extremist jihadists have hijacked the concept and have imposed it on uneducated, disenfranchised, impoverished, and gullible young people.

The sacred places of Islam include Mecca, Medina, Jerusalem, Wali shrines, the al Aqsa Mosque, and the Dome of the Rock in Jerusalem, and each Muslim country's revered mosques. Christianity and Buddhism have a frank hagiography of saints. Orthodox Islam frowns on physical aspects of hagiography—of saint worship, or worse, idolatry; but the religion has its hagiography, saints or *walis*, [friends of Allah]—nonethless. Although the strictest fundamentalists hold that the veneration of a *wali* can be construed as a lessening of the fervor for and worship of the One God—and in some areas prohibit the practice—it is still common. It is popular practice to make a pilgrimage of veneration and visitation of shrines that honor one *wali* or another. And the practice thrives complete with the sale of icons. There is an extensive literature with a plethora of details about the marvelous lives, sayings, and practices of the *wali*. Interest in these religious luminaries is particularly keen in the orders of Sufism and the Dervishes. Islamic eschatological belief is spelled out with clarity in the *Qur'an*. The principle eschatological concepts of Islam include:

1. Resurrection - physical reunion of body and spirit.
2. Last Judgment, Paradise, and Hell. Heaven and hell are clearly defined and separate divisions of the afterlife.
3. God alone makes the judgment and final disposition of the dead. Unbelievers—kaffirs, and all who apostatize from Islam—go to hell, a place of permanent torture and remorse, which is described in the *Qur'an*, "They are fuel for the fire." Those who go to heaven—especially martyrs for the cause of Islam—will be served by houris—beautiful and obedient girls.
4. There is no agreement regarding predestination and free will among Muslim sects. All agree that Allah allows free will to perform those actions upon which a Muslim will be judged, and all persons are permitted to do good deeds. Islam belief holds that all persons were born free of sin. One can only sin after puberty and can only then be charged. No person is responsible for the sins of others—including Adam.
5. True repentance by a Muslim is the door to forgiveness, which is within the provenance of God.

Scripture: The Prophet and early Muslims were somewhat tolerant of Christians and Jews within the Muslim jurisdiction, although those nonMuslims were always treated as second class citizens at best and were subject to restrictions, extra taxations, and separation from the believers. Other nonbelievers were treated with intolerance often to the extent of cruelty; it was not a crime to kill a kaffir—a nonbeliever. The reason for the preferential treatment of the Christians and Jews was that they were "People of the Book," i.e., their religion was based on written scripture as was the *Qur'an*. The *Qur'an*—literally, The Recitation—is the only accepted scripture, per se. The *Hadith*—sayings of the Prophet—is very positively regarded, and its word is almost "gospel" to compare it to the Christian counterpart.

According to the Prophet and his followers, the *Qur'an* was recited verbatim to Muhammad by the Archangel Jibrīl [Gabriel] as he was directed by Allah and is the unalterable word of God—the final divine revelation, the final testament. It was given to the Prophet bit by bit over two decades. The Recitation was in Arabic—the language of God and the angels—and can only be truly understood by reading it in the original language. Officially—and clearly in the *Qur'an*—*The Book* was not to be translated into other languages. Eventually, the religion spread so far and wide that it was impractical to require all believers to recite the surahs that they could not even understand, and tacit permission was granted for translations.

The *Qur'an* describes itself as a book of guidance, sometimes offering detailed accounts of specific historical events, and often emphasizing the moral significance of an event over its narrative sequence. The *Qur'an* is short—114 chapters or suras—and is difficult to read and understand for a number of reasons: it is not in chronological order; it is not ordered by subject; it is a mixture of poetry, prose, and allusion to events and concepts that are obsure to nonIslamic scholars even including a number of faithful Muslims. Copies of *The Book* are treated with reverence, including the devout performing a ritual washing of their hands before touching a copy. A worn or soiled *Qur'an* should not be used, and such a *Qur'an* may not be destroyed, but rather, is given a formal burial, including a funeral. Desecration of a *Qur'an* is blasphemy—a crime of the first magnitude—and to this day is greeted with impassioned street marches and even murders of available *kaffirs* if the actual desecrator is not available.

It is regarded widely as the finest piece of literature in the Arabic language; certainly no one in the Muslim world would challenge that statement who wished to prosper—or in some vicinities, to survive. Throughout the world, Muslims are indoctrinated from earliest childhood in *Quranic* studies, largely by rote, and often by memorization—since *The Book* is actually rather short. In more backward areas of the Muslim world, even illiterate individuals are known to commit the entire book to memory sufficiently to recite it verbatim. A person whose recital repertoire encompasses the whole *Qur'an* is called a *qari'*. A memorizer of the *Qur'an* is called a *hafiz* [*fem. Hafaz*—which translate as "reciter" or "protector," respectively]. Muhammad is regarded as the first *qari'* since he was the first to recite it. Recitation [*tilawa*] of the *Qur'an* is a fine art—one full of passion, spiritual highs, and theatrical drama—in the Muslim world. There are schools to teach proper pronunciation, syntax, and to insure that the reciter and the recitation preserve a continuous *isnad* [an annotated line of authoritative quotation] all the way back to Muhammad through *tawatur* [the

196

recitation has to be related by a large succession of people from one to another down the *isnad* chain, thus preserving authenticity].

Contrary to the convictions of the ardent true believers, the *Qur'an* evolved over a considerable period of time. Many of the original recitations reported by Muhammad were given verbally—he was probably largely illiterate—and the communications came to people who would eventually die and carry their nuggets of scripture with them to the grave. Several of the original "right thinking" followers realized early on that the precious sayings of Allah through his Messenger had to be recorded, and they made valiant efforts to do so. Unfortunately, there were several men who made records; many of those records were written on different sorts of parchments, tablets of stone, flimsy branches of date trees, pieces of wood, leaves, leather, and even bones, by Muhammad's companions. Adding to the difficulty, different men wrote different things about what the Prophet communicated as scripture.

The recordings of Muhammad's nonscriptural sayings—the Hadith—had an even murkier history. One of Muhammad's wives was entrusted with the text of the earliest text of the *Qur'an* at the insistence of the Prophet's companions. The *Hadith*—on the other hand—became a nearly impossible collection of sayings to verify, collate, and preserve. Several earnest believers made it their life's work to sort the authentic wheat from the spurious inventions—the chaff—of what the Prophet was purported to have said.

Hundreds of thousands of hadiths were evaluated over decades before a more-or-less official version was accepted. Hadiths were rejected because there was inadequate verification, because of conflicting doctrine, because of self-serving accretions to the growing mass of prophetic sayings, and because some of the so-called hadiths were obviously presented to guarantee the reporter a place in heaven at the Prophet's side or—more prosaically—an enviable and prestigious place in the hierarchy of the umma. The Hadith is not strictly considered to be scripture, but it is widely studied and wholly venerated in Islam.

There is considerable similarity between the *Old* and *New Testaments* and the *Qur'anic* beliefs. The *Qur'an* is considered to be the culmination of a series of divine messages that started—according to Islamic belief—with the messages revealed to Adam—regarded in Islam as the first prophet—and continued with the *Suhuf Ibrahim*—scrolls of Abraham, the *Tawrat* (Torah or Pentateuch) of Moses, the *Zabur* (*Tehillim* or Book of Psalms) of David, and the *Injil* (Gospel) of Jesus. The *Qur'an* assumes familiarity with major narratives recounted in Jewish and Christian scriptures, summarizing some, dwelling at length on others, and in some cases presenting alternative accounts and interpretations of events.

As a point of clarification, Muhammad is not the only prophet of Islam. He is, however, the last and by far the most important. The *Qur'an*—borrowing from the Jewish and Christian traditions—identifies a number of men as "Prophets of Islam." Muslims believe such individuals were assigned a special mission by Allah to guide humanity in the right path. Besides Muhammad, prophets such as Ibrahim (Abraham), Musa (Moses), and Isa (Jesus) are listed and described in the *Holy Book* of Islam. In fact, twenty-five prophets are mentioned by name in the *Qur'an*. In addition there is a hadith—*number 21257* in *Musnad Ibn Hanbal*—that mentions that there were 124,000 of them throughout history, and the *Qur'an* says that God has sent a prophet to every group of people throughout time. Muhammad is identified as the last of the prophets, the one sent for the whole of humankind; and who, in Islam, is called *Khatim an-Nabuwwah* [Seal of the Prophets].

The Hadith is a collection of sayings, acts or tacit approvals—validly or invalidly—ascribed to the Prophet Muhammad. Hadith (plural) are regarded by traditional Islamic schools of jurisprudence as important tools for understanding the *Qur'an* and in matters of jurisprudence, although they are not formally recognized as scripture. Classical Islamic scholarship states that the intended meaning of *hadith* in religious tradition is something attributed to Muhammad, as opposed to the *Qur'an*, which came directly from Allah. Hadith were evaluated and gathered into large collections during the eighth and ninth centuries by men who surrounded and followed the Prophet constantly and to other sayings that were disseminated by his companions with his tacit approval. The two main denominations of Islam, Shi'ism and Sunnism, have different sets of Hadith collections.

Early on, the companions recognized that many false and questionable hadith were being disseminated by either well-meaning or interpreting communicators, and it was apparent that control had to be established to preserve the purity of the Prophet's sayings. Therefore, it became mandatory and a technical part of every hadith to trace its trail from the original—Muhammad or one of his companions—to the most recent transmitter. The *isnad* of an hadith consists of a chronological list of the narrators, each mentioning the one from whom they heard the hadith, until mentioning the originator of the statement. In common current usage, a hadith and the Hadith serve as an Islamic "science" and a principle of "jurisprudence," which, for Muslims, both refer to religion, not a material science like chemistry or physics, nor a jurisprudence principle such as a mundane ordinary law, as might be of interest to outsiders.

By the ninth century, the number of hadiths had grown exponentially. Early Islamic scholars were faced with a huge corpus of miscellaneous traditions, some of them flatly contradicting each other. Many of these traditions supported differing views on a variety of controversial matters. Islamic scholars and lawyers became concerned about the evident fact that there were by then many hundreds of thousands of extant hadiths, more than would have been humanly possible for any man to have uttered, even if he spoke constantly day and night all of his life. Thinking clerics realized that folly was creeping in and recognized that a number of individuals had become facile at writing and transmitting forged utterances that sounded every bit as if they were the semiscriptural sayings of Muhammad. Many of those sayings were self-serving—designed to legalize behavior that may have come into question. Beginning in the mid-eighth century, the rulers of Islam encouraged an effort at compilation of verified sayings, an agreed upon corpus of tradition. Scholars had to decide which hadith were to be trusted as authentic and which had been invented for political or theological purposes. To do this, they used a number of techniques that Muslims now call the science of hadith.

Between 815 and 912, a great sifting and reclassification took place to order the purported sayings into the various aspects of belief and practice. A prodigious and indefatigable scholar named Al-Bukhari spent sixteen years traveling throughout the lands of Islam collecting sayings that were believed to be hadith. He brought back an astounding 600,000 of them. He began a very stringent sifting process and ended up with a very few—4,000—that he could verify adequately for his exacting standards of work—the *Sahih*—which was canonized by the Sunni Muslim leadership of the time.

The issue of "innovation" was invoked during the Islamic medieval period, and changes essentially stopped. *Ijma* [change] has been invoked from time to time since; but fundamentalists have always objected, and usually successfully. Some of the orthodox will permit *ijma* only for those principles invoked by the early scholars and teachers of the law.

As in many other aspects of the religion, the Shi'i have a somewhat different take. The Shi'is pay special deference to the principle of *ijima*, but the exercise of the principle is restricted to the ulema religious class and the Ayatollah. Sunni and Shi'i hadith collections differ because scholars from the two traditions differ as to the reliability of the narrators and transmitters. Sunni narrators who took the side of Abu Bakr and Umar rather than Ali—in the disputes over leadership that followed the death of Muhammad—are seen as unreliable by the Shi'i; narrations sourced to Ali and the family of Muhammad, and to their supporters, are preferred. Sunni scholars put trust in narrators, such as Aisha, whom Shi'i reject. Differences in hadith collections have contributed to differences in worship practices and shari'a law and have hardened the dividing line between the two traditions.

In the Sunni tradition, the number of such texts is about ten thousand. The Shi'i are more dogmatic and inflexible in their acceptance of hadith; only the hadith approved by Caliph Ali—the narrations preserved by the family of Muhammad—are considered reliable. The Shi'i consider that a great many texts and books of study of hadith by the Sunni tradition to be in a gray area, if not suggestive of "innovation," a major fault for any believer. Twelver Shi'i scholars do not believe that everything in the four major Sunni books is authentic and; in Islam, the schism appears permanent.

It is not particularly surprising that Western scholars take a more objective and historical view than do the scholars who are convinced believers. Modern Western scholarship has seriously questioned the historicity and authenticity of any hadith or any collection of hadiths because—objectively—all evidence indicates that most of the statements and traditions attributed to the Prophet Muhammad were actually written much later and constitute apocryphal material and even forgeries.

One of the most important traditions in Islam is the *Sharia* [the path or the law]. Efforts to convert the entire world, even forcibly, to Islam, to establish Sharia at the expense of freedom, democracy, and Western jurisprudence, and to usher in an Islamic theocracy, are major drivers of the spate of terroristic acts of the past fifty years.

Sharia deals with many topics addressed by secular law—including crime, politics and economics, as well as personal matters such as sexuality, hygiene, diet, prayer, and fasting. But, make no mistake, Sharia is religious law; westerners almost universally see it as arbitrary, and appeal is very limited.

Sharia courts—with their tradition of *pro se* representation, simple rules of evidence, and absence of appeals courts, prosecutors, cross examination, complex documentary evidence and discovery proceedings, juries, *voir dire* proceedings, circumstantial evidence, forensics, case law, standardized codes, exclusionary rules, and most of the other infrastructure of civil and common law court systems—have, as a result, comparatively informal and streamlined proceedings.

The efficiency argument for Sharia is offset in most Westerners' minds by the potential for bias on the part of judge and by the conspicuous lack of defendant protections considered to be among the fundamental underpinnings of civil and common law.

In addition, Sharia—based as it is on religion—contains elements that are basically unacceptable—even abhorrent—to Westerners. Slavery and polygamy have never been formally banned under the Sharia, but neither is practiced by any but a minority of Muslims. Among the Sharia rules and acceptable practices are punishments by mutilation and capital punishment by what are considered cruel and unusual means—e.g. stoning—of the convicted criminal—who may be convicted for a strictly religious crime such as adultery, sorcery, homosexuality, or bestiality. Westerners—for the most part—consider polygamy to be repugnant, one of the twin relics of barbarism, along with slavery.

Saudi Arabia comes close to having such a social system; in Iran, the *Sharia* or *Fiqh*—as interpreted by the Ayatollah—constitutes the law of the land. The Sharia is considered to be divine law with Allah as drafter, legislator, forbidder, rewarder, and punisher. Fiqh is understanding in the legal sense—God speaks, God commands, and man must submit and obey and must do so actively, not passively—joyfully, not grudgingly. Fiqh jurisprudence interprets and extends the application of Sharia to questions not directly addressed in the primary sources by including secondary sources.

There are four officially accepted schools of the law, and every Muslim must subscribe to one of them. The Hanafi, Maliki, Shafi'l, or Hanbali schools dictate how the Muslim is to perform his or her religious duties and how he or she is to interpret the law. The *sunna* is right conduct, and the Sunni branch of Islam considers itself to be the sole possessor of right conduct.

Sharia is derived from two primary sources of Islamic law: the precepts set forth in the *Qur'an*, and the example set by the Islamic prophet Muhammad in the *Sunnah*—from which the term Sunni comes. In practice—as accretions have entered over the past 1500 years—the religion has become increasingly more complex with multiple different schools of the law. The Sunni/Shi'i schism has increased and hardened with books of law on almost all conceivable practices of humans.

While Muslims believe Sharia to be the law of Allah, they are not monolithic in that belief. They differ as to what exactly it entails. Modernists, traditionalists, and fundamentalists all hold different views of Sharia, as do adherents to different schools of Islamic thought and scholarship. More enlightened and educated Muslims shrink away from the prospect of losing the rights and benefits afforded them in Western jurisprudence in favor of the concept of an immutable basic code based on religious thinking and literature.

There are several schismatic divisions in Islam. Ninety percent of Muslims are Sunni, and the Shi'i branch—located largely in Iran—is the most prominent of the minorities. Most of the Iranian Shi'ites are what is known as Twelvers, a topic that will appear as another essay further along in this trilogy. For the purposes of this essay, the Shi'i will be given short shrift. "Shi'i" is the short form of the historic phrase *Shi'atu Ali* [followers, faction, or party of Ali]. In contrast to other schools of thought, Shi'is believe—based on their interpretation of the *Qur'an*—that only Allah has the right to choose a representative to safeguard Islam, and no one else has any choice in the selection. God's representatives such as prophets and imāms cannot be elected by common Muslims. For that reason, Shi'is disown the election and selection of early friends of Muhammad, Abu Bakr, Umar, and Uthman ibn Affan by the people. Furthermore, Shi'is do not consider Ali to be the fourth imam—as the Sunnis believe—but rather, the first "Imam." Thus they say that Muhammad, before his death, appointed Ali as his successor.

Ali was murdered in 661 C.E. According to the Shi'i. There is always an Imam of the Age, who is the divinely appointed authority on all matters of faith and law in the Muslim community. Ali was the first Imam of this line—the rightful successor to Muhammad—followed by male descendants of Muhammad through his daughter Fatimah Zahra. Another seminal event in Shi'i history is the martyrdom in 680 CE at the Battle of Karbala of Ali's son Hussein who led a non-allegiance movement against the defiant caliph. Hussein came to symbolize resistance to tyranny.

Shi'i Islam embodies a completely independent system of religious interpretation and political authority in the Muslim world and holds differing beliefs to the Sunni; for example, while Sunnis believe the Mahdi will appear sometime in the future, Shi'is believe the Mahdi was already on earth, is currently the "hidden imam" who works through mujtahids to interpret *Qur'an*, and will return at the end of time. The shism has been great enough throughout the centuries of Islam's existence that terrorism, segregation, discrimination, and even wars have attended the inability of the two factions to agree on their disparate issues to the least degree.

As remarkable as it would seem, the Jesus of Christianity is also revered by Muslims as the coming messiah. Islamic tradition views Jesus as the promised prophet sent to the Semitic Jewish tribes living in Israel at the beginning of the common era (C.E.). Further, they believe that the prophet Jesus will return to the earth after the apocalypse—but after the arrival of the all-important Imam Mahdi. Jesus will defeat the Antichrist, the false messiah. Jesus is not the Son of God, such a relationship would be impossible for the indivisible Allah. Rather, Jesus is just one in a line of prophets, perhaps second in importance to Muhammad. Jesus will destroy all religions except Islam at his coming and proclaim al-Mahdi as the true leader.

There have been a plethora of claimants to the title "Messiah," including among Muslims. All of them were eventually denounced as frauds. To name a few of the Muslim claimants:

- Muhammad Jaunpuri (1443–1505), who traveled about Northeastern India.
- Báb (1819–1850), who declared himself to be the promised Mahdi in Shiraz, Iran in 1844.
- Mirza Ghulam Ahmad (1835–1908) of Qadian, 'the Promised Messiah' return of Jesus as well as the 'Mahdi,' founder of the Ahmadiyya religious movement. He preached that Jesus Christ had survived crucifixion and died a natural death. He was the only person in Islamic history to have claimed to be *both* the promised return of Jesus as well as the promised Mahdi.
- Muhammad Ahmad—The Mad Mahdi (1844–1885)—declared himself the Mahdi in 1881, defeated the Ottoman Egyptian authority, and founded a short-lived empire in Sudan.
- Sayyid Mohammed Abdullah Hassan (1864–1920) of Somaliland, engaged in military conflicts from 1900 to 1920 to establish himself as the Mahdi.
- Rashad Khalifa (1935–1990), an Egyptian-American biochemist, claimed that he had discovered a mathematical code in the text of the *Qur'an* involving the number 19. He later claimed to be the "Messenger of the Covenant"–essentially, the Mahdi—and founded the "Submitters International" movement before being murdered.
- Juhayman al-Otaibi (1936–1980) seized the Grand Mosque in Mecca in November 1979 and declared his son-in-law to be the Mahdi. He was corrected by the government of Saudi Arabia.

Sources: *Walden University Online—LookLex Encyclopedia*; *OpenCourseWare*, University of Notre Dame. *Faith, Practice, and Law in Sunni and Shi'i Islam. ugu.edu—University of Georgia online*; *Wikipedia.* Michael Axworthy, *A History of Iran: Empire of the Mind*; Ervand Abrahamian, *A History of Modern Iran*; Nikki R. Keddie, *Modern Iran: Roots and Results of Revolution*; Hamid Dabashi, *Iran: A People Interrupted*; Amnesty International, *Iran: Violation of Human Rights, 1991*; *Iran, Lonely Planet*, Andrew Burke and Mark Elliott,

2008, *Islam*, ed. John Alden Williams, 1961; *Islam*, 5th Ed, Cesar E. Farah, Ph.D.; Dore Gold, *Hatred's Kingdom: How Saudi Arabia Supports the New Global Terrorism*; Milton Viorst, *In the Shadow of the Prophet: The Struggle for the Soul of Islam*, Wilfried Buchta, *Who Rules Iran?* 2000.

> **"Then you erring ones, you that cried lies, you shall eat of a tree called Zakkoum, and you shall fill therewith your bellies and drink on top of that boiling water lapping it down like thirsty camels." This shall be their hospitality on the Day of Doom.**
>
> *The Holy Qur'an,* **56:56**

CAST OF CHARACTERS
[Most important continuing characters—*]

IRAN

Nawsheen Shakibaie	Afsoon's birth mother, fourth wife of Ahriman
*Ahriman Shakibaie	Afsoon's birth father, master of a tent hamlet near Qushchu, Kurdestan County, West Azerbaijan Province, Iran
*Fereshten Shakibaie	Ahriman's first wife
*Azadeh Shakibaie	Ahriman's fourth wife
*Afsoon Daastrup— Afsoon Mouradipour	Biological daughter of Nawsheen and Ahriman Shakibaie, adopted daughter of Neal and Brenda Daastrup. Mourapidour is a cover name
*Astera Shakibaie	Ahriman's third wife
*Yasmin	Wet nurse and surrogate mother to Afsoon
Kamin Shakibaie	Ahriman and Fereshten's third son, Afsoon's half-brother
Muhammad Shakibaie	Ahriman and Fereshten's son, Afsoon's half-brother
Shokofeh	Astera's servant

Farhad Sharifi	Shepherd boy, illicit lover of Astera
*Firudin Jamshidi	Afsoon's temporary paternal guardian in rural Kurdestan County, West Azerbaijan Province, Iran
*Mariella Jamshidi	Afsoon's temporary maternal guardian in rural Kurdestan village
*Nassir Jamshidi	Loving "brother" of Afsoon in rural Kurdestan village
*Elaheh Jamshidi	Daughter of Firudin and Mariella Jamshidi
Mozaffarian and Gorgani Jamshidi	Elder sons of Firudin and Mariella Jamshidi
Dina Jamshidi	Daughter of Firudin and Mariella Jamshidi
Fatemah Shakibaie	New—fourth—wife of Ahriman after death of Astera
The Dashnaksutyun	Armenian bandits
*Fereshte [angel].	Afsoon's beloved rag doll, made for her by Nassir
Imam Ali Abedi	Cleric who preformed FGMs
Imam Zamaani Fard	Cleric in Kandovan who conducted Dina's funeral
*Grand Ayatollah Ali ibn Abi Rahimi	Supreme Leader of Iran—the Agha, the SL
Saif-al-din and his wife, Parveen	Temporary guardians of Afsoon in Kandovan Village, Kurdestan County, West Azerbaijan Province, Iran
*Hassanzadeh Shakibaie	Eldest son of Ahriman and Fereshten Shakibaie
Shireen	Shakibaie slave girl
*The Bakhtiaris	Bedouin nomads from the Zagros Mountains

Mullah Haji Zamaani Fard	Circuit judge at Piranshahr jail
Shafiqah Kadivar	Afsoon's employer at a wool carpet factory in Amarrh, Iraq
Sergeant Naomeh Nikahd	Municipal police, Al Basrah, Iraq
Aisha Toskhani	Kashmiri Pandit woman in charge of humanitarian relief center, Al Basrah, Iraq
Dr. Sylvia Asad	Physician at the humanitarian relief center, Al Basrah, Iraq
Haji NaazemZadeh Harandi	Scholar, librarian, teacher at the humanitarian relief center, Al Basrah, Iraq
Roshanak Rahimi	Wife of Supreme Leader Grand Ayatollah Ali ibn Abi Rahimi
Ali Hosseini Mejazi	Chief of staff of Supreme Leader Grand Ayatollah Ali ibn Abi Rahimi
*Mohsen Shahamatdoost and successor Hormoz Okhavat	Presidents of the Republic of Iran
Yazid ibn Sarrafzaadeh	Chief of Staff of the Armed Forces of the Republic of Iran
*Moqtada al-Benizir & Ayatollah Ali Hossein Golzar his successor after al-Benizir was murdered. Aisha and Khadija	Head of the Atomic Energy Organization Iran (AEOI). His wife and daughter (a singer)
*Mullah Ali Salar Omidyar	Director of the Ministry of Intelligence and Security (MOIS)
*Behrouz Omidi	Director of the Ministry of Intelligence and National Security of the Islamic Republic of Iran (MISIRI) or VEVAK.
Abdul Qadeer (AQ) Khan	Smuggler of uranium enrichment and nuclear weapon technology to Muslim countries
*Hamid Hejazi	SL guard, Agent-Ex
*Daniel and Brenda Daastrup	Georgetown, Washington, D.C. Daniel is Neal Daastrup's brother, and Brenda

	his sister-in-law. They are the adoptive parents of Afsoon
Dr. Nawal El Mubarak	Egyptian feminist physician and surgeon who repaired Afsoon's recto-vaginal fistula
*Ali Mohamed Mustaffen	Director of the Central Bank of the Islamic Republic of Iran
Ali Muhummad Sharifi, Mahdis and Javaneh, Mojtaba	Iranian Foreign Minister, his wife and two children (singers)
Col. Dariush Aghdashloo	On-site commander of the Agha's private security force.
1. Daron Naderi 2. Ayatollah Mohammad Esmail Rahmanipour 3. Ali Hossein Rahnavardand 4. Bobak Larijani 5. Col. Darius Aghdashloo	The management of the SL's household and directors of his personal guard [SL Agha Rahimi's oldest friends, if the Supreme Leader of Iran's Muslims could actually have friends in the usual sense]: 1. Head of amputee war veterans 2. Currently a member of parliament 3. Director of IRGC intelligence 4. Head of the guard corps and member of the Security Council 5. Second in command to Rahnavard.
*Project *Jahannam Adur* [Hell's Fire]	Iranian project for manufacture of nuclear weapons, placing them in missiles, and delivering the missiles on Israel and the U.S.
*Elizabeth Dayan	American expat living in Iran, horse rancher, and spy for the Iran Nuclear Interdiction Project
*Elias, Zachariah, Elijah, Kelsey, Leopold, and Pearl Nichols-Dayan	Children of Elizabeth and co-conspirators. Elias is an active agent with Aaron Schmuel in Iran
*Rabbi Ya'akov ben Avraham	Persian Jewish rabbi who ostensibly is a loyal citizen of Iran and secretly becomes an agent for the American-run Iran Nuclear Interdiction Project. Member

	of Neturei Karta—Ultra-Orthodox Jews, a Jewish Sect that opposes both Zionism and Israel.
Esfandiari Razizadeh	Deputy of Moqtada al-Benizir, Head of the Atomic Energy Organization Iran (AEOI)
Razmara Tassoudji	Deputy of Moqtada al-Benizir, Head of the Atomic Energy Organization Iran (AEOI)
*Amir Vehrahrami	Chief engineer for research and development at the Bushehr nuclear plant
*Hormoz Mohammad-Bagher	President of Bank Sepah, Tehran
Cantor Avril Azaria	Jewish singer
Ali Hassan Zolein	Member of the Majilis who spoke of Israeli Trojan Horse
Ayatollah Ali Hossein Golzar	New head of AEOI after al Benizir's murder
Arash Behdad	Finance Minister of Iran

ISRAEL

*Major General Zwi Rosenstein	Deputy director Mossad
Zeev Rosenkranz	Chief of Tel Aviv Israeli mafia –"Kosher Nostra"
*Max Rosenstein	Zwi's brother and second in command of Kosher Nostra
*Moise Levinsky	Ranking Kosher Nostra officer
*Jacob "The Greaser" Cohen	Ranking Kosher Nostra officer
*General André Lansky	Director of the Mossad
David Henderson	Mossad agent and Krav Maga expert
Sergeant Ruth McGuire	Mossad analyst
*Levi, Miriam, Rebecca, Alice, Abraham, Constance, Michael, Harry, Daniel, Avril, Julius, and Elsie	Mossad Institute analyst group

209

SLHAN1__@# percent@*trickmagicphantom.	G.R. IV's Mossad login code
Antal Disraeli	Mossad *katsa*—case officer
*Elsie Silberberg	Electronic communications analyst, friend of G.R. IV

UNITED STATES

*Gideon Emmanuel Rothsberger, I, II, III, IV [G.R. I, II, III, IV]	Line of wealthy Orthodox Jewish bankers. G.R. III and IV are members of the *Sayanim*. I is deceased, II is CEO of Gideon Products Universal, III is president of Rothsberger & Company Bankers, and IV is senior vice-president of the bank. Part of the Iran Nuclear Interdiction Project
*Chava Dayan-Hershowitz Rothsberger	Mother of G.R. IV
Tahmineh and Leila Rothsberger	Twins daughters of G.R. III and Chava, and sisters of G.R. IV
Nathan Rothsberger	Uncle of G.R. IV who opposes him for the position of senior vice-president and president-elect of Rothsberger & Company Bankers
*Rebecca Hershowitz	Mother of Chava and grand-mother of G.R. IV
Dr. ben Schulberg	Chava's obstetrician
Joseph ben Aaron,	Rothsberger's butler
Ruth Kline	G.R. IV's nanny Abba Cogen
Abba Cogen	G.R. IV's *mohel* [circumcisor]
Rabbi Bergen	Rothsberger's rabbi
*Aaron Schmuel	School bully, later friend of G.R. IV, action agent of the DIA in the Iran Nuclear Interdiction Project

210

*Levi Schmuel	Aaron's father, member of Kosher Nostra
Rabbi Pinchas ben Yisroel, ha-Rav	Headmaster, Saint Francis Woods Hebrew Academy
Leopold Antal Lavigne	Dean of students, Saint Francis Woods Hebrew Academy
*Lt. Col. Shai Avitan	Martial arts instructor, IDF. Krav Maga expert
Professor Samson Bernstein	UC Berkeley Professor and tutor for G.R. IV in elementary and high school
Gilda Rogdonavich	Master's thesis *Gifted Child* about G.R. IV
President Tate-Waring	President of UC Berkeley
Tom Bradshaw	Senate Majority Leader
*Ali ibn Massoud	VEVAK contact agent in the Ali and the Twelve Imams mosque
Dr. Stephen Ammon Rhodes	UC Berkeley math professor for G.R. IV
Dr. Willard Lazar	Head of the department of computer science—G.R. IV's major professor at Berkeley
Dr. Stanley Protel Thatcher	Head of the MIT computer science department
Miriam bat Ezekiel	Message courier—member of the *Sayanim*
Dr. Kristina Shimazaki	G.R. IV's MIT major professor in mathematics
Drs. Leif Erik Nielson and Karl L. Nielson	MIT economics department co-chairs
*Rear Adm. Martin Torgelson	Assumed the office of DDDIA in 2011 when Neal Daastrup retired. The appellation "3D" stuck with Vice-Adm. Daastrup, so Torgelson became known as the Swede.
Rabbi Pinchas ben Yisroel, ha-Rav	Headmaster, Saint Francis Woods Hebrew Academy

Leopold Antal Lavigne	Dean of students, Saint Francis Woods Hebrew Academy
Professor Samson Bernstein	UC Berkeley Professor and tutor for G.R. IV in elementary and high school
*Howard Ryan, Glen Gabler, Agnes Maxwell Cunningham, Oliver Sandstone, Umberto Gonzales	Presidents of the U.S.
*Army Col. Avery Holmes and Navy Captain Victor Raylan	Heads of DARPA and the SSG-CNO respectively. [Defense Advanced Research Projects Agency and Strategic Studies Group for the Chief of Naval Operations]

SWEDEN

Jonas Zillacus	Ambassador to the United States
*Ali Nylander	Consular agent in charge of trade and economic affairs
Dr. Arvid Bergström	Counselor for Swedish defense
Counselor Ms. Sanna Kullberg	Special Advisor, Homeland Security Affairs
Magnus Bielvenstram	Minister-Counselor, Trade and Economic Affairs
*Johannes Hjerdstadt	Ostensibly, the undersecretary for embassy affairs. Actually, an agent of *FMUndSäkC* [Swedish Army Intelligence].
*Marta Olson	Agent of *FMUndSäkC* protecting Afsoon in Sweden
*Ingrid Hakkensdatter	Agent of *FMUndSäkC* protecting Afsoon in Sweden
Nick Staphanakis	DIA agent protecting Afsoon in Sweden
Michael Grodmore	DIA agent protecting Afsoon in Sweden
Hassan Tajbakhsh	VEVAK agent following/protecting Afsson
Mohammad Ali Nikookar	VEVAK agent following/protecting Afsson

212

Ayatollah Mammad Qazwini	Senior VEVAK agent in Sweden
Salar Sabeti	VEVAK agent in Sweden who first approached Afsoon at the University
Mohammad Ali Nikookar	VEVAK agent in Sweden
Ali Hossein	VEVAK agent in Sweden

FRANCE

*Miriam Shahnameh	Maiden name of Gideon's wife—opera singer
Elijah and Ruth Shahnameh	French Orthodox Jews, parents of Miriam
Gideon Rothsberger V and Ruth	G.R IV and Miriam R's children
Marius Duvalier	Elderly French singer

Gen. Gangjon Chung-a - North Korean General, Col. Dockko Yong-Jin, and Dr. Soung Hong-jik of the Institute of Atomic Energy.

Gideon Meier and Rudolf Ashensky - Mossad agents active in battles between Bakhtiari and Iranian army.

Bakhtiari Headman Saad ad-Daula Khan

The Iran Nuclear Interdiction Project, Project *Jahannam Adur*

AUTHOR CARL DOUGLASS, a former neurosurgeon turned full time author, writes with gripping realism because in all his books he has been there and done that in some measure. He grew up in a small town where fighting was the rule, not the exception. He was determined to escape the sameness of geography, intellectual outlook, and career prospects of the majority of his contemporaries. In complete naiveté, he applied to only one well-known major university for his undergraduate work, and to everyone's surprise, he was accepted. He found himself out of his league scholastically and had to work like a Hannibal to find a way or make one to succeed in that rarefied atmosphere. His goal of success was to become a neurosurgeon, and he did it. His career in academia and the military as well as his work as a medical humanitarian provided the background to produce the riveting tales that have made their way into his remarkable books.

214